Betrayed

The Arnaud Legacy, Book Two

LYNN CARTHAGE

KENSINGTON PUBLISHING CORP.

www.kensingtonbooks.com

To Mom and Dad,

*in gratitude for making history so interesting for us girls
and for helping us to understand that we could
"trip" with books.*

CHAPTER ONE

Enclosed within these pages you shall not discover a
comprehensive compendium of all secret societies, since by the
very nature of such a convening they wish their actions kept
furtive, unheard of. Yet the faltering speech of those who
withdraw, their lips compelled to speak despite their urged
promise to keep silence unto death, gives us some small glance,
as by the light of a candle briefly lit and then gusted out by
rogue wind, of the happenings in the caves, caverns, lodging
rooms, cellars and hallowed temples of those who have set
themselves aside for some earnest task.

—*Secret Cabals, Societies & Orders*

MILES

*I*t's cool to see the look on Phoebe's face. She's looking at Paris with her moss green eyes the way I did a few years ago when my parents took me: dazzled by the buildings she's seen a million times in movies and books. They look even more brilliant in person. The city bustles with beautifully dressed women, smokers hunched over their espressos at tiny outdoor tables—and everywhere the florid language unfurling.

There's the Eiffel Tower, an iron skeleton against the sky; a short walk later and we're approaching the Place de la Concorde, one of several city squares where the guillotine once sat. Phoebe's jumping around, literally, pointing at the Egyptian obelisk that came from Luxor by a boat towed by another boat, its colossal face etched with cartouches and hieroglyphics telling a tale we no longer understand.

"Egypt gave France this obelisk, and France gave *us* the Statue of Liberty. We should send someone a Mount Rushmore face!" she says. Our first stop this morning had been the miniature Statue of Liberty stationed on its own island in the Seine, like the full-size statue that sits on Liberty Island. I've never seen her so excited. We make our dash across lanes of traffic to reach the Egyptian antiquity in the center. She's relaxed and carefree, a Phoebe I haven't really seen before. She deserves a trip to Paris after everything she's been through. Her eyes snap from crêpe stand to patisserie, while her long auburn hair falls in waves against her white sweater. It's October, and we're all wearing an extra layer.

"Miles," she says, "Look at the buildings. They look so *French!*"

I have to laugh. "Apparently they *are!*" I babble out a quick explanation about how during Napoléon's era, an architect tore down all the cramped medieval houses and built the buildings we see today, with the balconies always at the second and fifth stories.

We've come to Paris with Phoebe's family. Our friend Eleanor's with us, too, and she's trying hard to keep calm. The cars roaring around the circular Place de la Concorde terrify her. Before this trip, she'd never left Grenshire, the small English town we're both from. Phoebe and her family, including her cute toddler sister, Tabby, are from the States. Tabby's currently enjoying Paris from her buggy—what the Americans call a stroller—as her mum negotiates the uneven Parisian traffic.

"Miles, weren't people sad to see their medieval buildings go?" Eleanor asks.

"I don't know," I answer. "Ask one of them."

"Them" being the ghosts that surround us, each intent on their own journey. A few seventeenth-century women wander past with market baskets . . . Why do they haunt this square? Bad vegetables?

Others are Revolution-era ghosts. One boy who looks about eight stands sobbing, his hands to his mouth, watching something we can't see: people being beheaded on the scaffold? He turns to run away, and it's clear by his path that he has to push around people who are no longer there. They escaped being haunted by this day somehow, and, in turn, haunting the square. In their coffins they merely rest, as the saying goes, in peace.

But there are others who aren't RIP'ing. I see them in line, holding hands with the people in front of and behind them, their faces twisted. Like the boy, they seem to be watching action on a platform above our heads. The fact that they're lined up makes me think they may be waiting their turn for the guillotine.

Horrible.

Phoebe, Eleanor, and I have trained ourselves not to pay attention—it's too upsetting. We notice and then look away. It's almost like reading a scary book and skimming over certain passages: we're aware they're there but we choose not to read them.

For those who can't see ghosts—like Phoebe's parents—there's nothing here to suggest the bloodshed once indulged in by enraged, breadless peasants. It's a nice municipal court. Just a plaque indicates the place where the guillotine stood, but Phoebe's stepdad Steven is *way* into his French history and starts to tell us details that make us queasy.

He's the kind of person who isn't embarrassed to pull out a guidebook and read aloud from it. Already on this trip, it's started conversations with strangers who overhear the bits he reads, which I kind of like, but Phoebe always looks like she wants to sink into the pavement.

"Grisly tidbit *numéro un*," says Steven. "Onlookers at the

guillotine would bend to dip their bread in the rivulets of blood that flowed from the machine."

"I scoff," says Phoebe.

"Well, if you don't have peanut butter, let them eat blood," I say.

"*Numéro deux*," says Steven. "One princess pleaded for her life so tearfully that the crowd began to call for mercy, but they killed her anyway."

"Steven, Tabby doesn't need to hear all this," says Phoebe's mum.

"It goes over her head," he says.

"No pun intended?" I ask. "Anybody?" Phoebe gives me a weak smile. "Aw, really?"

"You don't know that," Phoebe's mum says. "This is a sensitive child and she's been through a lot already."

"Mom?" asks Tabby. "Blood?"

"See?" hisses her mother.

"Well, let's keep going," says her stepdad, putting the book away into his messenger bag. "The Louvre isn't far."

"Was anybody killed at the Louvre?" murmurs her mother, and I laugh softly. I really like her.

After a brisk walk, we arrive at the Louvre, an ornate blue-roofed former palace that's now a museum. Phoebe's family queues up in the Louvre courtyard near the large glass pyramid to buy tickets for entry. A cluster of male ghosts in breeches and tricorne hats are actually standing *in* the pyramid. They've gathered in their era's courtyard, which predates the modern sculpture. They appear to be fighting, all roaring and yelling at the same time.

"I don't know if Tabby's going to have the patience for this," warns Phoebe's mum.

"She's doesn't," says Phoebe, "but I do!"

"What's inside?" asks Eleanor. Her pale gray eyes fasten on the pyramid, where one of the men has pulled a knife and the others back away from him. She's dressed formally, like always, in a dark dress with crisp, ironed pleats.

"Some of the most famous art in the world," I say. Her prim-mouth reaction is priceless: she doesn't care. "Don't you want to see the *Mona Lisa?*"

She hasn't heard of it. I can tell by her face.

"Eleanor, you don't know the *Mona Lisa?*" asks Phoebe incredulously. She blushes. I can tell she doesn't mean to embarrass Eleanor. Eleanor's background is different from ours, and I'd be surprised if she knew of such a painting.

"Is it a sculpture?" asks Eleanor.

"It's a painting," says Phoebe, without a hint of a smile. "By Leonardo da Vinci, a famous Italian painter. The painting's famous because the woman has a sly smile."

"That does sound interesting," says proper Eleanor, and I suppress a smile.

"It's okay not to like art," I say. "Not everybody likes everything."

I look back at the pyramid. The ghosts have disappeared, and now Phoebe's mum and stepdad are gently arguing about the price of admission. She doesn't think it's worth it if they have to leave after just a half hour because of their restless toddler. It's fascinating to watch their fight—mild assertions like "I'm just not sure it's the best idea" and "why not give it a try?"

When my parents go at it, it's like no word can be loud enough and delivered with enough vehemence. Phoebe's parents are like . . . hm . . . how to describe it? Like squirrels chattering over a nut they both want. Maybe they used to fight differently back when their lives were normal.

They decide they'll return tomorrow in the morning when Tabby's fresh. In the meantime, they'll hit a few of Steven's destinations. He wants to continue his self-directed tour of All Things Bloody and visit the Conciergerie, where Marie-Antoinette was imprisoned before her execution. It's a foreboding castle prison that looks like something German.

"I'm honestly not up for that, Steven," says Phoebe's mum.

"Well, do you want to look at Notre Dame, then?"

"A dark cathedral? Maybe I'm not the best Paris tourist," she answers. "I'd just like to *walk*. In the sunshine. Is that okay? Tabby's a few minutes from falling asleep anyway. I'll get some exercise while she sleeps in the stroller."

"Sure," says Steven. "You want to meet back here in an hour?"

"That's perfect. Thanks for understanding." She leans in to give him a kiss, and I see something great in their faces: that they get each other. I look over at Phoebe, and our eyes meet and hold for a minute. That girl is so beautiful. I reach out with two hands and tuck her hair behind her ears. The Paris wind has made it wild. She takes a step toward me, and her hair drifts up again in the breeze. I want to take her in my arms, but I feel strange doing it in front of Eleanor.

I look over at her; she's studying Phoebe's stepdad. "Do we divide and conquer?" I call to her.

"Well, we *know* who Phoebe's going with!" she says with a smile. "I'll keep an eye on him. In fact, I'm interested in that poor queen and what her prison was like." So she goes with him, and the rest of us stay with Tabby, after fortifying her with an orange juice from the small store on the corner. The juice makes her face bunch up from its bitterness.

The walk is glorious. Paris is a light city, ebullient, somehow . . . I don't know . . . *healthy?* My heart lifts as we continue to walk, even though Tabby asks five times in a row how much farther it is and Phoebe's mum starts to get cross.

She walks quickly, and the resultant bump in the buggy eases Tabby to sleep. Soon we're out of the tourist part of Paris and in neighborhoods where people shop for groceries, go to work, and ride the Métro back home. They're living regular lives like in any other city. The storefronts and buildings still seem uniquely French, but there are no visitors bumbling along with knapsacks full of cameras and sweatshirts. It feels genuine in a way I appreciate; certainly, Parisians don't pay daily homage to the Eiffel Tower.

Phoebe's mum doesn't say anything. She's deep in thought, walking rhythmically with her sleeping child in the buggy. I hope she's keeping track of where she's going, because I don't think I'd be able to retrace our steps back. She's jogged left and right a few too many times without leaving her trail of bread crumbs.

Although maybe we could find our way back using *ghosts* as landmarks: turn left where the woman lies in a fetal position sobbing, her skirts pulled up to her thighs—did she die in childbirth on a straw-strewn floor?—turn right where the woman in a fine gown, her face tranquil, holds up a bottle marked with a skull and crossbones in front of her face as if deciding.

Continue straight on past the elderly man, reclining on one elbow as he tries to write a letter while having a coughing fit.

There's nothing I can do about any of these people. I give them a sympathetic look and move on.

When Phoebe's mum approaches a building with a long

green lawn, she stops in front to sit on a bench and rest. She takes some deep breaths, and tears glitter in her eyes. Tabby's still asleep, her cheeks rounder as her jaw nestles down into her chest.

"Mom, are you okay?" asks Phoebe.

Her mum blinks rapidly, pushing the tears back. "You're fine, you're fine," she tells herself. She blows her nose with tissue she finds in the nappy bag slung across the handle of the buggy, then stands up. She looks with curiosity at the building in the distance: long, white, low-level. It's a historical site, and she pushes Tabby toward its gate.

A tour is already under way, so we join in. With a sinking heart, I see that it's a cemetery of some sort. "Here at Picpus, we keep eternal vigilant prayer for the victims of the Revolution," says a nun in a gray and white habit.

I look over at Phoebe. Seriously? We walked all the way here to get away from the Revolution!

"The prayer has gone on unceasingly for over two hundred years," she says. "You may donate to support our sisters in our labors. Here is the grave of the Marquis de Lafayette, a name any of you Americans will recognize." I look around: blank faces, but Phoebe's mum nods. The grave is a flat slab on the ground decorated with a metallic wreath gone green, surrounded by an iron fence. "He was instrumental in assisting the Americans with their own revolution, while here at home his wife's family was guillotined. It is thanks to their generosity that the memorial was established. We'll go over there now. Please follow me."

She leads our small group out to a field blocked out with two large rectangles. Gravel covers the surface of the grass over them.

"These are mass graves where the victims lie," she continues. "Brought by carriage from the guillotine at the Place de la Nation."

I stare. Below that gravel are hundreds of bodies, now nothing more than skulls and skeletons bearing a clean slice at the top of the spine.

"Why aren't there more ghosts?" I ask Phoebe. I do see a few wandering the grounds, imploring the Fates to change that which can't be changed. One man stands at the edge of the pit and repeatedly spits into it.

One question answered: they've been reunited with their heads for this stage of existence.

"Maybe they haunt the guillotine instead?" says Phoebe. "Perhaps the Place de la Nation is more haunted than the place we went with the obelisk. Or they haunt the house of whoever turned them in?"

"Or they found peace despite being so brutally murdered."

The nun's still talking. "We know of this site by the bravery of a young girl who secretly followed the tumbrels—the horse-drawn carts—under darkness of night as they carried her father and brother headless from the site of their execution."

I can't help but wonder . . . were heads reconnected to bodies? Did they gently arrange the bodies or were they unceremoniously dumped from the back of the cart?

Phoebe's mum looks pale. I can tell she's about to leave the tour and resume her walk with Tabby, but another woman on the tour, wearing a black and red chevron-striped dress, asks the guide a question.

"We've heard the legend about the woman whose lover dug her up," she says. "Can you tell us about that?"

The nun pauses. "It is possibly apocryphal," she says. "One

of those stories that arises out of the genuine tragedy and seems to illustrate it better than the tragedy itself."

"So it's true?"

Phoebe and I look at each other, and I snort.

"We don't know," says the nun gently. "But here is the story that has come to us through the years. A manservant who was truly devoted to his mistress tracked the tumbrel of bodies here and took note of where she was buried with the others. He waited until darkness fell, then dug her up."

"What about her head?" asks the tourist, an American, judging by her accent.

"He was able to locate it. As the story goes, he fastened it to her neck and stitched it on."

The entire group gives a gasp of shock, but with an under-layer of something gleeful for the morbid value of the tale.

I'm suddenly immersed in the thought of a woman who lost her life to the guillotine and lay underground for hours with other seeping, chilling bodies, and was somehow later brought back to life. What did it feel like as the servant stitched? Did she feel the pain? Was she numb, then filled with a rush of agonized nerve endings coming awake? As she walked again, upright after the forced, facedown recline on the guillotine, did her hands steal to her neck to feel the lim-its of that horrible circular gouge?

I shudder.

"He must've really been in love," says Phoebe.

I look at her, a faint dusting of freckles on her nose, and her lips full and inviting. "That's a pretty intense kind of love," I comment.

"And wouldn't it suck if she didn't like him?"

I burst out laughing. "Only you, Phoebe. Only you could come up with that."

"And so, after that, she continued to live?" asks the tourist.

"Impossible," the nun says firmly. "Only Christ can reanimate the dead."

Silence falls.

"It's just a legend," says the tourist.

"I think that's what I said to you when you told me about Madame Arnaud," Phoebe whispers. "And that turned out to be pretty goddamn true."

The next day, the family packs up to take the train to Versailles, the former French palace where three kings named Louis once lived. It's really the point of the whole trip. Phoebe's house, the Arnaud Manor in England, is based on Versailles and they want to look at the original to help fuel ideas for the manor's restoration. The Arnaud Manor is a wreck. Only a madman would live there, but her family seems bent on doing it up. If it were me, I'd let it go, but Phoebe's mum in particular really wants the project— something for her to focus on.

Of course, I don't have much to bring, but I hover around and watch the flurry of action required to get a toddler from point A to point B. Eleanor's in a good mood; she liked seeing the prison where Marie-Antoinette passed her last days. "There were dummies lying on the ground to look like prisoners," she tells me and Phoebe. "They had to pay for their own straw to lie on, and if they had no money, they lay right on the stones."

"France is kind of morbid," observes Phoebe.

"The whole continent," I say. "You spanking-new Americans think the world started in 1776. You forget there has to be an evolution of compassion. The Dark Ages were dark, and the Revolution followed on its heels."

"We had a dark period," says Phoebe. "Ever heard of slavery?"

"No," I say. "Could you explain?"

Phoebe hits me, but Eleanor looks curious. "We never heard about what was happening overseas. I don't think Madame Arnaud had much of an interest in the colonies."

Phoebe's about to tell Eleanor about the slave times in early America, but the family's out the door and we rush to catch up. They check out of the hotel and make their way to the Métro. I'm impressed by how easily this family navigates the streets of Paris. Steven has a *carnet* of tickets that covers everyone, and soon we watch the tree-lined countryside during our hour-long train trip toward the palace where kings lived in such vulgar opulence that after a few centuries the populace rioted. And, as they say, heads rolled.

During the train ride, Steven pulls yet another book from his messenger bag, but this one isn't a glossy guidebook of the sites. It's a black volume, very old, with a leather cover with stamped golden floral designs. It looks like the kind of book that should be called a *tome*.

"What is that, Steven?" asks Phoebe's mother.

"I pulled it from the library—I mean, *our* library, the estate library—before we left. It looked interesting, so I thought I'd bring it."

"But it's so old, won't you damage it carrying it around?"

"It's ours. And I'll be careful."

"So what is it?"

"A book about secret societies," he says. "I shall rub my hands together with glee as I finally learn what on earth is going on with the Masons."

She laughs. "Oh, Steven, you haven't heard about the Internet? I thought you ran a web-based company!"

"Touché," he says. "It didn't seem fair to just Google it."

"All right, well, share any juicy bits with me," she says, leaning her head back in her seat.

"Don't close your eyes yet," he says. "Let me do the open-book-and-stab thing."

He opens the volume at random, and the pages look like they could crumble with a heavy page turn. The letters are small and embossed deeply, and a menagerie of wild-eyed beasts crawls the margins, rudimentary lions showing their teeth, and monkeys, and things I don't think exist.

"That's a creepy book," says Phoebe.

"Let me," says her mum, and she grins as she arbitrarily points her finger to a paragraph on the left-hand page.

"Oh dear, not too interesting," Steven says, skimming quickly, his eyes moving back and forth. "This is a society that worshipped a particular boulder in Scotland."

"For how long?" she asks. "I would think that would quickly prove unpromising."

"It was established in the fourth century, but who knows if they're still around," says Steven.

"I found a pebble once that seemed wise," I say.

"Why am I not surprised?" says Phoebe.

"All right, we'll try again," says Steven. He gently closes the book and opens it to another page, his finger pointing to the right-hand side.

"Aha!" he says after he reads for a few minutes. "This is better. I'm in the middle of a prophecy."

"Oh, I love those," says Phoebe's mum. "Read it."

"But it's all in Old English. I'll have to bluff my way through it. 'On a stronde the king doth slumber, and below the mede the dragon bataille the wicked brike with bisemare from yon damosel—' "

"That one could've come true already and we wouldn't even know it!" says Phoebe's mum.

"'—and the goodnesse undonne for she who bitrayseth. But an thee seche they of the ilke lykenes and lygnage, for a long tyme abide thee to come thereby the thre wyghts'—I'm just making it up here pronunciation-wise," says Steven.

"I'm good now; you can stop," says Phoebe's mum.

"It might as well be in Russian," Phoebe says.

"Is there anything in there about secret societies in Grenshire? That'd be fun," Phoebe's mum says.

He opens the book to the back. "There's no index."

I look over his shoulder. Too bad. That might be very helpful information, *beyond* helpful, really.

He continues reading out snippets from the book until even I lose interest and stare out the window. It turns out sometimes secrets are only interesting to those who hold them.

The station is in the small village of Versailles, and we pull in to see lines of tired people waiting to board the train; they must have spent the night after their long day of sightseeing. The village is just another French town. You can't see the palace from the station. We get off the train and Phoebe's mum buys a fizzy drink from a vending machine. She drops a single euro coin and it rolls under the machine. Tabby lies flat on the ground before anyone can stop her to extend her little arm underneath to retrieve it.

"Gross, Tabby!" says Phoebe.

"Thank you, sweetie," says her mum, hugging Tabby when she stands, presenting the coin proudly. She wipes invisible public-space germs off both of them afterward as Steven stands there, smiling.

The family checks into their small boutique hotel, placing

their bags on a faux Louis XIV dresser. Phoebe's mum takes Tabby into the bathroom while Steven and Eleanor look out one window at the unassuming view and Phoebe and I look out the other. It's a nice day, with the kind of hefty clouds painters love. We see a quiet street with other homes and a couple walking their bikes next to each other so they can chat without the wind taking their words. It's nowhere near as noisy as Paris was.

Phoebe's mum comes out for her purse, brushes her own and Tabby's hair, and reapplies lip gloss. "Ready to go?" she asks.

At Tabby's insistence, we take the rickety, glacially slow elevator down to the lobby although it's faster to take the stairs. She likes the cagelike effect when the metal grille gets pulled across the door. Then we're back in the sunshine, making our way on foot to the palace itself, thronged with people from all nations. It takes about ten minutes to start to see a sudden swarm of people and the palace rising up ornately. It seems everyone arrives from the train, and our detour to the hotel means that they all beat us here. The lines to enter are massive, and I hear Phoebe's mum groan. They snake around, hundreds of people taking photos while they wait.

The chateau's exterior is enormous, almost impossible to describe, and I watch Phoebe's dad try without luck to get its entirety into his camera viewfinder. He takes a picture of his wife and Tabby and about half of the hulking structure. Like the Arnaud Manor, it's shaped as if one side of a rectangle is missing, stretching long in the main body, with two wings that flank it on either side. It's luxurious in its large windows and grand architecture. Gold glints, even at the exterior, which is prey to weather. Looking up, I see a row of statues at the roofline, former kings wearing their chain mail and swords, with squat crowns perched on their heads.

I remember this, the monumental black and gold gates guarding the front cobblestoned courtyard. I can recall my mum's coo of amazement. I stand for a minute in the memory: my father—who hates crowds—walking with his shoulders up around his ears while Mum twirled around a bit like a princess in a movie to see all sides of the vista presented for her enjoyment.

"Okay?" asks Phoebe.

She must see the pain on my face; I've never been good at hiding my emotions.

"I'll be fine," I say.

"What is it?" asks Eleanor. Her good, strong face is instantly concerned for me. Sometimes I worry she has feelings for me; a few times a hug with her has turned a little too intense.

"I was here before with my parents," I say simply, and she nods compassionately.

"I'm so sorry. I do remember you saying that."

I look again toward the courtyard and my parents aren't there: no beloved humping of shoulders from discomfort, no girlish twirling. It's just hundreds of strangers who trample the courtyard, brought here by the chance to see golden interiors, French finery, velvets and brocades—and the place where one family pushed it too far.

History marches on. Touring Versailles can be done in one day, but hurriedly. Phoebe's parents are smart; they've decided to tour the grounds today and come back tomorrow for the palace interior.

At the side yard—if you can use the word *yard* to describe

literal acreage—we tour the Orangerie, where the exotic orange trees were planted in a parterre, a totally artificial garden form. I notice, as I always do, the ghosts. They always seem so caught up in their own repetitious behavior. I'm not sure who else they're aware of. If they bothered to look around, would they wave at me? Coo at Tabby in her buggy?

"We could do this, couldn't we?" asks Phoebe's mum, pointing to young orange trees in boxes and the swirl of grass cut in floral patterns.

Steven smiles. "So long as we have a good measuring tape to keep all the lines straight," he says. He takes a bunch of photographs of the elevated beds in their intricate patterns.

As we walk around, he regularly reads aloud from the guidebook, which probably would've driven me crazy if it were *my* dad, but somehow it's okay when someone else's does it.

The Grand Canal stretches its wide ribbon of water. In the reign of Louis XIV, Phoebe's stepdad informs us, naval "battles" were staged here with cannon fire and ships literally sinking as the nobles, heady on wine and bonbons, cheered and laughed.

The canal is deep and man-made, its edges pristine concrete trimmed to perfection. "I'd love to swim laps here," says Phoebe. "You'd never have to turn at the end of the lane. The lane just . . . goes on."

Along the canal, statues are placed at regular intervals, like the ones in the backyard of the Arnaud Manor. Goddesses planning their next dalliance with humans, young men with muscular legs and laurel wreaths in their hair. They are each different but brought into compliance by standing atop duplicate stone podiums. Everything at Versailles falls into line: there is strict attention to detail here. No plant can flourish unpruned, no tree can simply grow—it has to be adjusted to grow a certain way, to match the other trees.

"Here's a good anecdote," says Phoebe's stepdad, one finger in the guidebook keeping his place as he reads aloud. " 'The king would stroll through, and upon his return an hour later expect a completely different configuration of flora, which servants would work feverishly to make come true, digging out old flowers and hurriedly embedding new ones already in bloom.' "

"Busywork," says Phoebe's mum. "Quite the honey-do list."

There are outdoor "rooms" off the main walkway, set off by thick hedges. In one of these, Phoebe's family pauses. We're surrounded by an arcade of trellised flowers, and in the center of the private area—for once, we have lost the other tourists and have this space to ourselves—is the gigantic statue of a man, or half a man, really, struggling to emerge from the ground.

It's shocking, this sculpture: his face is twisted in distress, his beard a sinuous uncoiling mass that shows how much he moves, wrestles, struggles. He is clawing his way out of the earth.

"It's the giant Enceladus," Phoebe's stepdad informs us, quickly reading. "He was buried by a mountain brought down upon him, and this sculpture shows him struggling to the surface."

"Good Lord," says Eleanor. "Whoever would bring a mountain down upon a giant?"

"Maybe another giant?" asks Phoebe.

"Wonder what he did to deserve it," I say. I look at his face: Was he truly a victim? Or was he the recipient of a blow he deserved? Eleanor lingers to look at the statue, bending down to examine it across the water of its moat until she is almost hidden from view.

I notice Phoebe's family has left the grove, so Phoebe and I start to follow them.

"Eleanor, we're leaving!" I call. Then something makes me blink.

The very air seems to change.

It's like the light gets brighter . . . or is it dimmer? It's wavering. The light falters and then stills.

I see a woman ahead of us in a vintage gown. Her elaborate silver skirts extend straight out from her hips as far as her arms would be able to stretch, before they take the corner to fall to the ground. Her dark hair is in one of those absurd upsweeps that tower far above her head. She strolls with a man in equally lavish breeches with golden embroidery and a white shirt with dangling sleeves. They're clearly historical reenactors roaming the grounds. We can't see their faces from behind.

"Etienne, *mon chéri*," she says to him, and leans her head back for a long, lingering kiss from him. It lingers so much they stop walking and face each other. It's then that I get a good look at her profile, as does Phoebe.

Holy crap.

It's Madame Arnaud.

I thought we killed her.

Phoebe throws herself into my arms. "Oh my God," she says. Frantically, I pull her backward, and we huddle near the arcade. There's no escape route except the one they block. I crane around to look for Eleanor but don't see her. We can't do anything except hide and wait for them to leave.

Phoebe shakes, holding my hand tightly.

Please don't let them see us.

The woman smiles at her lover. She and Etienne nibble at each other with the slowness of lovers who don't know they're being watched.

"But we killed her," Phoebe says, her voice breathy and terrified.

I try to understand what I see.

"I wonder . . ." I whisper, ". . . if it's her ghost, playing out the happy days of her youth."

"But they're not filmy," she protests.

She's right. They're solid-looking people, such that I had originally thought them actors. There's nothing transparent about them at all.

The woman's long neck is reminiscent of one I already admire, slender and graceful, and she gives the man kisses I, too, would like to receive. She's a dead ringer for Phoebe—Phoebe with dark coloring rather than her auburn hair. It's Madame Arnaud, before she became evil. She's just a contented woman in a beautiful gown on a sunny day with her lover. No one would ever guess, looking at her now, the horrible acts she was capable of.

Etienne's hands span Madame Arnaud's waist and begin to creep up her bodice. How far will these lovers go, not knowing their display is forever recorded for those who can see them? He walks her backward to the arcade a few feet away from us and tilts his head down for an extended kiss. I can almost see her legs collapse under her, through the voluminous skirts.

Phoebe and I, still hunched on the ground, crawl backward away from them. I scan the garden for Eleanor but can't see her. Thank God there are tons of flowers and thank God Madame Arnaud's distracted.

All we can do is wait.

"Could this really be the same person?" Phoebe whispers. Madame Arnaud's face is alight with pleasure. She looks happy, beautiful, untouched by the deeds she will later commit.

"Ah, Etienne," I hear her murmur drift, wholly French in its rich syllables.

How long is this going to continue?

And how far?

If they sink to the grass and get on eye level with us, the jig is up. We'd have to take advantage of their surprise to bolt out of the grove as fast as we could.

"Phoebe, we should be prepared to run," I whisper to her. "They might—"

I'm interrupted by a peal of laughter, a glassy chime from Madame Arnaud. She pushes down her skirts from Etienne's hands as he steps back, abashed.

"*Va plus lentement pour le prix,*" says Madame Arnaud, showing her bright teeth, and some portion of my brain, schooled for so many years in French class, translates: "Go more slowly for the prize."

She slings a single arm around his neck, gives one emphatic kiss on the lips, and dances away, casting a delicious look behind her as she goes. Phoebe and I are left with his aftermath, his scrubbing his face with his hands, his low laugh of appreciation.

"*J'aurai ce prix,*" he says. *I will have that prize.*

After he leaves, we call and search for Eleanor and realize she must've left earlier with Phoebe's family. We catch up with them, relieved to see they're just walking, with Madame Arnaud and Etienne nowhere in sight.

"What happened?" Eleanor asks. "I couldn't find you."

"You didn't see Madame Arnaud?" Phoebe asks incredulously. "You had to have walked right past her!"

"Madame Arnaud was *here*?" Eleanor stops short. "But . . . my God . . . she's still alive?" Her forehead develops a network of wrinkles above her large eyes. Her hand leaps to her heart.

"Her ghost, we think," I say quickly. "With a man named Etienne."

"Then you believe she remains dead?"

"She better be," Phoebe says grimly.

"She's a strange version of herself," I say. "She's flirty and *happy*."

"That doesn't sound like her at all," says Eleanor, still frowning.

"She was kissing him," I say. "There was nothing scary about it. Other than who it was."

"They made out, then they left," says Phoebe.

"Did she say she was off to murder some children?" asks Eleanor in a brittle tone. I can tell she doesn't approve of our relaxed attitude where Madame Arnaud is concerned.

Silence falls. There's no good answer for that one.

Eleanor straightens up. "Well, let's just hope it was a distinctly onetime honor. We'll stay away from the grove and its horrid, buried-alive statue."

"Agreed," I say. "So where are we all headed?"

"To the Hameau," Eleanor says. "Tabby is being a quite good girl, and the family stopped to eat a snack on the grass. You were gone awhile."

"Why didn't you come back and get . . ." Phoebe's voice trails off. She and I both know what Eleanor was thinking: that we deliberately lost the group, that the people who were kissing were us.

"I did try to find you," says Eleanor. "I concluded you didn't want to be found."

It's awkward, because what she says could've easily been true. "Not the case," I say.

"What's the Hameau?" asks Phoebe, changing the subject. She's blushing.

"It's Marie-Antoinette's play farm," says Eleanor, "as your stepfather explains it. The queen wanted to get away from the court and live as simple countryfolk do. She kept lambs and a dairy, but she perfumed the lambs and milked the cows with a porcelain bucket. She couldn't quite get it right."

"It's actually kind of cool," I say. "There are no animals now, but it's like visiting a really calm, really fetching farm."

Phoebe tries to hide the fact that she's laughing.

"What?" I ask.

"I've never known a guy who used the word *fetching* before," she says.

"I'm British, what can I say?"

"You're not just British, you're calm and fetching," she says in a deep voice.

"Don't mock me," I warn.

She flashes a huge smile at me. When she throws her head back like that, her auburn hair tumbling back from her strong face, I just want to . . . I just want to touch her more.

"Eleanor, do you find Miles calm?" she asks.

"As calm as a millpond," says Eleanor promptly, and I throw her a look of admiration. How'd she come up with that so fast?

"And do you find him . . . *fetching?*"

Eleanor blushes, but again responds quickly. "He indeed fetches many things. He is an excellent carrier of goods."

We all snicker. It feels good after everything we've been through. Just being away from the Arnaud Manor is its own holiday, let alone visiting one of the most impressive estates on earth.

Acting on some instinct I can't explain, I run toward Tabby. A kid like that should be playing chase. She's walking by herself, having finally let go of her mum's hand. We're in the long, tree-lined avenue that parallels the Grand Canal. Every tree perfectly placed, everything just so for a king. I pummel toward her at full speed and at the last second, I veer to the side. As I fly past, I look at her face. Will she pick up my energy and surge after me?

She doesn't see me. She's lost in some toddler reverie. I imagine to her these trees are monumental and will appear in her dreams for years to come.

"Will no one chase me?" I implore.

That's all it takes for Phoebe, and instantly she's at me, so I dart into the trees and thread back and forth through them like a human needle going through fabric. Phoebe whoops and nearly tags me a dozen times; she's fast, but I'm faster. It isn't until I round back and look that I see that *Eleanor* is running, too.

She's outside her comfort zone, her skirt impeding her progress, and her hair falling out of . . . a braid? I hadn't noticed she'd adopted that hairstyling, something a step down from her typical tight bun, and I see how pretty she is when her face is open and she's outside herself.

I circle back around and let her tag me; I have to. Then Phoebe and I are chasing her, and I glance at Phoebe so we lope a little, slow our pace, so the chase continues.

"I can't breathe," Eleanor calls back to us.

"No rest for the wicked," I shout back and she performs a clever maneuver, dashing behind a tree at the last minute so we have no choice but to run past her.

"Darn her," says Phoebe. "She's using intelligence to compensate for her lack of speed."

"I have speed!" Eleanor protests from behind us. She staggers a few steps toward us, then bends over to put her hands on her knees. Have athletes done this throughout time? Is there something in our genetic code that causes us to adopt that exact posture? She takes heaving breaths while I grin at Phoebe.

"We need to get you some running shoes," says Phoebe.

"Intriguing idea," I say.

"I could never wear those ghastly things."

I pretend to rear back at the insult she's offered both Phoebe and me. "You're becoming more outspoken every day," I comment.

"The colors are just so garish. I prefer brown and black, thank you very kindly."

"The thing is, brown and black just aren't very *fast*," says Phoebe cheekily.

Eleanor plops down onto the ground, her legs spread out in front of her. The casualness of her stance is stunning. The Eleanor of a few weeks ago could have never sat so informally. And as I watch, she blinks hastily as she looks up at Phoebe and then at me.

"I've never done such a thing," she says. Her voice is raw, tear filled.

Phoebe instantly kneels down to her and takes her hand. I remain standing, feeling awkward. I hate it when people cry. I never know what to do.

"What do you mean?" asks Phoebe softly.

"I've never run. I've never chased, never felt that— that playfulness."

"I'm so sorry," says Phoebe.

"My life has been so sober and dark," says Eleanor. "Even without Madame Arnaud's influence, I still would have lived a constricted life. No one expects someone like me to run through the trees."

Phoebe gives her a big hug, and I wander off to give them some privacy. The random fate of what family you're born into! For some it's a carnival of good luck and for others the desperately unfair dungeon below the fairgrounds.

I look back at Tabby and her parents, far behind us after the spurt of our racing. She's so small and helpless at this distance. She was born into the carnival that morphed into the dungeon. Poor little kid.

CHAPTER TWO

Daily, Marie-Antoinette selected her outfit from a book entitled *The Wardrobe Book of the Queen*. In it, the gowns were described and a small sample of the fabric included on the page. Marie would take a pin from a pincushion and prick her day's choice.

—www.historicalcostuming.com

When I turn my head and look forward again, I see Madame Arnaud with Etienne. She's wearing a different dress although he appears the same. They're doing exactly what we did, chasing through the trees. Her bright scarlet dress makes a really pretty (dare I say *fetching*?) sight among the stark black trees. She's fast, like Phoebe, and Etienne is doing something interesting: he succeeds at tagging her, but she keeps going. Their game has different rules.

Phoebe catches up to me and we study the frivolity of the ghosts in the distance. She remarks drily, "Can you believe this is really the same person?"

Etienne finally seizes Madame Arnaud and kisses her. Once again, we're stuck watching a PDA that we didn't sign on for.

"Hey, where'd my family go? Where's Eleanor?" asks Phoebe. She cranes to look behind us. They're gone. Did they peel off the pathway?

The light has changed, and the trees appear diminished. Wait, that's not quite right. They're not just diminished, they're *smaller* and thinner. I whirl around and look; everything is the same but slightly altered. The water in the canal is bluer. The dirt pathway is less well traveled, not as defined. It's starting to dawn on me . . . this path hasn't been traveled by millions of tourists; it's only been traveled by hundreds of courtiers.

I look at Phoebe's face and get confirmation. She's looking around wildly and starts to run back down the path. "Tabby!" she screams.

I run to her. She whirls around to grab my arms, panicked.

"I think we went back in time," I say. "We're not seeing Madame Arnaud's ghost . . . I think we've gone back to the time when she was *alive*. That's why she's not filmy."

Phoebe goes pale. Well, paler. "Miles, that's crazy."

"You were thinking the same thing—look at the trees!"

"I know," she says, "I *know*, but it's just so crazy."

"I can't think of any other explanation. We're just . . . we're in the past."

"But no one else came with us?"

I pause and shake my head. "Just us. Like in the grove. Maybe they were too far away."

"But Eleanor was near us last time."

"Why didn't she come with us, then?" I say.

"I'm asking *you*!"

"Maybe we're . . ." my voice trails off. What am I trying to say? We're special? Different?

"Yeah," she says hollowly. "Maybe we're 'lucky.' So how do we get back?"

We both look at the people who seem to have brought us here, but they're not paying any attention to us. Etienne has now positioned Madame Arnaud on a bench near the canal, kneeling before her and pushing up her skirts. She's not stopping him this time. It's getting extreme pretty quickly.

"It's all going to be fine," I say hoarsely. "It's mad, but it's all right. I mean . . ."

"*What?*" says Phoebe. "How is this going to be all right?"

"We get to see Versailles when it's still happening."

"Are you kidding? I would take a documentary over this *any day.*"

"We might see royalty," I say. "We could deliver some advice to Marie-Antoinette!"

Begrudgingly, because I can tell she's trying not to panic, she manages to smile. "Yo, make sure everyone has enough bread, lady!"

"Ah, good rally, lass!" I say, enjoying the blush that rises on her face for me calling her such a name.

"Avoid snarky comments about cake if at all possible!" she adds, turning her face so I don't see her pleasure.

We go silent. There may be danger here for us, even if Madame Arnaud hasn't turned bad yet. And how *will* we get back? If we don't return soon to keep an eye on Tabby, Phoebe's going to lose her mind.

"Are you all right?" I ask.

"I don't know."

We stand there at a loss. Another couple approaches, this time two men in their finery, wearing high heels and their hats the size of suitcases. Phoebe and I step off the path and into the trees. The men are solid, living.

"Oh my God, we're totally in another century," whispers Phoebe. "I don't think I like it."

They speak an antiquated, fast-paced babble of French,

but I'm fairly fluent and catch a few phrases here and there. ". . . with everyone off to Paris, we may explore where we couldn't before . . ." and ". . . our chance to see the chateau . . ."

I frown. Was the palace ever deserted?

"What are they saying?" Phoebe asks.

"It sounds like the court has gone off to Paris and just a few people remain at Versailles," I say.

"That's odd," says Phoebe. "I bet my stepdad knows why."

After they pass, we get back on the path and I look toward the palace in the distance. What king lives there? Does a pleasant queen stroll languidly inside, or a doomed and sad one?

"Should we continue on toward the Hameau?" I ask. It will mean trying to skirt past the lovers. "Do you think your family is still walking in their time period?"

Phoebe doesn't answer.

It's eerie to think they're here, just hundreds of years later. When we return to the present, will they have lingered where we left them or will they already be at the Hameau? Or maybe days will have passed for them and we'll miss their voyage back to England.

Or maybe . . . we'll never leave.

We stay shielded by the trees while we pass Madame Arnaud and Etienne, still kissing on the bench . . . and perhaps a lot more, based on the grunts and sighs. I try not to look.

We walk for about five minutes, when the air starts to shimmer. That's not quite right. It's not that it shimmers, it *changes*. Almost like the way it feels when the sun goes behind a cloud . . . and when it comes back out.

"Thank God," says Phoebe. "I think we're back."

The path beneath our feet is wider, harder-packed dirt now. The sculpted trees are much larger, the water in the canal a different shade of blue.

Phoebe bolts forward, running to find her family.

"The good news is, our trips never last longer than, what, twenty minutes? Half an hour?" I call out as my strides bring us neck and neck.

"Our *trips*? Is that what we're calling it?"

"You got something better?"

Soon enough, we see the group: Tabby, her mum and stepdad, and Eleanor. When we draw level, Eleanor tries to avert her head from us. I see that her eyes are red. She's been crying, pretty hard.

"Eleanor!" I say in shock. "What happened?"

"Nothing," she says, her voice filled with the sadness she's hiding.

"Everyone's okay?" I ask. I look around. The family's now a bit ahead of us, stopped in front of the Grand Trianon, another chateau. Monarchs are never satisfied with just *one* palace on the grounds. Tabby's back in her buggy, and everyone looks calm.

"Yes!" says Eleanor. "Everyone's fine."

"You're not," I say.

"Miles!" says Phoebe. She shakes her head at me.

"Of course I am," says Eleanor. "Let's stick with the family, shall we?" She plasters on an artificial smile and walks off briskly. From behind, her skirt twitches because of how fast and determined she's walking. I have the feeling I did something wrong.

"Miles," whispers Phoebe. "She thinks you and I snuck off to be alone."

"Seriously? Is that what she's really thinking? So we should tell her what happened!"

"That might hurt even more," she says. "Imagine how that feels for her."

Staring ahead at Eleanor, I mull it over. For some reason, she's not tripping with us. It makes sense that Phoebe's family doesn't—but Eleanor should. Why doesn't she?

"Just act like nothing happened," says Phoebe.

"But . . ." I stop short. Phoebe's right. There really isn't any way to talk about it without hurting her feelings.

"And nothing did, really."

"Nothing happened? We went back in time!"

"Yeah. And we saw two men walk by. *Wow!*"

I stare at Phoebe's eyes, unsure what's going on. Is it too scary for her to think about what it would've meant if we'd become lost in time—forever separated from her family? Is she genuinely protecting Eleanor's feelings?

"Good point," I concede. "All right. But I wish we could make her feel better."

We continue along with Eleanor and the family, passing the Petit Trianon on our left, yet a third palace. Marie-Antoinette took it over for her own, Phoebe's dad tells us, after Madame de Pompadour died before getting a chance to live there.

"Madame de Pompadour," Phoebe says, raising a single eyebrow. "That can't be her real name."

Then we reach the Hameau and its familiar outcropping of buildings around the lake: a waterwheel at the mill that seems diminutive and adorable rather than an actual source of power, the tower of a half-sized lighthouse, other rustic buildings that look medieval and half-timbered.

Eleanor breaks out into a gentle smile, and I'm relieved she seems to be over her sadness.

"I could totally live here," says Phoebe. "I'd just lie on my back and stare at the clouds."

"I'd be happy here, too," says Eleanor wistfully.

An irony occurs to me, that maybe Marie-Antoinette thought the same, that the placid farm with its manicured lawns could resurrect a happiness in someone so bruised by circumstances. In fact, she had been here at the Hameau, reading in the rock grotto, when word came to her that a mob was on the march from Paris to seize her and her husband, Louis XVI. She had hurried back up to the chateau to locate him, but he was out hunting. The events of that day must have been so panicked, the last day of true serenity—if indeed she found it here. She and her family, including the returned Louis, had walled themselves up in the palace, but still the mob attacked at night while they were in bed and captured them.

I lift my gaze to the meadow on the other side of the lake, where I see what must be Marie herself, with a girl of about seven, her daughter Marie-Thérèse. I look around quickly, but this isn't a trip. Their bodies are somewhat transparent, and I still see tons of visitors with cell phones and holding up their iPads to take pictures, like protestors holding picket signs.

Marie-Antoinette wears a gauzy white dress with a blue sash, and a floppy straw hat. I think it's the outfit from a painting that caused a big sensation when it was unveiled. Because the gown was so loose fitting and non-regal, it didn't match up to the stiff, brocaded, jeweled gowns expected of queens. I remember my mother showing me this on the computer before we came here. The portrait had to be re-painted, with more suitable couture.

The girl wears a similar white gown. She carries a pair of scissors and bends down now and then to cut a stalk of a perfect flower, which she lays carefully in the basket her mother carries. Their sense of leisure is palpable. This girl's pleasure in her mother's company is, too. Roomfuls of noblemen and duchesses couldn't make her smile the same way the butterfly does, as she lightly runs after it.

Phoebe and Eleanor are watching, too. "What happened to her, the little one?" asks Phoebe hoarsely.

"She lived," I say. I don't tell her the rest of what I know: that she was imprisoned with her family at the Tuileries and then the Conciergerie that Phoebe's stepdad so delighted in visiting. That she had been part of an escape plan, a carriage ride that brought the family to the borders of Austria, only to be betrayed, some say, by the scent of her mother's perfume.

And of course, that she was orphaned by the guillotine, and in her prison chamber likely heard its blade plummet onto the necks of her father and, months later, her mother— each time, the horrible roar of the crowd joyful to see them killed.

That she was separated from her brother and could hear him through the hallways screaming as his captors tormented him. That when the news passed to her that he had died under mysterious circumstances, she must have known it was only her luck to be born as a girl that had spared her from the same fate. Her brother could have been king, but she would have been passed over for her uncle in line for the throne.

All that terrible fate, all that agony, is entirely unforetold as she walks with her mother in the meadow, cutting blooms as they please, the scissors' cuts neat and clean as that of the guillotine blade her parents will meet.

"She lived?" Phoebe repeats dubiously. She's been watching my face the whole time.

I look over at Eleanor. Does she know this history? But she's not listening, looking over at the two Maries, her face concerned. She's used to worrying about children.

"Yes," I say abruptly. "They even tried to reinstall her later after Napoléon's empire fell."

Still, I think Phoebe can tell I'm not saying everything I know. "Then I'll just enjoy watching her cut flowers," she says softly.

We trail Phoebe's family around the outcropping of nine thatched-roof cottages that constitute the farm. Phoebe's stepdad snorts when he reads from the guidebook that the dairy is called the "Dairy of Cleanliness."

"I'm guessing she had a wet nurse instead of nursing her own babies if she thought milking was 'clean,'" says Phoebe's mum.

"And get this: she had porcelain cups made, molded *from her breasts*, to drink the milk from."

"Well," says Phoebe's mum. "I'm sure men enjoyed that."

Inside we see marble walls, not the typical vista for cows. The Swiss cows who produced creamy milk are no longer here. I imagine the Parisian mob slaughtered them and enjoyed steak for the first time in their lives. We see the dovecote, essentially a chicken coop the size of a single-family home, and the Marlborough Tower. Phoebe's stepdad points to the worm-ridden wood selected for the buildings to make them look instantly old at the time they were built, and the way a craftsman had painted cracks on the plaster between the beams, manipulated to look rustic for the queen's eye.

The queen's house and billiard room are accessed by an outdoor winding wooden staircase that is rickety and fragile, with some steps completely missing. It also looks madly cool. I want to climb it. Tabby wants to, too, but there's a short picket fence around the base to stop people. None of these buildings except the marble dairy can be entered.

I wink at Phoebe and Eleanor and point at the door at the top of the staircase.

Their reaction? *Textbook.*

Eleanor shakes her head, and Phoebe grins.

I hold out my hand to Eleanor, but she shakes her head again.

"No?" I ask.

"I don't think so."

"Why not? We won't hurt anything, and it'd be so cool to see! They always lock up the good stuff."

"I like it when we all six stay together."

"I do, too, but just for a few minutes," says Phoebe.

"Please let's keep together," says Eleanor. "It's not completely safe here. You two saw Madame Arnaud!"

"Literally, just for a minute?" I plead.

She answers by walking away. Phoebe's family has already drifted along to the next building.

"I'm game," says Phoebe. "But make it quick. I don't want to hurt Eleanor."

"In and out," I promise.

We have ways of getting in. It's cool to see the opulence inside, a faint haze of dust floating above these objects: grand settees, porcelain flowerpots with the queen's *MA* initials. We walk in awe past these once-loved items, now accessible only to museum staff. We dart across the second-floor gallery connecting the billiard room to the queen's house. Let's see: grand salon, a dining room . . . but no bedroom. Drat. I had the wrong building, didn't I? These weren't the queen's sleeping quarters.

"Looking for something in particular?" Phoebe asks.

"I was just wondering where the queen slept," I say innocently.

"Wait a minute . . . Is that why you were so adamant on getting in?"

"Nothing whatsoever at all to do with it." I look at her blankly until she slides into a knowing smile.

"You had plans?"

I reach out and touch one of those slightly curling locks of her auburn hair. Very, very gently, I tug it. She takes a step closer to me.

Our eyes lock.

I could almost swim in those green depths, with the darker flecks around her pupil, widening even as I look. Something in her eyes pulls me in, makes me forget everything else in the world. I inch my fingers up that same lock of hair to get a new grasp, and tug again. She comes closer.

We're almost touching, but not quite. Her lips part, but I don't move. I want to kiss her so badly, but I also love this moment of suspense when we both know we're going to but haven't yet. I slowly incline my head toward her, and she tips her face up, glowing, beautiful, touched by the half-light from the clouded windows.

She closes her eyes and I study the way her lashes, long

and honey-colored, flutter slightly as she waits. I let go of her hair and move my hand to her jaw. I take one step closer and feel her against my chest.

She opens her eyes and looks up, wondering why I'm leaving her hanging. My own eyelids lower in response and I bend to her, our lips about to touch.

She runs her hands over my arms up to my shoulders in a smooth caress that is possibly the best thing I've ever felt.

Then I hear it.

"Miles, come to me."

A plaintive voice I haven't heard in a long time.

"Miles, I can't stand it . . . I can't handle this—I miss you—"

I'm in Gillian's bedroom, which looks like a stage set with a spotlight on her. *Gillian* with her golden hair in that short punk hairdo, wearing layers of black clothing, her eyes outlined in dark, thick eyeliner.

She's sitting on the floor with a candle set before her. It's the only source of light, which explains the dramatic lighting. She's pulled the curtains so I can barely see the two friends there with her. God, I'd forgotten about them: Lily and the one that I thought never liked me. I struggle to come up with her name.

Avery.

That's right.

Avery, Lily, and Gillian, sitting with their legs crossed, forming a rough circle around a thick red candle sitting in a tea saucer. All of them are crying.

"I want to talk to you," Gillian says in a voice so raw that I instantly kneel next to her to take her in my arms. It doesn't work. My arms go through her. "I can't believe I'll never see you again."

"Send us a sign, Miles?" pleads Avery. "Make the candle flicker?"

They're doing a séance for me.

No, no . . .

I lean forward until my forehead touches the black and gray carpet, but that's just an illusion my mind feeds me— because I can't touch anything other than Phoebe.

Gillian's so beautiful—and so destroyed. I've never heard her sob like this before. "I love you so much," she says. "I just can't believe that you're gone. Miles, come to me. Say something."

Gillian was with me when I died. I'd been driving and she was buckled up in the passenger seat. The car had drifted into a ditch and rolled, and I fell out and hit my head on a rock. I hadn't been wearing my seat belt for some reason . . . why not?

Gillian had scrambled out of the car and come to me, there stranded against the rock, my head dripping with gore, blood streaming so heavily I couldn't see until she wiped my forehead for me. She had sat with me, holding my hand and telling me over and over, "You're going to be fine."

But I had heard her frantic call on her cell phone as she lost control and told whatever emergency responder was on the other end of the call that she could see a gash in my skull and that she didn't know what to do, how to keep what was inside, inside.

I remember thinking *I've lost my mind . . . literally* before my eyes drifted closed on that sight of beautiful Gillian willing the world to move faster, to get an ambulance to her boyfriend before he died on that remote country road, surrounded by wildflowers and beauty on the other side of a bridge.

"I'm here," I say to her, lifting my head so our eyes are on the same level. "Can you hear me, Gillian?"

She continues crying. She hasn't heard.

I inhale and look around the circle at the half-lit faces. No one sees me. Lily and Avery are exchanging a glance between each other, like a how-long-do-we-let-this-go-on? kind of look.

"Gillian!" I say urgently, right in her face.

I've seen Phoebe successfully reach Tabby after many attempts, after a lot of practice: but only Tabby. We've learned—me, Phoebe, and Eleanor—that the living aren't all capable of connecting with us. Only special people can, like Tabby.

But I'll keep trying. Maybe Gillian *is* capable. It seems if she's holding a séance, if she's called me to her, she's as receptive as she ever could be. She *wants* to hear from me and in some way expects to; what better moment could there be?

I reach out to try to touch her cheek; that had worked with Phoebe and Tabby. My hand hovers over her skin and . . . penetrates it. She doesn't react.

I feel the tug at my chest that signals another arrival.

It's Phoebe.

She arrives, standing in the center of the circle. If she were really there, her boot-cut jeans would catch fire from the candle. She looks around, bewildered. "Miles, where are we?"

"We're back in Grenshire," I say. "This is Gillian, my . . ."

I gesture toward Gillian, her face now ruined by crying, the mascara blotched all around her eyes. Lily has given her a tissue, but Gillian's erratic wipe at her eyes only moved the makeup around, not off.

Phoebe sinks to her knees between Lily and Avery, and

now all three of them stare worriedly at Gillian. Real girl, ghost girl, real girl. Phoebe is only slightly less vibrant than the living girls, but with the contrast I can see the paleness, her insubstantiality.

"This was your girlfriend," says Phoebe.

I nod.

"And she's trying to talk to you."

"She's trying, and I'm trying, but we're not connecting."

I brace myself, waiting for Phoebe's reaction. She'll be angry? Jealous? From her perspective, I left her hanging to come see Gillian. We were about to kiss, and here I am trying to talk to my old girlfriend.

Phoebe's eyes fill with tears. "I can't imagine how she feels," she says. "Losing you. My God."

I look over at Gillian, now hyperventilating and trying to regain her breath. Her body heaves out of control. She really loved me. And . . . I loved her.

"Unreal," I say, and again lower my forehead to the ground. Gillian's pain is almost unbearable.

I feel Phoebe's arm stretch across my back. Thank God that she and I can touch. She's literally all I have now.

"I'm so sorry," she whispers.

I've never been the crying sort, although I cried when I told Phoebe I was dead. Our huge epiphany. Now tears prickle at my eyes, but I think I can school myself to not let them spill.

"Gillian?" says Avery quietly. "I think this isn't working." Beside her, Lily nods, her face wet with tears.

"We all miss him, too. Not the way you do, but we miss him. We can try again, but I don't think he's coming today," says Lily.

Gillian nods. She sits there staring into space as the other girls blow out the candle and put it back on her dresser. They open up her curtains and let the muted sunshine of an over-cast England afternoon back into the room.

"What do you want to do?" asks Avery.

"I want to make him a cake," says Gillian. "I want to make him a glorious chocolate cake. With seventeen candles."

"We'll help you," says Avery firmly. She waits a beat, then adds, "And believe me, girlfriend, we'll help you *eat* it."

Gillian lets out a weak laugh, exactly what Avery was an-gling for. Avery pulls her up to standing and the three girls hug together, tightly. I stand there watching them, feeling like I've done something wrong.

I let Gillian down. I was the jerk who got her to fall in love with me, and then I died.

"Miles?" asks Phoebe. "Do you want me to go back? I was just checking on you. You disappeared and I—"

One look at her stricken face and I am wrenched in two. Phoebe's hurt in a whole different way. "Stay," I say. "I need you."

And instantly she's in my arms, and I nuzzle down into the vulnerable crook of her neck. God, she's incredible.

By the time I lift my head again, Gillian and her friends are gone. From downstairs, I hear the cupboard doors open-ing and closing, and them chatting. They're really making me a cake.

"Happy birthday, Miles," says Phoebe quietly.

"Thanks," I say. We disengage and I watch Phoebe look around at Gillian's room, the pottery she's painted in glossy black and the abstract art on watercolor paper. Again: black. Even before she became a griever, Gillian was attracted to the dark side. She wouldn't be caught dead in pink.

I cringe at my own thought.

She wouldn't be caught dead in anything, because she was smart enough to wear her seat belt. I start replaying the events of that day, trying to figure out what made me not click in. If I'd been driving a newer car, rather than my beat-up vintage Mini Cooper, the seat belt chime would've alerted me. I wonder briefly if my parents have thought about that, if they've wished they'd taken a firmer hand in helping me pick the car I bought with my own money. A newer model. A son still alive.

I'd still be going to school, hanging out with Gillian, still mad about her.

Instead, I fancy an American I never would have met if I hadn't died. Odd how the biscuit crumbles.

"Do you want to go downstairs?" Phoebe asks. "I feel kind of weird in her room when she's not here."

The eternal sense of trespassing, of eavesdropping. Will we ever get over it? Living people think they're alone and say and do the strangest things. True privacy is only for those who know who else is in the room with them. I'll forever be the observer who learns the unpleasant, unsavory things people thought were hidden.

"I don't know," I say. "I don't want to watch them make a cake I can't eat."

"Do you want to go back to Versailles?"

I wander over to the dresser, where there's a picture of me and Gillian, a candid snap Lily took. I'm clowning in the picture and I wish I had a normal face on. Is this all Gillian has to remember me by? The twisted face and bulging eyes? I guess we took a bunch of selfies that live in her phone.

Live. Pictures live, but I don't.

"Not right now," I say.

Phoebe nods. I see what she's feeling, it's written all over her face. She wants me to go back with her, *choose* her, but I'm also so confused by what just happened that I can't comfort her.

I'm in my girlfriend's bedroom. Is she my ex-girlfriend? We never broke up.

"I think I should go," Phoebe says. "You can stay and . . ." Her voice trails off.

Next to the framed photo there's a notebook I gave Gillian—it's about the size of a playing card, with a cool blackbird design on the cover. It fitted in her pocket and was for drawing scenes as she walked around. She's not carrying it with her anymore.

I flash to a memory: Gillian and me at the women's dress shop in Grenshire, which geared itself to those over the age of seventy. Gillian was trying to buy a hat without laughing. A black hat, of course. I don't even remember what she called it, but it had a name she knew. She didn't want to buy it because it was so expensive, but she pulled out that notebook and quickly sketched it.

If I could touch this notebook—but I can't—and turn the pages—which is now impossible for me—I'd see that hat again. For some reason, this brings the sense of loss for me to an indescribable high pitch. More so than seeing my girlfriend crying over a candle. Unbelievable. Over the thought of a drawing of a *hat*.

Phoebe hears the strange pattern of my breath as I struggle not to cry. She hesitantly hugs me from behind.

"Maybe we should both go back," she suggests.

I nod. "Okay."

"You're ready?"

I look one last time at the notebook and the photograph. I might never see them again. I might never see Gillian again. The girls had said they'd try to reach me again, but I've been warned now. I might be able to resist the pull. I will hear her voice and stay put. I don't want to go through this again. It's too hard.

"Yes," I say. "I'm ready."

CHAPTER THREE

Join our men's swim team in our first meet of the season, 3 P.M. today. Everyone to wear blue in memory of our fallen teammate.

—Emmons School Facebook page

We're back in France.

Phoebe wisely guided us, not to the queen's house, but to her family and Eleanor, now exploring the Temple of Love, a circular Greek temple with a statue inside its open-air layout.

"Are you quite finished?" asks Eleanor crisply, her face flushed.

I hang my head. I know what she thinks Phoebe and I have been doing this whole time, which honestly . . . we might have, if Gillian hadn't had her séance. I'm scared at the thought that I was so carefree. I had found a new normal in my death, had fallen into Phoebe with careless happiness.

"Whatever you think we were doing, we weren't," says Phoebe flatly.

"Well, what on earth was going on while I've been playing nursemaid to your sister?"

Phoebe softens. "Eleanor, oh . . . oh, dammit. You're not obliged to watch Tabby. You never need to think you have to be a babysitter."

"I'm unfamiliar with that term," says Eleanor stiffly.

"She means childminder," I say.

Everyone's feelings are getting hurt. Phoebe's sad I had a relationship with Gillian, and now Eleanor's sad I'm having one with Phoebe. "Sorry, Eleanor," I add. "We didn't mean to be gone so long." I pause, trying to find the right words. "My girlfriend Gillian, from when I was alive: she was holding a séance just now and called me to her. That's where we've been. Back at her house in Grenshire."

"Oh dear," Eleanor says. "I'm so sorry. I've lived through that, too. I barely remember it. But I recall the sting."

"Austin tried to reach you after you died?" asks Phoebe, referring to Eleanor's boyfriend when she was alive, back in the 1800s.

"Yes, he did, as well as my parents, many of their . . ."
She's frowning.

"Who were those people?" she asks herself.

I don't have an answer, but Phoebe jumps in. "What do you mean?"

"There were people always over at our cottage and they were very concerned to try to reach me after I died. But I don't know . . . why. I haven't thought about it for centuries."

"Maybe it has something to do with our situation," says Phoebe. "Whatever it is that keeps us as ghosts. The thing we have to accomplish to move on."

I instantly have a strange reaction: both excitement at the idea that I could find peace and move on from this half realm, and terror at the idea of everything ending. No more Phoebe. No more *me*.

"I'll try to remember more," says Eleanor. "In the meantime, you've just had a shock. Are you quite all right, Miles?"

I look away.

"His girlfriend was trying to reach him for his birthday," Phoebe says. "She and her friends were burning a candle and calling out for him. They didn't know we were there."

"That is a true shame," says Eleanor. "You want her to feel some peace."

"I did say good-bye to her at the time," I say grudgingly. "But maybe not in a way she understood."

"Really?" says Phoebe.

"She was on the phone with emergency personnel and they kept her on the line, but when I felt like I couldn't hold out any longer, I looked at her eyes and I thought she got it."

Eleanor and Phoebe are both silent.

"I couldn't talk," I explain. "I was physically incapable. But I thought she saw it in my eyes."

Phoebe sighs. "It seems like she might've missed that, Miles. And for sure, she misses *you*."

"Do you think she has anything to do with our situation?" Eleanor asks.

I shake my head emphatically. "No, I don't think so. She just had the misfortune of getting involved with someone who died."

"So did I," says Phoebe. She's joking, but I see the sadness behind it.

I try to imagine some alternate sixth-form college in my mind, the Emmons School of the Living and the Dead. At this school, I attend class with Gillian and Phoebe—and Eleanor's there, too. I have a hard time picturing her in the school uniform rather than the long black dress she wears with the crisp white apron covering it, and her old-time hobnailed boots. I work at it until I can visualize her, her hair loose over her shoulders rather than in a braid that dangles from under the cap she sometimes discards. She's the kind of girl who would get a lot of attention if she wasn't dressed so severely. Instead, she was born into a life of service in a wretched time period, and thought very little of herself.

It's frightening to think of Gillian and Phoebe walking into that classroom together. Would they hate or like each other? As a new ghost, I'd spent a lot of time trying to break up with Gillian after I met Phoebe—"breaking up" because I wasn't clear on the fact that I was dead.

I imagine one would be my girlfriend and the other just a friend, but how would I configure that? *Which one?*

Maybe neither. Enter Eleanor.

Crap. I shake my head. Life (uh, *death*) was already complicated enough without adding another romantic interest into the mix.

As I look at Phoebe, I realize that the intensity of my feelings for her have been special from the start. But if the circumstances of our being dead were taken away—if we were healthy people attending school together—would it be so intense? I don't have a way to judge.

And it's a useless puzzle anyway. I can't have Gillian and so it doesn't make sense to figure out if I would have chosen her or not.

"Enough of this," I say. "What's been happening while you were the nursemaid?" I wink at Eleanor to soften the blow of throwing her own words back at her.

Predictably, she blushes.

"Well," she says. "Everyone's okay. But I've noticed something."

"Yes?" Phoebe asks.

Eleanor turns to Phoebe. "Your family seems sadder than usual today. Something's bothering them."

★ ★ ★

Of course Phoebe wants to catch up with her family and see what's going on. They've been in sight the whole time, but now Phoebe scurries over to listen in on their conversation.

The Temple of Love isn't too exciting, but it does have about ten steps that let Tabby go up and down endlessly, giving her something to do while her parents talk. They're talking about what to do tonight, where to eat. Steven's found something in the guidebook, but he doesn't know if it's special enough.

"It'll be fine," says Phoebe's mum. "Well, it won't be fine, but it will be our version of fine."

Steven, Phoebe's stepdad, wraps his arms around her, standing at the top of the temple, and gives her a long heartfelt hug. Things won't ever be fine for them; Phoebe's with me now in the world of the dead.

"I wish I could take a picture of them," says Phoebe. "It's such a great picture how they're framed by the temple, but Tabby's too young to take it."

"She'll start taking their picture before you know it," I say.

"Yeah—but will they be hugging at the Temple of Love ever again? This is one of those once-in-a-lifetime shots."

"From what I've seen," says Eleanor, "so much time is spent taking these photographs and not enough time experiencing."

"Sorry if this sounds ignorant," says Phoebe, "but did you even have photography when you were alive?"

"I don't know," says Eleanor. "It certainly wasn't introduced at the Arnaud Manor. Perhaps in other, more lively cities."

Too soon, Tabby is bored with the steps. They resume walking, this time to the theater where Marie-Antoinette and favored courtiers performed in plays that showcased them to great advantage. It's a small space that seats about a hundred, but what's extraordinary are the painted backdrops, elaborate scenes of the French countryside.

"This looks a lot like a mural in the part of the Arnaud Manor where Madame Arnaud lived," says Eleanor.

There's a velvet rope to stop most people from climbing to the stage, but the three of us go up there without a second thought. We turn and look at Phoebe's family, and I wonder what it was like for Marie-Antoinette to perform in the light shed by gas lamps: her audience was receptive and flattering, but the wider audience of France was not. Perhaps too much was asked of her; she didn't have the fortitude to be a queen. She was just a young Austrian girl plucked too soon from her family, before she developed a true sense of herself.

The light dims and I wonder for a second if someone has adjusted the lighting on the stage. Then I notice no one else is here anymore; the tourists have vanished. The fabric on the seats in the audience is a different design and the wood gleams brighter.

Phoebe and I—but not Eleanor—have gone on another "trip."

To the side, in the wings where the curtain hangs pendulous in its golden rope, whispering starts. It's from people who weren't there before. Phoebe bolts across the stage and leaps back down to the main floor of the theater.

I don't need to hide: Madame Arnaud has never been able to see me.

She's not with Etienne. She's speaking with another woman, taller and stronger-looking than her, although they look somewhat similar. The other woman's hair is swept up into a grand cushion of starched and powdered hair and, unbelievably enough, a small model of a ship appears to be riding the white waves of her pompadour. The two women hold an intense, hushed discussion. Clearly in their time period they did not want to be overheard and had seized a moment in the unused theater to talk.

"She's stolen all that was meant to be mine," Madame Arnaud is saying, and my mind races to translate as quickly as she speaks. "She drank from the vials that were my destiny . . . She's spoiled it all . . ."

"But you drank as well," says the taller woman.

"I did, yet she has tampered with my fate. It has been altered. She's now Sangreçu, and she was never meant to be!"

"Giraude, calm down. It can all be sorted out. She may have toyed with things, but the prophecy is much larger than a woman stealing from her sister."

Giraude?

I whip my head around to look at Phoebe. Wasn't Madame Arnaud's first name Yolande, not Giraude?

"I wish it had been as poison to her," says Giraude bitterly. "Why didn't it act as such?"

"She will only get what she is meant to get. She has overstepped, but she cannot take your fate from you . . . if this is indeed your fate."

"She has already, in part. She's Sangreçu."

"Only time will tell how long that will last."

"Can you stop her?"

"She has tricked me, too, Giraude. She gained ancient secrets I thought I was telling *you*. I ought to have set up a word, something only we two knew."

"Make one now," Giraude commands. "We shall stop the leak."

"What shall I choose?" The other woman cocks her head to the side, and I see she's displeased.

"It matters not, just something she'd never guess. And from now on, promise that if you entrust secrets to someone you believe to be me, you will first ascertain it *is* me."

"Now *you* are overstepping. Never instruct me."

Giraude looks down, and even in the dimness I see her hands trembling. "I apologize."

"I have been around for many, many, many centuries, Giraude. You call me Athénaïs now, but I have held other names and lived other lives. Your frustration is like a flea biting at my elbow."

"But I'm part of the prophecy, aren't I? Isn't my life bigger than just . . . me?"

Athénaïs looks at her with pitiless eyes. "I'm not certain you are part of the prophecy after all. You don't seem to have a big enough spirit."

The two women survey each other for a long moment, then Giraude narrows her eyes in anger and slips back into the darkness backstage. Athénaïs stands there for a while, then vanishes.

Instantly, the light changes and I can hear Steven pontificating about something. Tabby's pulling on her mother's arm while she tries to look sincerely interested in what her husband is saying. I jump down off the stage with Eleanor.

Eleanor looks at me and Phoebe urgently. "I saw this time. I watched you two vanish and then reappear. Was it Madame Arnaud again?"

"Yes," I say at the same time Phoebe says, "No."

"I have a theory," Phoebe says.

"I'm all ears," I say.

Eleanor looks at her strangely.

"I mean, I'm interested to hear," I amend. "It's a saying."

"So, that's not Madame Arnaud. It must be her twin. The other woman, Athénaïs, called her Giraude."

Ah yes. That makes sense, why she seemed so fun and silly while with Etienne. It was another woman altogether.

"And Athénaïs said Giraude's sister looks enough like her to trick her," Phoebe adds.

"Perhaps this Giraude never left France. Only her twin traveled to England," says Eleanor.

"And the vials she drank from?" I say. "The one thing we know Madame Arnaud drank . . . well, was this a better version of it?"

"What was that strange term she used? 'Song resoo'?" asks Phoebe. "It seemed to be related to the vials."

"I took a lot of French," I say. "Blood is *sang*, which sounds like *song*. The other part of the word could be *reçu*, the past participle of *recevoir*, to receive. So: someone who received blood?"

They both register distaste.

"I had hoped that was just Madame Arnaud's strange habit," says Eleanor.

"And now it's part of some kind of prophecy," says Phoebe glumly. "A whole bunch of blood-drinkers. How wretched."

"She mentioned a prophecy?" asks Eleanor.

"Yes . . . Giraude wanted to be reassured that she was part of some prophecy, but Athénaïs wasn't exactly agreeing," I say.

"Did they say what the prophecy was?"

I shake my head.

Phoebe's family is filing out of the theater. We follow them back out into the sunshine. Although Eleanor seems disturbed, I'm bristling with our discovery. It's not Madame

Arnaud at all! We've got the "good twin" and so maybe Tabby's not in danger here. We're just reviewing pleasant scenes from Giraude's past.

Not too shabby. It turns out the Madame Arnaud who terrorized the village of Grenshire had a pretty decent, sexy sister.

I turn to Phoebe with a grin, but then I see her gaze directed toward her mum and the smile falls off my face.

The parents look tired and drawn. They're sad, just like Eleanor said. They make efforts at bright talk for Tabby, but I also see Phoebe's mum's hand snake around behind Tabby's body to fiercely grab her husband's. They're silently comforting each other.

What's going on?

CHAPTER FOUR

The oeil-de-boeuf window is a small oval one in the shape of a bull's-eye (as oeil-de-boeuf translates). At Versailles, such a window may be found in the antechamber to the king's room, where courtiers were forced to cool their heels as they awaited the chance to see him.

—*Nooks and Crannies of Versailles*

We all backtrack to the grand marble courtyard at the main entrance and exit the grounds. We continue along to the dinner place the parents decided on after some back-and-forthing with Yelp. "We'll have to behave really nicely in here," cautions Phoebe's mum to Tabby as we stand outside the tiny establishment in a narrow alley. "Do you think you can sit down and be quiet while we're here?"

I step through the glass-paned door to take a look inside, and understand why she's anxious. It's very intimate and adult with tiny clustered tables, each setting with a delicate wineglass at the ready: not the place for toddlers. Especially American ones, who everyone knows are louder. Back outside, I'm tempted to say this to Phoebe, but she's aware of that sadness Eleanor picked up on, and I don't think she's up for being teased.

After Tabby nods, her parents straighten up and enter the restaurant the traditional way. Steven holds the chair for Phoebe's mum as she sits, and Tabby crawls into her lap. Usually, they would encourage her to take her own chair, but this time Phoebe's mum rests her chin on Tabby's head and nuzzles her.

The menu is a small blackboard on the wall with a handful of options, all written in French. After a small bit of conferring, the parents order two *steak frites* and a *croque-monsieur* for Tabby.

"It'll be great to go back tomorrow and see the inside of the palace," says Phoebe's stepdad after the waiter steps away.

"Oh, I know. I just wish Phoebe could see it."

"Fee," says Tabby.

She's only repeating her beloved sister's name, but Phoebe's mum lifts her shoulders and opens her eyes wide.

"Do you see her?" she asks.

I look at Tabby's large eyes. Does she? She has before. But Tabby's twisting around to look up at her mum, not her sister, with a worried expression. I think that she, too, is getting her head around that overall sadness. What's going on with Phoebe's family today?

"She would've loved it," says Phoebe's stepdad. "I bet she would go crazy in the gift shop, too."

"She'd buy one of everything," Phoebe's mum agrees.

Phoebe looks at me, outraged, and I stifle a laugh.

"Is this how they see me?" she asks. "Seriously?"

"I like to think about her racing Tabby around on the grass," says Phoebe's stepdad.

Whoa. Had he sensed in some unconscious way the chasing that had taken place along the canal earlier?

I notice that Phoebe's mum barely eats, maybe a handful of bites, before she sets down her fork and knife for good.

"Want some cake for dessert?" she asks Tabby. "If you can finish your dinner, I'll let you have some."

Tabby doggedly works on her *croque-monsieur*, which her father cuts up into small pieces for her as she eats them. She's too young to point out the hypocrisy that Phoebe's mum isn't finishing *her* dinner.

"What was your favorite thing we saw today?" Phoebe's stepdad asks Tabby.

"The worm."

Eleanor laughs. Must've been something that happened while Phoebe and I weren't there.

"The Belvedere," says Phoebe's mum. "I want to make one at home to match it."

"There might be one already!" says Phoebe's stepdad. "We haven't explored all the grounds yet."

Phoebe gives me a funny look, and I realize she doesn't even know what the Belvedere is. I visited the round pavilion with golden paneling when I came here with my parents, but she missed it while we were in the queen's house and at Gillian's.

I glance guiltily at Eleanor. She catches my eye and I know she's thinking the same thing.

"I liked the theater," Phoebe's stepdad says. "I like thinking of Marie-Antoinette putting on plays. Today they'd be all over YouTube and maybe she wouldn't have lost her head."

Phoebe's mum laughs. "The Internet could've changed history in many ways."

He finishes, his plate a clean moon. "That was really good," he comments. "You didn't eat much."

"Can't."

He nods.

The waiter in his white apron covering his hips takes away all the plates and Tabby starts chanting, "Cake cake cake cake."

"Can you say it in French, sweetie?" her dad asks. "It's *le gâteau*."

She repeats, "Le gat toe," and he gives her the most delighted smile.

"Perfect!"

Phoebe's mum orders *gâteau au chocolat*, but they're out. The waiter apologizes and they order the other dessert, *tarte aux pommes*, an apple pie. As soon as he walks away, he goes to the chalkboard and uses the flat of his palm to wipe away the word *gâteau*.

"Sorry, Phoebe," her mum murmurs.

"Why?" asks Phoebe aloud.

Her mum takes her purse off the back of her chair, puts it on the table, and unzips it. She takes out a small, carved wooden box that says *Phoebe Irving* on it in silver, cursive, embedded lettering.

"What is that?" Eleanor asks. I can't bear the look on Phoebe's face, so I quickly look away.

Tabby touches the box. "That's a good girl," praises her mother. "You're being so gentle like we talked about."

Phoebe's mum takes out an envelope and props it up against the box. It's addressed:

Phoebe Irving

c/o Anne and Steven Arnaud

Auldkirk Lane

Grenshire, England

"Oh my God," chokes Phoebe. "It's from Bethany, my best friend back in California."

Now Phoebe's mum takes out a ziplock bag. Inside are

tiny pastel candles and a piece of paper. I lean over to see that it says, *Est-ce que je peux avoir une allumette pour ces bougies?*

"What's the note?" asks Phoebe's stepdad.

"I Googled the French for 'Can I have a match for these candles?'"

"You think of everything."

When the waiter comes with the *tarte*, she holds up the piece of paper for him and he smiles broadly and pulls a lighter from his pocket. Of course. Everyone in France smokes.

Phoebe's mum quickly inserts the candles, counting aloud for Tabby's sake. Tabby joins her for the first ten.

There are seventeen.

It's all coming clear to me.

"I can't sing it," whispers Phoebe's mum, her voice tear filled. "But I want Tabby to have that experience. Kids love birthdays."

There's no one else in the restaurant, but Steven starts singing the "Happy Birthday" song in a really soft voice as if he's trying not to disturb other people. Tabby joins in, and with a tremulous smile, so does Phoebe's mum.

Phoebe turns away, into my arms. She's holding me so tightly it almost hurts. I'm glad to feel that sensation: I can still feel a vestige of physical pain. Something to be grateful for.

The waiter hovers nearby, happy in the shared celebration, but he's frowning. When the song ends, he asks, "Too many candles for her?" as he gestures to Tabby.

"It's our other daughter," says Steven. "She's not with us anymore."

"Well, she is but she isn't," says Phoebe's mum, pointing to the engraved box.

The waiter looks stricken. He bows to them and leaves.

"That box contains my ashes," says Phoebe in a low voice, her face still pressed to my chest. "She keeps it in their bedroom closet at home—I mean, at the Arnaud Manor. I've always avoided that closet but couldn't figure out why. I knew, but I wouldn't let myself acknowledge it."

"Oh, Phoebe," says Eleanor. She rubs Phoebe's back gently.

Tabby gets to make the wish and blow out the candles for her missing sister. In the smoke drifting up, Phoebe's mum asks, "Tabby, is Phoebe here?"

"No."

"We're celebrating her birthday today. Do you think she knows it?"

"Not."

"We love and miss you," says Phoebe's mum to the air. "Dear Phoebe, how I *miss you.*"

I know how upset Phoebe is because she doesn't turn in my arms to look at her mum. She's not trying to reach Tabby to send a message. She's buried in the only thing she has: me.

We should leave. It's too sad to watch this. But where would we go? My own parents are probably doing their own version of a birthday remembrance for me, and I honestly don't think I can handle that. I'm here to watch over Tabby. I helped protect her from Madame Arnaud, and I'll continue keeping her safe until we three understand what our role is and why we don't move on to another realm. We can't physically intervene since we're ghosts, but we can watch and strategize when Tabby's in trouble. There's nothing I can do to help my own parents. Useless son. I'm dead.

Then it hits me.

Phoebe and I have the same birthday.

That must mean something.

It may be part of why we don't "graduate" to the next

stage of our death, part of the work we have to do. Why fate threw us together, her always driving with me in my car, the way we always met up at the pool.

"I miss you, too," says Steven. A world of melancholy is in his voice.

"Me, too," says Tabby.

"Happy birthday," says Phoebe's mum. She silently cries as she opens the card from Bethany.

"Don't, Mom," says Phoebe, muffled in my shirtfront. She can hear the envelope being torn open.

"'Dear Phoebe,'" she reads. "'I couldn't not send you a card. I hope your family is doing okay. I think about you all the time. I look at pictures of us and I wish more than anything that you were still here. I don't really talk to anybody. I don't have a best friend anymore. I want you back. Happy birthday.'"

And that's the end of that. Steven plonks down a handful of euros and her mother silently puts her collection of items back into her purse.

"I was too ambitious," says Phoebe's mum through her tears. "I honestly thought we might be able to celebrate. To find something good in it."

"There's no guidebook for this," he says. "We just have to do the best we can."

He picks up Tabby while her mum uses a napkin to wipe as much food off Tabby's face as she can. The waiter comes up and hands the euros back to Steven.

"Please," he says in stilted English. "We wish to treat you tonight. So sorry about your daughter."

He nods over to the kitchen, where the chef has come out and stood by the door. He bows deeply to the Arnauds.

Steven looks at the bills in his hand for a long time. "Thank you," he says finally. *"Merci beaucoup."*

"You are so kind," says Phoebe's mum.

As we leave, another group comes in, loud with frivolity and youth. They are going to deplete the wine list and make the poor waiter wipe more things off the chalkboard. They're attractive, three girls and two fellows in their midtwenties, out for a fun night. They're French. They must live here, maybe they even work at the chateau. They start pushing tables together; more are coming. They're laughing hard at something, or maybe just at their good fortune.

I grip Phoebe harder and think, *This could've been us in a couple years.*

If only.

We return to the hotel, a boutique-type room on the second floor. The furniture makes a small pretense to the Louis Seize style, with curved legs supporting the mirrored vanity. Phoebe's mum busies herself with locating Tabby's pajamas and toothbrush in their shared suitcase. Steven tries to read his secret societies book, and I lean over his shoulder, hoping to learn something, but he stays on the same page for ten minutes. He's not reading. Eventually he gives up the charade and closes the book.

"You two have the same birthday," says Eleanor when Phoebe's calm.

"October twentieth was a very auspicious date," I say.

"All the best people are born then," says Eleanor. I almost want to stop and give her a high five, not that she'd know what that is. She's made extraordinary steps in the short time we've known her. Born in the 1800s to become a servant in the Arnaud Manor, she's developed a wry sense of humor she simply wasn't capable of when we first met her.

After the family is asleep and we sit looking bleakly at one another, Eleanor stands up and comes to sit next to me. "Can we go see your family?" she asks. "It's your birthday, too. Maybe they left something for you."

"Like those offerings of fruit and sweets people leave at altars?" I ask. "My parents aren't like that."

"How do you know?" she persists. "This is the first birthday since you died, right?"

I nod.

"I'd like to know them," she says. "We'll go with you."

"It's not necessary," I say. "I don't need anything from them."

She just looks at me.

"And they don't need anything from me."

Now Phoebe's on her feet. "Let's go. Eleanor's right. I've been so self-involved. You haven't seen your parents in . . . how long?"

"I don't know. Can you sit down?"

"Just a check-in," she urges. "We don't have to stay. We'll look at them, make sure they're okay, and blast off."

I don't want to. I don't think it's going to do anything except make me feel a hundred thousand times worse than I already do. I'm an only child, so my parents aren't even parents anymore. I can't stand to go see how quiet they're going to be, watching the telly without speaking to each other.

"Maybe next year," I say.

In the morning, everyone seems to be making an effort to act encouraging. Steven compliments Phoebe's mum on her shirt and she seems pleased.

"I ordered it online," she says. "There just isn't much available for women's clothing in downtown Grenshire."

"There isn't much 'downtown' available in downtown Grenshire."

They laugh. Phoebe's mum packs the nappy bag for today's outing, letting Tabby pick the nappy designs she wants (Minnie Mouse holding balloons).

A short walk later, we're back at the chateau. We briefly queue with the tickets Steven bought the day before, and we've lucked out that it's not so busy. We middle-class ghosts will get to penetrate the king's inner sanctum, an opportunity many nobles would've killed for back in the day.

It almost seems you have to make a special, dramatic inhale upon entry. If you have air in your lungs, that is. If not, you just pretend. The halls are touched with gold, open and spacious, with statuary everywhere.

The place is also, I have to add, completely haunted.

Not only are there today's tourists, pressed so closely together that they block one another's view of everything, becoming grumpy although this is the vacation they've saved up for and they're hell-bent on *enjoying* it . . . but there's an equal number of ghosts. Some panicking, others calmly reenacting their days of blissful, ostrich-in-sand affluence, walking slowly in their finery.

It's claustrophobic to a high pitch and visually stressful, such a volume of bodies. I feel like I'm looking at a life-sized Hieronymus Bosch painting.

One ghost woman dressed in a lacy rose-colored gown runs shrieking through the hall, her face tormented and terrorized. She enters at one end, runs through, and exits—then instantly she's back at the beginning again. She's on an endless treadmill and I pity her . . . she's been doing *this* since 1799?

"What on earth was her role?" asks Eleanor, her face stricken. "She's running from the mob of angry peasants?" I wonder aloud. "Maybe she's running to warn the royal family?"

"And she's guilty forever because she didn't make it there?" asks Phoebe.

"Who knows what her story is?" says Eleanor. "Perhaps she was cut down in the next moment. Maybe there was just one person chasing her in the middle of the night, bent on harming her, not even related to the Revolution."

I watch her cycle a few more times. I think Eleanor's initial guess might be right; there were people pursuing her once, but they're not here now. They found their final rest somehow—or maybe they're haunting the site of even worse crimes. If there is ever a definition of hell, this is it: eternal panic without resolution. For this poor ghost, being caught would probably be an intense relief.

I look around to see who of the living is aware of her. There's one older man with a gray beard who watches her with horror and excuses himself from his companions with a few quick words. He exits the hall without noticing me, Eleanor, or Phoebe. Who knows what he'll see in the next room? I think grimly.

We slowly move with the crowd through the rooms of state with their enormous portraits of prior kings in fur and jewels, with furniture that doesn't look comfortable although it does seem obvious craftsmen took their time carving the wood, tufting the upholstery, and embroidering it with gold.

Everyone wants to see the same thing, and after we walk with shuffled half steps through many chambers—absolutely no one here can walk at a regular pace—we see it.

Marie-Antoinette's bed.

It's set in the center of the room as if it were a stage. And in some ways it was, including when Marie gave birth, laboring in front of dozens of courtiers determined to be there for the historic birth of a hopefully male heir.

The bed is so wide six people could rest in it, a ménage à six rather than trois. We've caught up with a tour already in progress, and Phoebe's family nudges close to hear better.

"Notice the door to the left of the bed. It's left ajar for us to see today," says the English-speaking guide, a tall brunette wearing a red scarf twisted around her neck, which always looks so French. "But when closed, it blends into the wallpaper and becomes invisible. It's a hidden passageway through which the queen fled that fateful day the palace was invaded. Despite the temporary reprieve, she was captured and brought to Paris with the king and their children."

I hadn't remembered that detail from my last visit here. We didn't have the benefit of the guide, and probably our eyes had just glossed over it as a small door without meaning.

"Marie's lady raised the alarm," says the guide, "and she fled through the interior hallway, which connects with the oeil-de-boeuf chamber, and then on to the king's room. He wasn't there; he was looking for her in another hallway. Eventually they were reunited with their children, and just in time. Rioters killed two of Marie-Antoinette's Swiss Guards as they tried to prevent the mob from entering her chamber."

She continues on, describing how they howled and ransacked, and even stabbed Marie's bed. I try to imagine how it feels to have hundreds of people running through your house, calling for you, terrifying your children, loud and violent.

Just as our collective attention shifts away, I see a tiny bolt of blue—the fleece jacket Tabby's wearing, as she slips through the secret door.

I bolt over the velvet ropes restraining visitors, although that's just a reflex. I could go through the ropes; I'm made of air.

"What?" calls Eleanor, but Phoebe—eagle-eyed for anything that has to do with her sister—is already ahead of me, dashing through the door and into the slender, interconnecting hallway.

Part of my mind registers the fact that it's pure dead brilliant to be able to go where people aren't supposed to—just like with the queen's house at the Hameau—but I'm also terrified about Tabby being separated from her parents. If she gets into trouble, none of us ghosts can help her. All we can do is watch.

"Tabby!" Phoebe's yelling but Tabby doesn't react. How could she?

We sprint after her. I'm surprised how fast her little legs can carry her. Down the hall, there's no end in sight. Yet, out of the gloom a door opens.

It's Giraude, bearing a lamp.

Tabby comes to a halt just in front of her and even though there's a half second where I pause—because after all, she looks like Madame Arnaud—I catch up to her. Out of the corner of my eye, I see Phoebe bending down to pick up her sister, but her hands go through her.

We keep forgetting.

As Phoebe straightens, Giraude looks her full in the face. A look of hatred comes over her instantly.

"You're not the firstborn!" she screams at Phoebe.

We all jump backward, and Tabby lets out a cry and begins running back toward Marie-Antoinette's bedroom, a bright rectangle in the distance.

"It was never to be yours!" Giraude continues, her eyes angry and intense.

We run after Tabby, sprinting away from Giraude, although of course she can't see me. I don't know if she can see Tabby. I whip my head around to see if she follows us.

In her confusion, Giraude drops the lamp and it shatters. A fire erupts in the pool of oil on the floor. I stop, thinking her skirts will catch fire. She dances backward. I'm distracted by the light changing, the hallway's paint losing its luster.

Phoebe's mum is here in the secret passageway with us.

We're back in the present day.

"Tabby! Oh my God!" says her mother. She scoops Tabby up and the little girl's arms and legs go fiercely around her body. She's clinging, terrified.

"If it makes you feel better, she's not the first child to find that door irresistible," says a museum guard. He's wearing a blue blazer with an official Versailles badge on the breast pocket. "I try to keep an eye out, but this one just moved too fast." He speaks English with only a very light French accent. He's been dealing with tourists for a long time, I gather.

Behind him is Eleanor, her face serious and concerned, and behind her—actually occupying some of the same space as her—is Tabby's dad.

The parents retreat back to the public area of the chateau, leaving us teens in the dark, except for the light from the faraway door.

"What was she yelling at me, Miles?" Phoebe asks, her voice ragged.

"Who?" asks Eleanor. "I didn't hear any yelling from the passageway."

"Our favorite seventeen hundreds twin," I report. "And she was saying, 'You're not the firstborn.'"

"But I am!" protests Phoebe.

"And why on earth would she care?" asks Eleanor.

I know exactly why she cares, but just as I'm about to say it, a more pressing thought darts into my mind.

I turn and look back at where the lamp had been dropped. There's no sign of it, the fire or the ashes or the shattered glass. It belonged to another time period.

I'm remembering something else about that moment. Something disturbing. Something that will cause a lot of problems if it happens again. I see again that split second where Tabby reacted to Giraude and ran away at her roar of anger at Phoebe.

"Tabby came back in time with us," I say slowly.

CHAPTER FIVE

The potted trees at the Orangerie provide a startling display of abundance, albeit confined and controlled.

—*Nooks and Crannies of Versailles*

*I*t's a terrifying thought, that Tabby is prey to hurtling through time like we are. What if she travels without us? *What if she gets stuck?*

"Oh my God," says Phoebe. "That's not cool. That's so not cool." She walks forward a few steps, then pivots and comes back to us, pacing like a dog. I almost wish I hadn't said it. But it's something we need to be aware of.

"A child goes, but I don't," mutters Eleanor.

"She's an Arnaud," I point out. "Don't take it personally."

"I *wish* you could go and not her!" snaps Phoebe. "Even if that's Giraude and not Yolande, I don't want Tabby anywhere near her!"

"I'm so sorry, of course, of course," soothes Eleanor. "It's foolish to be jealous of such a dangerous ability."

"Is that what you think?" I ask, marveling. "It's not an ability—it's something that's done to us."

I get it now. She's not just jealous that Phoebe and I have a romantic thing going on. She thinks we're more skilled somehow. Like we drew the lucky time-travel card and she got the seven of clubs.

"It doesn't feel good to not have control," says Phoebe. As if unable to bear the thought, she starts walking down the hallway toward Marie-Antoinette's bedchamber. "I want to stick tight to my sister."

She's almost at the door where one portion of the thousands of people crowded into the palace today is squished, and she turns around to look at Eleanor and me with a frown. "What does Giraude care if I'm firstborn or not?"

I resist the urge to glance at Eleanor. Phoebe has always challenged the truth that she looks like Madame Arnaud. I temper my voice to sound gentle. "She must have thought you were her sister. That you'd stolen her destiny, just as she was telling Athénaïs."

Phoebe stands stock-still. Behind her is so much commotion from the visitors shuffling around the room and trying to get a good camera angle of the bed, but there's a sliver of quietude here in this secret passageway. "She thinks *I'm* Madame Arnaud?"

I nod. "I think so, Phoebe. Although they're twins, Giraude must've been born first."

"No wonder she looked at me like she hated me. So each time I trip, I'll have to make sure she doesn't see me. I don't want to take the revenge that's meant for somebody else."

She looks so reflective there, way older than the sixteen she was when she lost her life. Maybe I'm looking older now, too.

"Don't worry," I say. "She can't touch you. You're . . ." My voice trails off.

"I know that, Miles. I know what I am. I can even say it. You ready? *Dead.* That's what I am. *Dead dead dead.*"

I'm not prepared for the intensity radiating out of her. She's someone else.

"Can *you* say it? Can you visit your parents? Nope! You're too busy denying it to pay them a visit."

"Phoebe, you're saying things you don't even mean," says Eleanor in a low voice.

"I'm dead," I say flatly.

"Oh, well, there you go," Phoebe says. "You managed it. I'm dead, you're dead, she's dead. It's like a festival of deadness. So you don't need to remind me, Miles. I got it. Believe me, I got it."

"I'm thoroughly aware of that," I say. I try to keep the coldness out of my voice.

Unsuccessfully.

"And since I know I'm dead, you don't have to school me that Giraude isn't supposed to be able to touch me. But the thing is, Miles, the rules keep changing on us. Things are upside down and tilted the wrong direction, so if one day Giraude happens to grab me and I feel it, I wouldn't be a bit surprised. You don't know all the rules. You don't know how this world operates, because it isn't really operating. It's gusting along however the hell it wants. All we can do is watch and try to keep our footing when the tilting starts."

"I never claimed I—" I begin angrily. I stop short when I see the tears glistening in her eyes. I hold both my hands up in the air, a gesture of submission. I step past her and Eleanor into the vibrant press of people in Marie-Antoinette's bedroom.

Light streams through the floor-to-ceiling windows. Everything is golden. People here breathe, every moment their chests lightly lifting and falling. It's a gift. It's a bloody gift.

I sense the tremendous pressure of their hearts. In every body, there's something wild and yet restrained, following a rhythm as it throbs in absolute muscular power. Nothing is as strong as a heart for its consistent labor. Even as the bearer sleeps, it pounds out its cadence. It never stops from the moment it starts when we're inside our mothers' bodies . . . never stops.

Until.

It stops.

She's right.

Eleanor's right.

I need to see my parents.

Just as I imagined, the telly's on. But as I walk closer to them in that warm, firelit room with the scent of peat I can just barely catch, I see that they're not alone.

Dad has given up his armchair to a visitor, joining Mom on the sofa. There's an awkward silence. Why are they watching the television, not something you typically do with a visitor?

I glide into the center of the room to see who it is. Their eyes stare through me to the screen beyond.

It's a girl my age. I don't know her.

Did they adopt her? A replacement for me? Who is this?

She's got long brown hair and an attractive face, but it's set in an unpleasant sneer. I want to slap her. No one should be around my parents with that face.

"Do you mind if I head upstairs and take a nap?" she asks.

"Not at all; you'll find everything you need up there, Raven," says my mother, and I can hear the relief in her voice.

As the girl leaves, I watch my parents' faces. They share a long look with each other, and my father heaves a large sigh.

"We won't have to see Raven Gellerman again," he says quietly.

"Perhaps the one silver lining in Miles's death," says my mom.

I wait to see if more tidbits of information arise, but they return to watching the telly, morose.

I go upstairs, where the girl is in my room. A suitcase sits at the foot of my bed; she's planning to spend the night.

She walks over to my dresser and examines each of my things without touching them: swimming trophies, photographs, an Eiffel Tower model we bought in Paris. She lifts her eyes and looks at herself in my mirror.

She looks for so long that I start to feel myself drifting back to Phoebe. But then she speaks.

"Guess you weren't the one we thought you were after all, Miles."

The room suddenly feels icy. Does she know I'm here?

"All these years of checking up on you . . . and for nothing. You rolled your car and you're a statistic in the churchyard now. So much for the prophecy."

The prophecy *does* involve me. I want to rip open the room, make her notice me, have her *tell* me. *What is the prophecy?*

She glumly places her elbows on my dresser top, bends over, and puts her chin in her palms. "You were so cute, too!"

"Hello?" I say.

"Last trip to Grenshire for me," she says.

"Can you hear me?" I ask.

"Farewell, Miles Whittleby. Congratulations on a very poor showing. I'll report back that this lineage just isn't working. Unless of course your parents happen to have another child."

I rear back, shocked.

"But based on the shell-shocked lack of intimacy I see downstairs, I think this is a dead end. Literally."

"Are you aware of me?" I ask.

She continues to stare into the mirror and begins to braid her hair, twisting her head slightly to watch her progress. Either she has no idea I'm here or she's the most unselfconscious girl I've ever seen. When she reaches the bottom of the braid, she holds it in place for a moment, admiring. She lets go and the first part of it unravels, then she undoes it as swiftly as she did it. She puffs out her hair into a cloud of brown waves and makes a sexy face into the mirror.

Yeah. She has no idea I'm here.

"It's the worst system ever, Miles, and maybe it let you down. Nobody's really into secret societies dating back eons. It's hard enough to get people to join the debate team, let alone our group."

I listen closely. She's letting go of information now, things I need to hear. Was I supposed to be part of this society? Maybe when I turned eighteen? But she doesn't look eighteen yet, either.

"So we're back to the beginning, back to paperwork and family trees. We must've missed something."

She turns away from the mirror and goes to my bed. Every ounce of me revolts when she pulls back the covers and gets in. That's my *bed*.

"Such high hopes," she says as she turns off the bedside lamp and closes her eyes.

I use intention to find Phoebe and return to Versailles. She's back at the Orangerie with Eleanor, and her family is nowhere in sight. I instantly see why. Phoebe and Eleanor are sitting on the grass next to each other. Eleanor's arm is around Phoebe, who's crying. They've withdrawn because Phoebe was so upset.

They both look up at me.

"I'm so sorry, Miles," says Phoebe. "I can't believe the crappy things I said to you."

"I'm sorry as well," says Eleanor. "I was the one who invented the upsetting proposal."

"It's okay," I say. "Really." I lean over and take Phoebe's hand. "You were right. I was supposed to go check in. My parents are beyond sad, which I already knew . . . but I saw someone in our house, a stranger to me."

They straighten up, and Eleanor's arm comes off Phoebe's shoulders. "Tell us," says Phoebe urgently.

"Her name's Raven Gellerman and she's part of some secret society. She said that I was expected to be part of the prophecy, but apparently by dying I negated that. It must be the same prophecy Giraude was talking about."

"What is the society based on?"

"No idea. She was our age. It was really strange. You'd expect an old, white-haired man to be part of a secret society."

Eleanor looks thoughtful. "I wonder if she is part of the group Austin's family was part of." Austin was a stableboy at the Arnaud Manor in the 1800s, and someone Eleanor had found—abbreviated—love with.

"Tell us more about Austin," Phoebe says.

"His family was really interested in the pagan lore in Grenshire. They met with others, I think at times of the year harkening to the pagan calendar, like the solstices and such."

"Did they happen to meet on October twentieth?" I ask.

"Maybe. I don't know. To be honest, Miles, the centuries

have passed with such slowness that I forgot things, specific tools the living use, like dates."

"Were *you* born on October twentieth?" I ask.

There's a long silence. "I don't know. I don't know if I ever knew or I knew and forgot. My family was poor to a degree you and Phoebe can't understand. There were no cakes. There was no celebration."

I feel awful pressing, but I think it's important. "Do you think you were born in the fall, at least? Do you have a sense of the time of year?"

"My birthday was not marked," she says. "My arrival was not cause for celebration for my family. As a girl, I was a burden, simply another mouth to feed. As soon as I was eligible for service, they thrust me out into the world."

I take her in my arms, and Phoebe hugs her, too. One strange mishmash of bodies on the grass.

It is heartbreaking to have a loving family and lose them. It's perhaps equally heartbreaking . . . maybe worse . . . to have a family that doesn't love at all, and keep them.

"It was dazzling the way Austin's family treated me," she said. "They loved their son, and they loved me. For the first time in my life, I felt wanted. I felt like I had some value."

I'm about to blurt that the value they may have seen in her was related to the prophecy, but realize before I say it how cruel it would sound. They found value in her because she's a good person. Because they liked her.

Eleanor's hands smooth out the apron across her lap, then she crinkles it all up.

"I think sometimes what my life would have been like if I'd worked at a regular big house. Even a cruel mistress would have been fine. Austin and I could have married, and I could take on laundry or sewing or some other means of supporting our family. I'm sorry, your tragedies are so much more recent. I've been mulling over my loss for hundreds of years. But seeing you two and the way you feel about each other—it brings it back. It makes my pain fresh again."

"It's all right," I say. "We want to hear about it."

But I can feel myself growing distant. I don't like it when people cry. I just . . . I have a hard time with it. But I want to be better about it. Girls show their emotion and that's a good thing. It helps them work through hard stuff.

"Austin was devastated," she says. "I watched him grieve. I watched his family try to figure out how to move forward."

"Did he stay on as stableboy?" Phoebe asks gently.

"Oh no! No one stayed on! They all left."

"Oh," I say. "That's how the manor house fell into disrepair and was abandoned."

"Yes, all but Madame Arnaud left."

"Did he marry someone else?" Phoebe asks.

"If he did, I have blocked it out because it is too painful to contemplate," says Eleanor.

"How could he?" I ask. "After knowing Eleanor, he wouldn't have been able to find anyone else to match her."

Eleanor squeezes me extra hard, and as if on a signal, we all disengage. We sit in a row watching the living come into the Orangerie and then leave. Like they're a program on the telly we just can't turn off.

"We should get back to Tabby," says Phoebe.

We rejoin the family. They're slogging through the chateau. It's clear that Tabby's runaway adventure stressed out her parents. Steven's not reading from his guidebook, and his wife isn't bothering to take photos. They're just mechanically doing the tour. And Tabby's bored. This isn't really fun for kids unless they can jump on the monarchs' beds and sit in the gilt chairs.

We're now in the infamous Hall of Mirrors, a long hall with symmetrical pairings of windows with mirrors, so the whole thing is flooded with light.

I feel that light change.

It's subtle, but I've learned to pay attention to it in the last few days. We're tripping.

The sunlight in Giraude's time period fell into the palace differently. Maybe the windows were cleaner—or less clean. Maybe the place wasn't quite as mobbed—or maybe it was more mobbed. I look to see who came with me through this journey: of course, Phoebe, and thank goodness, not Tabby. Eleanor—I feel a little pang of sadness that she doesn't come.

We're still in the mirrored hall but it's changed. The chamber's empty and it's nighttime. Just a few flames encased in glass globes on stands light the room.

"Why are we here?" asks Phoebe. "It's just us?"

I put my fingers to my lips. I can hear something.

Whispering.

Phoebe and I move to the edges of the room, where it's darker. We don't want Giraude noticing her. We track the sound of the whispering.

In a niche, two women sit. It's Athénaïs and . . . I look over at Phoebe. Is this Giraude? Now that we are aware she's a twin, I don't know.

"The king adores you," says the twin. Her eyes move down Athénaïs's body, lingering as a lover's eyes would do. I see Athénaïs almost imperceptibly alter her position to enhance her appearance. That sucking in of her stomach Gillian used to do when her photo was taken, and the accompanying straightening of posture and pushing out of her breasts. She's preening.

"What do you do to make him love you so much?" continues the twin. She smiles in anticipation.

"He may be a king, but he's just a man. And men have always found me fascinating," says Athénaïs. Somehow she gets away with this conceited statement—even with me. She's got that superconfident air that seems based on fact rather than wishful thinking.

I look over at Phoebe. She can't understand their French, and it's going too quickly to translate for her. She looks on edge, probably concerned about Giraude seeing and attacking her.

"You are beautiful, beautiful beyond any woman I've ever seen," breathes the twin. "Is it just that? Or do you know ways to please the king?"

"I am a courtesan," says Athénaïs. "I'm no wife. I'm the pleasure he finds when he slips away from her sausage-shaped arms. I let the night unfold as he wishes."

"What are his wishes?" asks the twin.

"Aren't you the coyest thing! Are you going to steal my secrets and seduce him yourself?"

"I would never dare," says the twin hotly, bending away from Athénaïs with a look of indignation. "And I would never succeed. You have his heart."

"A man can be tempted," says Athénaïs.

"Not one so thoroughly satisfied."

"He is that," said Athénaïs. "He would never say that he wasn't. I make sure he is brought to the pinnacle of his earthly pleasure many times before I let myself sleep."

"It must feel incredible to have a king at your beck and call."

"It gives a certain sense of power. But, Giraude, we have a power that outlasts far longer than his time on the throne."

I look over at Phoebe. Did she hear the name Giraude in all that riotous French? I mouth the word, and she silently shakes her head at me.

"And that is what I want to hear more about," says Giraude.

"In due time. I'll tell you things when you need to hear them."

"But I'm dying to know now. What does it harm?"

"I don't know yet if you're the one to take my place in our ancient lineage."

"But I must be! All the signs are as you said."

A silence falls. Athénaïs doesn't have an answer and she graces Giraude with a gentle smile. "Patience, my dear. Patience is the quality of character that lets a woman gain a place in the king's bed and be as powerful as the queen . . . or more so."

"I will try," says Giraude. "But now that I'm Sangreçu, I'm anxious to learn everything."

"You feel the rush of that blood throughout your body, don't you?" says Athénaïs. "I remember how it felt the first time."

"It's like every heartbeat is a drum played in my ear," says Giraude. "Every inch of my skin tingles. I feel more alive than I ever have."

"I envy you that first moment," says Athénaïs.

"Tell me how you do it, please! How did you create the vials?"

Athénaïs laughs gently. "That is very deep, ancient magic that was taught to me by someone I left behind long ago."

"Who?"

"All in due time."

"You have more vials somewhere?"

Ooh. Wow. This is important stuff. I drop my eyes to the floor to focus better. I listen as if someone's telling us how to save our own lives.

Maybe in a sense she is—but with an adjustment. Telling us how to save our own *deaths*.

"There are of course more vials. I have a cache."

"So if I find myself in need, I may find refreshment here at the palace?"

"A little farther flung. I must keep it out of the hands of wandering courtiers who may stumble across it while looking for privacy."

"Are the vials in Paris?"

"All in good time, my dear."

"Who else knows? Does the king?"

"We Sangreçu are a very special, select, and *small* tribe. He is not a member, no," says Athénaïs.

"You have given me something you did not even give him!" exults Giraude. "You have favored me above him!"

"In this regard, that is true," says Athénaïs.

"You cannot know how much this affects me," says Giraude. "I admire you beyond what I may tell you."

A look passes between them. I know that look.

"You are so beautiful," says Giraude. "I wish I could take the king's place."

"Shhh," says Athénaïs. "Many kinds of love are observed in this palace, but I am the mistress of the king. It would undo me."

Giraude reaches out her hand to Athénaïs's cheek and Athénaïs permits her to lingeringly trace her jawline. "Where are the vials kept?" she asks softly.

"You pray to know the answer," says Athénaïs.

Giraude seems to hear or understand more than I do, because she looks very pleased as she says, "I believe I know that place."

Athénaïs takes Giraude's hand from her face, but with seeming reluctance. "But you are not to go there without my permission," she says. "I shouldn't have told you."

"I am your confidante, your mirror, your heir," says Giraude. "Why would I do such a thing?"

"We neglected to set up a secret password," says Athénaïs. A brief frown crosses her face. "I ought to have . . . before I told you, I ought to have . . ."

Giraude smiles easily. "It's me, you can rest assured. From now on, why not use the word *sister*?"

I see the frown appear again just for one moment, then Athénaïs is smiling again. "I am terrible at keeping secrets from such an eager face. You are an extraordinary protégée, and I relish and cherish each moment we spend together."

Again the look between them.

"As do I," says Giraude.

Athénaïs continues on, but the light changes again.

I grab Phoebe's hand as we trip. I don't need to—but there's still some fear she might not come with me. I don't want her to get stuck in the past with an angry Giraude who thinks she's Yolande.

We're back in the present day and the hall is teeming with visitors, people checking their reflections in the many mirrors. I hear English, French, German, languages I can't identify. It's a blur of sound.

"Miles," says Phoebe, "I don't think that was Giraude."

"No?"

"I think that was Yolande pretending to be her."

"How could you tell?"

"It's just a feeling. Something subtle."

"Well, you've had a lot more face time with her than I have." I'm starting to mull over how effectively she tricked both Athénaïs and me, but now Eleanor's with us, and without thinking about it I drop Phoebe's hand.

That's weird. Why did I do that?

"Where were you?" asks Eleanor.

"We tripped again," says Phoebe.

"Can you hold my hand next time? And I might be able to go when you go?"

"Yes, we'll do that," I promise. "I'm sorry."

She's really trying not to be upset, but I can see that something shook her up. "What is it?" I ask. "What happened while we were gone?"

"Nothing happened," says Eleanor. "Don't worry about that."

"But?"

She hesitates and throws a strange look at Phoebe.

"I had a strong wave of emotion come over me," says Eleanor. "Nothing I've ever felt before. Almost like someone else's emotions were being poured into my body."

"And what was it?" asks Phoebe.

"The feeling that you betrayed me," says Eleanor.

"What?" I say.

"Me?" asks Phoebe.

"Yes."

"Eleanor . . . no! I would never do anything to hurt you and you must know that. Miles and I . . ." She pauses and blushes. "We've known each other a little longer than we've known you. But we don't mean to exclude you. When we go back in time, we have no control."

"It's not that," says Eleanor, looking at her intently. "You and Miles are an item, as we would say back in my era." And now it's Eleanor's turn to blush. I might be a little warm in the cheeks, too. "But it's something between us. Something that happened before."

"We didn't know each other before," says Phoebe slowly.

"I know. That's why the feeling is so confusing."

"Please know you can trust me," says Phoebe. "Maybe . . . maybe I remind you of someone who betrayed you a long time ago?"

"Perhaps," Eleanor allows.

"I won't ever screw you over," says Phoebe with an earnest face. She takes both of Eleanor's hands in hers. "We've been through too much together."

"Screw me over?" asks Eleanor. "I am not a bottle of wine."

I groan.

"It means . . . I won't be disloyal," says Phoebe.

"To you, wine, or beer," I add.

Eleanor smiles tremulously. "I know that. I know you're true."

It seems like everything's okay again, but I'm worried about that feeling Eleanor had. Something caused it. What if it makes her turn against Phoebe? We're all in danger here. We don't understand the prophecy or our role in it—or if we even *have* a role in it.

"Tell us if you feel that again," I say abruptly. "We'll talk you down."

"Talk me down?"

"It means, we'll . . . What does it mean, Phoebe?" I appeal to her. Words are not my forte.

"It means we'll stay with you until the feeling passes. We'll comfort you."

"Yeah, that," I say.

"I am grateful," she says. "I appreciate your kindness. Now—while I was feeling such vile sensations, what were you experiencing?"

I bring her and Phoebe up to speed on what Athénaïs and Yolande spoke about. The family is ahead of us now, and we drift through the crowds of people to be reunited with them. The long day registers on all their faces. Steven holds Tabby balanced on one hip, perhaps so she won't run off again and perhaps because she's tired from all the walking.

"Let's get some air," says Tabby's mum. "I know this is your thing, Steven, but Versailles is wearing thin on me. Can we go outside and eat our lunch?"

Easier said than done, but twenty minutes later we're all out in the sunshine again. They buy *jambon baguettes* from a vendor with a red and white striped umbrella protecting his cart. To eat, they stretch out on the lawn near the famous fountain showing the horses rising up from under the water's surface.

"I bet you anything Tabby's going to fall asleep right here," says her mum.

"Fine by me," says Steven. "I could spend an hour here reading the guidebook. Why don't you take a nap, too?"

"That would be heaven," she says. She stretches out, props her head on her folded arms, and almost instantly she's asleep. Steven holds Tabby in his lap and sings softly to her until she winks out, too. He reads his book, holding it open on the grass with one splayed palm. I notice with amusement that each page turn requires a feat of engineering with only one hand.

So we ghosts linger, too. I'm aware now of wanting to include Eleanor, so I make us sit in a triangle of sorts rather than a row. That means that I'm the sole person facing the drunk bloke heading toward us, lumbering and lurching.

CHAPTER SIX

As with any good palace, there are secret passages to
aid a monarch in escaping—and to assist him in
secretive amorous pursuits.

—*Nooks and Crannies of Versailles*

*H*is stumbling approach would have tipped me off, but his bottle in a brown bag is an even bigger hint. He's red-faced from all the drink in him, and a crooked snarl shows he's a belligerent drunk, not a happy one. And he's heading right toward our happy little bereaved family.

"Guten Tag!" he roars at Tabby's dad, who instantly lets go of his page in the book to put his index finger to his lips and make the accompanying "shhh."

He lets go of a string of German that I don't understand, but he's clearly waiting for an answer and isn't moving along.

"I'm sorry," says Steven. "I don't speak German. I can't help you."

The man spins around in a circle as if to ask the world, *What's wrong with this man?* He drops onto the grass and points at Tabby's mum. She wakes up because of the torrent of foreign expletives or whatever it is he's saying.

"Steven, who is this?" she asks, alarmed.

"No idea. He just came up and sat down."

"Well, let's go!" She hurriedly gathers up their things while he, ungainly, manages to stand up with Tabby in his arms.

"Can you get my book?" he asks Tabby's mum.

But the drunk man has grabbed it. He's growling and spitting out that chopped salad of a language that we call German. I'm really glad I took French, but it occurs to me at this moment that it might be helpful to know German, just to know what his problem is.

"Let it go," says Tabby's mum. "I'll buy you another copy. Let's get out of here." She walks over and takes Tabby right out of her husband's arms and sets her down on the ground so they can all move quickly.

I see on Steven's face that he doesn't want to back down. That's his damn book.

"Give it back," he demands.

The German man turns and hurls the book as far as he can. Given his state, that's about two feet. I can't help it; I laugh. Tabby and her mum are now walking backward from the scene in progress. Eleanor and Phoebe are with them.

"Pick that up and bring it here," says Tabby's dad. His voice is pretty authoritative—I have to hand it to him. This is the man I would've had to make polite small talk with if I were dating Phoebe in a real way, in a living-person kind of way.

"Steven, he's not going to do that. He doesn't even understand what you've said. Let it go and let's get moving! He doesn't seem like the healthiest individual to be standing around talking to!" says Phoebe's mum. She delivers the last line with a bit of humor I have to admire.

"I bought that on special order," protests the dad. "I want it back."

"Then swallow your pride and go pick it up. I don't think the descendant of Nazis is going to deliver it to you."

Oh no. He might not understand English—but *Nazi* is a

German word. The man wheels around and starts heading toward Phoebe's mum now. She's pissed him off. He's loudly enumerating her faults in a way that is somehow getting its message across.

It's showtime.

Steven starts running, and he tackles the drunk effortlessly. They both land on the grass.

"I wish I could get the book for him," says Phoebe, "and bring it to Mom. Goddamn corporeality."

I watch the rolling around with a certain amount of pleasure. It's clear no one's going to get hurt. A bunch of tourists are now standing around watching, and predictably a few people pull out their phones and start recording it. I try to picture the YouTube title, "Manful fighting at Versailles" or "Tourists get entangled."

I glance over at Tabby's mum, and my smile vanishes. It's been a tough couple of days for her. She's tried to figure out how to mark her dead daughter's birthday, she's had her other daughter bolt away from her and go temporarily missing in a foreign country, and now her husband is fighting an inebriated prat.

"We're going," she calls out to her husband. "We'll catch you later. I'm going to take Tabby to get some ice cream."

I can tell he hears her, but he's too embroiled in his current situation to respond.

"I'll have my cell on," she offers as she walks away.

I get it. I wouldn't want my kid to watch that, either.

Finally, the men rise, panting. Steven points one last time to the book, and the man, defeated, actually goes and brings it to him. He mutters some words which I guess are German for "I'm an idiot." He slinks away and I wonder what his story is. Is he a local who comes to the beautiful grounds of the palace to get drunk? Or is he a genuine tourist who shouldn't have brought his bottle?

Steven unruffles the pages of his guidebook and turns to look for his family.

"They went to get ice cream," I remind him, but he doesn't hear me.

I stick with him as he runs his hands through his hair and tries to regain his breath. Maybe this fight was good for him. A, he won it, and B, he got to pummel out some of his grief. Drunks should always pick fights with bereaved people.

"Nicely done," says Phoebe, and we smile at each other. Eleanor looks uncomfortable.

"I hate men who drink," she says. "So many lives I saw ruined for a man who couldn't stop himself."

Steven brushes grass off his trousers and shakes his head like a dog coming out of water. He begins to walk in the direction his family went. I grin as I imagine the huge banana split he's going to reward himself with.

He doesn't limp, but I can definitely see signs of older-man-coming-off-adrenaline-surge in his gait. He's going to be fine.

I turn back around to Phoebe to say something clever, but behind her, I see someone approaching whose face makes me freeze.

It's Giraude.

Haggard, unhappy, pale. She wears a black choker necklace around her neck and clothing that seems less ornate than things she's worn previously. She looks careworn.

I notice: the light *doesn't* change. I can still see tourists milling around us. This is no happy interlude from the past that we traveled back to watch. This is real. And it's happening now.

Giraude's still alive.

Eleanor, who was halfway between us, runs to Phoebe and pulls her toward me.

"What?" says Phoebe, stumbling at the other end of Eleanor's strong arm. "Are you okay?"

"Don't look behind you, miss," says Eleanor, reverting back to servant-speak in her panic.

Of course Phoebe looks and halts, frozen. I can't see her face, but I can see Eleanor's, a study in determination. This is what made her a valuable part of the Arnaud household all those years ago: her commitment to her duty. Which right now involves pulling Phoebe away from a dangerous intruder.

I take a few running steps and am with them. It's too late to get away from Giraude, but at least I can fortify Phoebe with some attitude. The trick is not to be scared.

"Looks like she has the gift of long life, just like her sister," I say drily.

"That can be fixed," says Phoebe, and I whistle in admiration.

Giraude walks straight to Phoebe, bristling with anger in her every step. Her face is locked in a sneer. "I will control myself enough to deliver a message," she says in French.

"I have . . . no idea what you just said," says Phoebe.

Giraude's laugh is a snarl. "You think to flummox me," she says in English. "But I know this sharp, percussive language. I've learned it over the centuries by listening to the visitors and studying the pamphlets they discard on the grounds. I knew one day I might go to England, where Athénaïs believed you went."

"That's . . ." Phoebe can't bring herself to say "good." She looks at me with desperation, and unheard by Giraude, I reassure her.

"Don't worry," I say. "Learn what you can, and if it gets scary, intention yourself away."

We can always move ourselves somewhere else—just not back in *time*. That part is controlled by someone else.

"I cannot believe your audacity to show your face to me," says Giraude, continuing in English. "But since you have, I can make good on a threat. The threat you robbed me of the chance to give so many years ago."

"That wasn't me! I didn't rob you of anything!"

"*Taisez-vous!*" shrieks Giraude. "*Shut up!* Be quiet and listen . . . I've waited centuries to tell you this." She pauses, lowers her head, and looks up at Phoebe with her eyes half-coins. Her voice also drops in pitch as she says, "Give me the vials or I will murder everyone you care about."

Phoebe's eyes expand.

"You can leave anytime," I remind her. "I'll stay here and watch Tabby."

"I'm not Yolande," says Phoebe. She's still scared, but she knows she has an escape route. She stands up straighter and puts her hands in her back pockets. "I look like her—I look like you! But I'm not your sister. I don't know where the vials are."

"Please don't insult me. I know you. I've known you for centuries. You've adopted the dress and customs of this generation, but I know you."

"Seriously!" says Phoebe. Her eyebrows are lifted high, and I can see the effort she's making not to turn and run. Her legs tremble. "My name is Phoebe Irving. I was born in the United States in 1999. My stepdad is an Arnaud."

"How do you explain this?" Giraude asks. She points to the mole in Phoebe's cleavage, a beautiful perfect dark circle just at the place her right breast begins to swell.

"My mole?" she asks in disbelief.

"Your mark of beauty."

"I was born with it . . . What can I say? Your sister has the same mole in the same place?"

"Stop with this ruse," snarls Giraude. "You have stolen *everything* from me. I was meant for higher things, and you diluted my inheritance. I want the vials. You get them to me or I will kill. I've done it before and I can do it again."

"I'm a descendant," says Phoebe, and I realize this is the first time she's acknowledged that she may be a true Arnaud, not just a stepdaughter of an Arnaud. "I'm an Arnaud, I guess, but my mole is just a coincidence. I have no idea where the vials are. I've never drunk from them."

"You are not Sangreçu?" For the first time, Giraude looks disconcerted.

"*No!*"

Giraude cocks her head to the side, studying Phoebe's face with a frown.

"I'm a ghost," says Phoebe. "I died. Your sister wasn't even able to touch me. You try!"

Giraude reaches out a tremulous hand to touch that mole and we watch it go straight through Phoebe's chest. Giraude gasps.

"You are not Yolande," she says. She sinks to the ground, her skirts forming a circle around her. "Where is she?"

"You don't have to worry about her anymore," I say. "Whatever she stole from you, she's lost it, too." But she doesn't hear me, doesn't see me. Only Phoebe, her descendant, is visible to her. So Phoebe repeats what I've said.

"You knew my sister," Giraude responds. "Then you have her secrets. You know where the vials are."

"No! I keep telling you. I don't know," says Phoebe.

"The only chance I have in this world is to drink again. *You find those vials!*" She rises and now, if anything, she looks *more* angry. Maybe we should've let her keep thinking Phoebe was Yolande. It gave us a position of power, I realize belatedly.

"Want an example?" she says. "I am in earnest." She turns her head and it's like a hawk hidden in a tree looking at all the sweet little starlings flying around carelessly. She scans the tourists, and thank God Phoebe's family is long gone, somewhere enjoying ice cream. One person stands out. He's alone. He's walking really slowly. He's even lurching.

Her gaze fastens on the drunk German tourist. She hones in on him and begins walking toward him.

How is this going to work? She's in 1700s dress, with full skirts and her hair a towering concoction. But guess what—everyone's bent over their phones reviewing the footage of Phoebe's dad kicking the bloke's ass. No one seems to notice Giraude.

She walks right up to the German and with an iron grip snags him and pulls him behind a thick bush. I hear his one cry, then eerie silence.

"What do you think she's doing?" asks Eleanor.

I don't answer. She knows.

The quiet with which Giraude does it is almost worse than if he were screaming.

We wait.

Only one person emerges from the foliage. She stares at us and the skin on my back contracts with chills. She's as bad as her sister.

Pure evil.

She wants the vials, and all we know about them is the cryptic thing I heard Athénaïs tell Yolande.

She turns her back to us and walks toward the chateau. Within a few seconds, she's hidden from view. It makes sense. She has walkways she's developed, secret ways to walk among the visitors. She's kept herself hidden since the 1700s as the palace went through all its changes: from monarch's palace to destroyed revolutionary example to museum to restored splendor.

Where are the vials?

CHAPTER SEVEN

The fireworks at Versailles intended for the date of Louis's marriage to Marie-Antoinette were canceled due to a storm. The postponed fireworks, held in what is now the Place de la Concorde, resulted in a fire. Panicked Parisians attempted to flee the square but were blocked on three sides by the statuary and colonnades that were part of the display. Those who managed to escape via the fourth side (largely blocked by parked carriages) found themselves on the banks of the Seine at a time when few knew how to swim. The mob behind pushed in many who drowned. Certainly an inauspicious start to a doomed reign.

—*Sparks and Sizzles: A History of Fireworks*

We're not going to leave Tabby's family. Giraude's a killer. This is game-changing.

Eleanor is hugging Phoebe, and together they're shaking. "I can't believe it," says Eleanor. "She's terrifying. She's the very image of Madame Arnaud."

"That's how twins work," I say, but my attempt at levity goes sour when they ignore me.

"She's going to kill Tabby," says Phoebe in a broken voice.

"No. No way," I say emphatically. "Not on my watch."

But that's all the power I have: to watch. I have no corporeality. I could reach out to stop Giraude, and my ghost hand would go right through her. She doesn't even see me. I'm nothing to her but cold particles of air.

"Phoebe, no," says Eleanor. "She doesn't know Tabby. She picked that man because he was in her way, and slow moving, and stupid."

"There's nothing to connect you with Tabby," I add. "I don't reckon she remembers her from that moment in the passageway."

"That was hundreds of years ago to her," Eleanor says soothingly.

"But Tabby probably made an impression because she was dressed as a child of today, wearing jeans," says Phoebe. "And she was with me, who she took for her sister. *And* it caused a small fire."

She disengages from Eleanor, her face stark and alarmed.

"I'm sorry you're scared," I say. "We'll protect Tabby with everything we have. You might call Giraude's attention to her by staying so close, so maybe we should keep a healthy distance from now on."

"I agree," she says, shivering. "Let's keep them in our eyesight, but not be *with* them. We can't protect them if she zeroes in on them. You saw her hand go right through me."

I nod grimly.

"So let's find them," she says. "But not too close."

Intention comes so easily to us now, and we find ourselves inside a patisserie where Tabby is indulging in *une glace au chocolat*, chocolate ice cream. Her mom and dad each drink from a tiny espresso cup and seem to be sharing a plate of *macarons*. It's not usual for me to want food or drink anymore; it's just not something that I feel. But looking at those circular confections held together with sweet ganache . . . I crave them. I wish I could experience them on my tongue, melting away, just one more time.

I lift my glance from the plate to see that Phoebe has moved herself outside and is looking in at us through the window. We're too close, should Giraude happen by. But Giraude can't see me or Eleanor, and I reason it's important to hear what the family is next planning to do. I hold up my finger to Phoebe to gesture that we'll be out in a minute, and she nods.

After listening for a few moments, I learn that Steven is trying to convince his wife to return to the palace for the nighttime fireworks. Eleanor looks at me, startled.

"No, go to your hotel. Go, go, go," I chant.

"It's the experience of a lifetime," he argues. "When else do you get to see a replica of the fireworks Louis XIV arranged for his court? It's going to be spectacular. Plus, Tabby loves fireworks."

"I'm tired," says Phoebe's mum. "I don't know if I want to stay up late to see those and then walk to our hotel in the dark. And, Steven . . . you were in a fight today! I'm still reeling from that."

"I'm fine," says Steven. A smile teases at the corners of his mouth. He's proud.

"Maybe we can promise ourselves we'll come back in a few years?" she says.

"Do you really want to do this again?" he says. "Next time, Italy. Let's do Versailles to the hilt and cross it off our list for good."

"You make a good point. I don't know if I'll want to return, it's so overwhelming."

"Well, we did get some great ideas for the gardens' restoration at the Arnaud Manor," he says.

Tabby has reached the last spoonful of her ice cream. She climbs down from her chair and crawls up into Steven's lap, the whole time perilously holding the spoon in her fist.

"What's going on, little one?" Steven murmurs.

Tabby responds by bringing the spoon to his mouth.

"For me?" he asks.

She nods. He opens his mouth and eats the last bite. "Thank you, Tabby," he says. "Why did you give me your last bite?"

"No fight," she says.

"I promise."

"It was all she could talk about on the way over here," says Tabby's mom. "It scared her to see you rolling around with that man. Yet another reason not to return to Versailles for the fireworks. Who knows if we'll run into him again?"

"I won't fight again, sweetie," says Steven. He looks up at his wife. "Listen, if you can handle a few more hours, then we'll be done with Versailles once and for all. Plus . . ." He shifts in his seat, moving Tabby from one leg to the other, for some reason looking guilty. "Plus, I already bought tickets and it wasn't exactly cheap."

She laughs. "Well, that happens. Fine. We'll go to the show. Want to see fireworks tonight, Tabby?"

Tabby's answer is a gleeful banging of her spoon on the tabletop before her mom stops her. Oh crap. So the idea that they'll make their way to the hotel safely and we can relax is just not happening.

"We're in trouble," says Eleanor to me suddenly. "Because even if Phoebe's family makes it back to England safely, Giraude's going to keep killing people here. We can't let that happen."

"What do you suggest?" I ask.

"This is our 'graduation,'" she says. "We have to kill Giraude."

I stare at her. "Let's take this outside," I say. "Phoebe should hear it."

We intention to the sidewalk outside. "Eleanor's had a brainstorm," I announce.

"Yeah?"

"Well, it has occurred to me that we do have some sort of responsibility for the vile threat Giraude made," says Eleanor.

"How are we responsible?"

"Because we know about it and can prevent it."

"We can't prevent *anything*," says Phoebe. "All we can do is hope my family gets back to England safely."

"We are the only ones who know what Giraude plans," says Eleanor quietly. "And she wouldn't have threatened those plans if she hadn't seen us."

"Seen me, you mean."

"We are a team," says Eleanor.

"So . . . what do you suggest we do?"

"That's the surprising part," I say. No one laughs.

"We must kill her. She's our responsibility. We understand who she is and how to kill her."

Phoebe and I share a pained look. *Again?* she seems to be saying with her eyes. It wasn't so long ago we were preparing for another murder.

"Or we could get her the vials," protests Phoebe. "We can try to find them. Then she'll subside to the outskirts of Versailles for another few hundred years, right?"

"And then she emerges again to put people in danger."

"If we've 'graduated,' she won't be our responsibility," I say.

"We're the only ones. It's up to us. Whether the danger is now or a hundred years from now."

"We might not be the only ones," says Phoebe. "Remember that girl who visited Miles's family? She's part of that society . . . there are others who know. They probably even know more than we do."

"But they aren't here," says Eleanor.

I look at her with newfound respect. Meek servant wearing black? I don't think so. "Remember, you were the girl

who stabbed someone to the point that the mattress underneath was destroyed," I say. "You're cut out for this."

Back when Eleanor was alive, she assassinated Madame
Arnaud. It's unfortunate that the house resuscitated her and
sent her on her merry way.

Eleanor shakes her head. "No, not cut out for it. I don't
like this life," she says. "This death, I mean. I didn't agree to
any of this."

"But you're willing to do what's right," I say. "I admire
that."

"There's a guy lying in the bushes cooling until some
groundskeeper comes across his body," says Phoebe. "I guess
it's up to us to stop that happening to anyone else."

"It seems we've reached accord," I say. "We just have to
start rolling out our whens and hows."

The door behind us opens and Phoebe's family is exiting
the patisserie. We fall into an uncharacteristic silence as we
pad silently behind them, keeping distance between us. Their
pace is languid, and after a while I realize they're just wandering to kill time—I wince at my own mental wording—
until the fireworks display.

They pause to put Tabby back into the fold-up buggy that
has a carry strap like a purse. The mom has been carrying it
on and off all day. Then their pace quickens without the
toddler-sized steps slowing them. We follow them back
through the front gates of the palace but they slip along past
and toward the long walk to the Hameau. How do they have
the energy?

"It feels so good to walk," says Phoebe's mum. "It's a med-
itation for me."

Steven nods. "And we need peace."

I reach out and take Phoebe's hand. We're thinking about killing someone and they're lost in memories of the girl who would've turned seventeen yesterday.

"Will there ever be peace?" Phoebe asks. "I mean, really? It's never going to end."

"It *will* end," says Eleanor. "I have faith."

"We killed Madame Arnaud. We were good, and then they took this trip to France and we're in trouble again. What happens next year when they go to Italy or back to the States or to Ireland? Are we just going to find evil people we have to kill wherever we go?"

"I don't believe so," says Eleanor.

"Me, either. I think this is it. Madame Arnaud had a twin, and we don't hear anything about any other siblings."

Phoebe wrenches her hand out of mine. "I wish I was back in San Francisco and none of this ever happened!" she yells. "I hate British accents and signs written in French!"

"You have culture shock," I inform her. "And actually, you really like my sexy accent."

Although she's deeply upset, I find it ever so slightly . . . just a sliver . . . amusing. She's got culture shock on top of being dead. This girl needs an infusion of American pop culture.

"I wish I had a hot dog to hand you," I say.

"You're an idiot," she says.

"And some crisps, oops, I mean potato chips . . ."

"Seriously, hot dogs and potato chips are America to you?"

"What else is there?"

"Miles, you're not helping her with this insensitive talk," says Eleanor, but as I look at Phoebe's eyes flashing at me indignantly, I know I helped her out a lot. I shook her out of her spiral of sadness.

"At least we keep our teeth straight!" she says.

"Now that's a stereotype and you know it," I say. "Check out this glossy row." I lift my lip and show her my teeth.

"One of the lucky and the few," she says.

"And you think the Day-Glo glare from Americans' bleached smiles is anything but painfully artificial?"

"I've never bleached," she says.

"Oh, you will, American, you will," I promise her.

She stops, puts her hands on her hips, and collapses into a bout of laughter that includes perhaps eight percent crying.

It's intense, I'm telling you what, this being dead. It doesn't ever end.

Eleanor gives me a baronial look of scorn that makes me think again, as I often have, that she has something royal or special in her background. She wears an apron, yes, even now, but she's no one's serving girl.

"What?" I say to Eleanor. "I cheered her up."

"Let's look at the rock grotto again," says Tabby's dad.

We've been walking for a long time now. Phoebe's no longer mad or sad or whatever complex cocktail of emotions described her a half hour ago. Tabby's fallen asleep in her buggy.

The grotto's another thing Phoebe and I missed yesterday, but I remember visiting with my parents. It's a man-made rock with carved entrance and exit, and a peephole for Marie-Antoinette to see people coming. She was reading on a stone bench inside when they brought word to her that a mob was coming from Paris for her and her family: the beginning of the end.

We cross a rickety bridge over water to approach it. It looms above us, a dark rock with many secrets. As we approach the metal bars that now block the entrance to the grotto, I sense it coming.

The wavering. The rock developing shadows, then brightening.

I whirl around and look at Phoebe. I'm too far away to grab Eleanor as we promised . . . and it looks like Phoebe is, too.

"Grab her!" I yell. "The light is changing!"

Eleanor's face looks panicked, and she runs toward Phoebe. But not fast enough.

We're tripping.

Just me and Phoebe.

I scan the area, pulling Phoebe off to the side. I can't see anybody yet, but that doesn't mean they can't see us.

The entrance is now open, the metal grille gone. We enter a cave of sorts, a narrow passageway that smells of dampness, of objects kept from the sun. Seems like the best place for us to hide. The walls are dark with moisture, and I think for a moment about how tortured Marie-Antoinette must've been, that she preferred to crawl into so forbidding and primeval a place rather than linger with the golden furnishings of the palace.

From farther inside the cave, I hear a moan. I share a glance with Phoebe and we carefully and slowly twist around the corner.

The lovers are here, standing pressed against each other, kissing like crazy. Etienne is lifting Giraude's skirts and this time she's not stopping him. He hoists her up, and her legs encircle his waist. Her legs are beautiful, muscular, and end in slippers so thin they show her individual toes curling.

They stop kissing as she leans back in a swoon and he pulls her bodice to the side. He furiously works at her buttons and laces to get to her breasts.

"The mole!" whispers Phoebe.

My first thought is that it's a trick. We know the French royals painted beauty spots or even pasted on brown circles, moving them around to please the eye. Possibly Giraude has created a mole where her sister has one. But then Etienne speaks and I realize it's a betrayal.

"Giraude must never know," he mutters. "You promise?"

"I promise," Yolande breathes. "I've wanted you for so long . . ."

"She won't give it to me," he says. What a liar.

"I will!" she says exultingly. Her face is filled with passion and also triumph. She's seducing her sister's lover.

His hands disappear under her skirts to take off whatever undergarments prevent him from moving further, and of one accord Phoebe and I move backward around the corner so we can't see them anymore.

"Awkward," mouths Phoebe.

I whisper into her ear, "I've always noticed a variety of yogurt at French supermarkets. Do Americans enjoy yogurt? If so, what kind?"

She shakes, holding in her laughter.

"Another thing I've been puzzling over," I whisper. "How much emphasis do you place on making your handwriting legible? Is it even important in this era of keyboarding?"

She waves her hands in front of her face to make me stop, her face bright with suppressed amusement.

Around the corner we hear the cries of ecstasy; it seems Etienne and Yolande may have taken things to a whole new level. Phoebe puts her hand over her mouth, and I'm just about to suggest we vacate the grotto when the cries behind us are overcome by another sound, a sinister buzzing. A black cloud bolts past us. Phoebe and I both leap to the wall and flatten ourselves against it. The smudged blur goes around the corner.

"What was that?" gasps Phoebe, her eyes wild.

Although every instinct tells me to run, I want to see what happens. I peer around the corner to see hundreds of hornets descend on Etienne.

"No!" cries Yolande. She bats at the insects, but only gets stung for her trouble, shrieking and jumping away each time.

Etienne has leapt away, his trousers loose at his hips, and Yolande scrambles against the rock wall to keep her balance. The hornets completely hide his face with their black and yellow, writhing bodies. Their wings waver in frenzied time with their stinging. He's wearing a black, moving mask.

"They can't get us," says Phoebe. "They're his. It's his fate."

I can't help myself, though, from stepping backward, keeping myself between Phoebe and the hornets.

Yolande is screaming as loudly as Etienne, and she has pulled off her fichu to flap at the hornets and get them to leave him alone. It doesn't help.

In another moment, it's over. Phoebe and I back up as the hornets come toward us again, but they have no interest in us. They fly off as quickly as they had descended. Etienne's face is unrecognizable, a swollen mass of throbbing bites. There's nothing human about it. He sinks to his knees and falls flat on his face.

We watch in horror as Yolande crouches to touch his wrist, seeing if he has a pulse, and then howls in anger. "It's the work of Giraude," she says as she rises. Phoebe jumps back out of sight, but I remain there to see what transpires. I'm invisible to Yolande.

Yolande's face is tight. She isn't necessarily heartbroken, and she sheds no tears. She didn't care for Etienne other than to screw over her sister.

"So your love is dead, poor dear sister," she says as she smooths her skirts and begins undoing the damage to her elaborate hairstyle. "You have taken a knife to your nose to spite your face."

Phoebe takes my hand as the light readjusts, and the noise of present-day visitors penetrates again, people lining up photographs and selfies and sharing snacks from their backpacks. People peer in through the grille, not seeing us.

"Unbelievable," says Phoebe. "Do you think he was really dead?"

"I don't think they had antihistamines back then," I say.

"What a way for it all to end," she says in disbelief.

"Kind of makes you rethink the safety of getting so close to someone," I joke just because there's nothing we can do about it. "I won't ever touch you again."

Eleanor shows up, her face stricken. She's heard what I said.

"I'm sorry," I say quickly. "I tried to reach you but we weren't close enough."

"It is simply unfortunate," she says, "that I am not prey to the same magic you are. But what a lovely rock chamber."

She's so polite, the fault of her century and her social standing. I don't know what to say to that. I myself am still reeling from all the changes. Eleanor's known she's dead for a lot longer than I have. I'm not comfortable yet. And I hate feeling guilty for things that aren't my fault.

"So what happened?" she asks. "Or did anything?"

Phoebe looks at me unhappily. "A lot happened," she says. "Yolande was fooling around with Etienne. Somehow Giraude knew and sent hornets to kill him."

"So much for chasing each other through the trees," I say.

"But why not kill both of them?" Eleanor asks.

"A bit of sibling loyalty?" says Phoebe.

"Versailles was hard on lovers," I joke. Both girls give me a stare.

I sigh. "What's our plan? Vigilance followed by fireworks?"

"That's about it," says Eleanor. "Unless you'd like to vanish for a few hours."

"It's not our fault!" says Phoebe. "I tried to run to you! You saw me trying!"

"I did," says Eleanor glumly. "I saw that. I'm just wishing we were treated the same."

It wasn't so long ago that Eleanor treated us like we were in a social class above hers. She was a servant and we were not, but she has made leaps and strides toward a sense of self-worth. I'm dying for the day she finally discards her cap.

"Me, too," says Phoebe. "I wish the magic whisked you along, too. But maybe it's best you stay and look after—"

I can see where her sentence is going, and I can see the scowl starting on Eleanor's face. She's meant to watch over Tabby, a nursemaid, a governess, while we play at leisure. She's still the help, and she doesn't get what we get. I'm breathing in, preparing to do some damage control, when the light doesn't change so much as it goes dark instantly—

I whirl around and grab at Eleanor, but I'm still too slow—
and Phoebe, too, reaches out her hand to me, but I'm
gone—

I'm gone . . .

And back with Gillian in her bedroom.

CHAPTER EIGHT

The Sun King attended mass in the chapel every morning, and each day a new musical work was performed, composed specifically for the half-hour service.

—*Nooks and Crannies of Versailles*

*I*t's just her this time. Her and a candle.

   She's not crying but there's an intensity in her face that seems even worse.

   "Miles," she's whispering. "Miles . . ."

   "I'm here," I say. "What do you want to say?"

   "Miles, do you think about me? Where are you? What is it like?"

   I feel like an idiot, but I answer her in steady tones. "Of course I think about you," I say. "I'm still here, some version of here. I'm just not completely here."

   "I miss you. Your birthday was hard. Do you even know it was your birthday?"

   "I knew because you called me to you."

   "School is weird. Everyone thinks of me as your girlfriend still. Everyone's always hugging me. Reminding me."

   I don't say anything.

   "Did you know your locker is all decked out? All these messages scrawled on it and photographs and lipstick kisses? I couldn't remember your combination."

   Neither can I.

I hope there's no tuna fish sandwich in there slowly decomposing.

"I have so many memories of you. I miss you."

"I miss you, too," I say softly.

"My mom and dad want me to apply to university. That seems like I would completely leave you behind."

"You should," I say. "You should go to university. You should have your life."

Poor Gillian. Her lower lip is trembling and she's fighting tears again. She's completely dyed her hair since yesterday to flame red. She matches her candle.

"I need to make some fresh starts," she says.

"Okay," I say.

"It's year twelve." She says it with such a pang that I realize there's a whole missed year of our life together. We were supposed to go to the prom together, we were supposed to either plot to go to university together or talk each other into staying and working or traveling. I've always kind of fancied the idea of going on safari. I guess I can do it now—using intention, I could be on a safari in the next second—but without really experiencing it.

Gillian and I will never get a flat together, never have another row, never kiss. I'll never have her lips on mine again. She's lost to me . . . or more like, I'm lost to her. I'm vanished to everybody except Phoebe and Eleanor. I'm the original lost boy.

"Do you remember Chris Chadding?" she asks. "Of course you do. What a stupid question."

But it's funny—it takes me a few moments to remember him. The dude on the outskirts who doesn't talk much. Dark hair and always slouching into his oversized T-shirts.

She pulls out a school photo from her back pocket. She

briefly reads the inscription on the back, too quickly for me, and turns it back to the front. *Oh yeah, him.*

"He likes me, Miles," she whispers. "Is that okay? Is that okay?"

Oh, poor Gillian.

But I have to admit, something's rising in me, too. *That was fast*, I think. Did you mourn me for all of what, two months? I'm not even sure how long I've been dead.

I look contemptuously at the photograph of Chris. The photographer must've made him sit up and have good posture. He looks decent. Maybe the time I've spent dead, he's spent working out and getting better-looking.

Something else arises. Who's taken my place on the swim team? Who's the fastest, who's the leader?

So glad I meant something to you, Gillian, I think bitterly. Was yesterday's birthday séance really just softening the blow before this? How had she changed so much just in twenty-four hours, or had she? Maybe Chris's photo was in her back pocket the whole time.

"Take him, I don't care," I say aloud. "Be my guest."

"I'm really sorry," she says. "I wish I had a way to know you were okay."

"I'm fine! Things are totally going my way!"

"I'll never forget you, Miles. You were really special."

"Present tense, harpy!"

Now I don't like myself, either. It's not her fault. She should move on . . . maybe just not so fast. But the fact is, crying over a candle isn't going to change anything. Maybe a few kisses with Chris Chadding will make all the difference. Gillian will be good for him, and she'll heal and forget me and I'll just be that sad thing that happened before her A-level exams.

"Miles?"

It's Phoebe.

"Hey," I say briefly.

"You okay here?"

"You're not the only one who wants to know," I say.

"Who's he?" Phoebe's looking upside down at Chris's photograph as Gillian sits looking at it.

"My replacement."

"Seriously?" Phoebe's eyes widen. "You haven't been . . ."

". . . dead very long! I know!"

"Sorry."

"She wants permission to date him. From me, the dead bloke."

Phoebe smirks. "I say, big thumbs-up!"

Reluctantly, I laugh.

"Eleanor's probably super ticked off I'm here, but you were gone long enough I got worried."

"Thanks for checking on me."

"I feel awful sometimes," she says, and while she talks I'm aware that Gillian's in the background crying over the photograph. "But she's right. It's like we're linked in a way that doesn't include her. I wonder if we've had other lives or other . . . I don't know . . . representations of ourselves. Maybe I did betray her once."

"Well, you're nice to her now," I point out.

"I get worried that once we figure everything out, that's it."

A long silence falls. "I know," I say. "It's scary to think about it all ending."

"She's had a couple hundred years to mentally prepare," Phoebe says. "But I'm not ready to let go."

I nod. "Especially when we don't know what the next stage is."

"It looks like the universe wants us to kill Giraude. We're like the twin killers. It would make a great show on the Discovery Channel."

"On what?"

"Oh right, I forget you Brits only get three channels."

"Take it back!"

"Sorry," she smirks.

"So . . . how do we go about it?"

"Same trick twice?" She's thinking about how we fought off Giraude's sister in England.

"I don't know how we'd arrange that again."

"Or do we just get her the vials?" she asks.

"Right—because that's so easy! Because they've been kept hidden for hundreds of years, but we'll just waltz in and immediately locate them!"

"If we could direct our tripping," she muses, "you could overhear more secrets. Or we could even see where the vials are."

"Athénaïs said, 'You pray to know the answer.' Do you think it has to do with a religious place?"

"There's a chapel in the palace," she points out. "Should we go poke around?"

"Might as well. Let's grab Eleanor on our way."

I turn my attention back to Gillian. She's stopped crying and she's sitting there on the floor with her chin in her hands. She looks like she's in deep thought, her eyes focused on nothing. Not necessarily bad thoughts, either.

"New hair," comments Phoebe.

"New hair for a fresh start," I say wryly.

I'm moved by this quietude in Gillian. She was always loud, always punk rock, always sassy and funny . . . it's different to see her sitting so quietly. Did my death steal her loudness forever? Such that she'd consider someone like Chad for a boyfriend, so lanky and such an outsider?

It makes me think about myself, too, and what I was. The kind of person whose girlfriend had bleached punk hair and wore combat boots . . . but I shouldn't define myself by my girlfriend. I was the kind of person who wore a thrift-store leather jacket, who drove a beat-up old Austin Mini, who hated the songs on the radio and sought out his own music. Someone who did okay in school but wasn't averse to bunking off lessons now and then to go make out in a field on the other side of a bridge.

It hits me that I should try to communicate with her, try to find a way to let her know it's okay to date Chad and let me go.

I look at her empty hands. Could I hold one? Could I put something in her hand? A pen that I'd write a message with?

"Miles?" whispers Phoebe. "I'm going to go now. I'll check in with Eleanor and my family. Come whenever you're ready."

"Sure," I say. I smile uncertainly at her, and she's gone in an instant.

I feel so lonesome suddenly. Gillian's here but she has no idea I'm with her. I'm nothing. I'm a disturbance of the air. I wonder if I make a cold spot, like they always say about ghosts. I'm the effing draft in the room.

I stand up and walk around, trying to touch stuff, unsuccessfully. I spend a while with her pencil cup. I really want to communicate. I attempt to knock it over so pencils roll, but I'm like a useless rock-and-roll star trying to kick over the guitar stand but too drunk to aim correctly.

I crouch next to Gillian and talk right into her ear. "Can you hear me? Nod if you hear me."

I repeat that a few times at varying volumes.

She doesn't hear it.

She's looking at the candle, probably wishing she'd never been paired with me in chem lab, the whole reason we got together. We bonded over protons and neutrons, our elbows digging into the slightly malleable black rubber of the table-top. She should've been paired up with Chad and then my death would've been just that kind of thing that happens to someone you *know*, but not someone you thought you might spend your life with.

I remember her putting her pen in her mouth, then spitting it out with the most outraged face. She'd forgotten she'd stirred our chemical compound with it. She didn't have laboratory-safe practices, that girl.

"Go ahead, Gillian," I say. "You can resume your life. This was just a blip."

She leans forward. She's mesmerized by the flame of the candle. On impulse, I lean next to her and blow.

And the flame bends for a second before returning to vertical.

"Holy sweet Jesus!" I screech.

And she reacts, too. "Oh my God, are you here?" she asks, her eyes wide, so wide.

I bend over and blow again, and the flame bends.

I get it. I'm the drafty cold-spot ghost. I can move air. It's not much, but with a candle burning, it's *something*.

"Do that again," she commands.

I blow.

"Oh man," she says, and she jumps to her feet and runs to her door, yanking it open.

Not cool, Gillian. I'm not some demon.

I hear her pummeling down the hallway and down the stairs. She's terrified.

Of me.

I throw my face into my hands. When is anything ever going to feel good? This is just the cretaceous layer of crap atop the sedimentary level of shite, crowned with more crap, laid on top of endless strata of bollixed-up-itude.

Thanks, Gillian. I needed that. It wasn't enough to bleakly contemplate my own death and your replacement of me with some dude with bad posture; now I feel so *great* knowing I'm an object of fear, too.

Wonderful!

Effin' candle.

Her house'll burn down if I don't extinguish it. So I lean over, fill my not-lungs with her air, the air she's privileged to breathe, and blow the jones out of that candle.

Dark.

Buh-bye.

Cheerio!

Back in France, Phoebe's family is hanging out on a blanket waiting for the fireworks display to start. Eleanor and Phoebe are talking earnestly as I arrive, and they stop midsentence the instant they see me.

I'm in no mood.

I sit with my back to them, staring out at the green lawns tinged with blue as twilight falls.

Tabby is the only one with any energy. She's darting out in forays from the blanket, running to a particular bush and back, over and over. Add a stick to the mix and she'd make a great puppy.

I think about the German man hidden behind one of these bushes, waiting for the world to notice he's gone. But I don't see yellow police tape anywhere; there are some lonesome people in this world who can vanish without a soul paying heed.

"Can't you see if they'll refund the tickets?" Phoebe's mum is saying. "It's hours yet and she's already manic."

"It won't hurt her to have one late night in her life," says Steven.

"It might hurt me," says Phoebe's mum. She's joking, but she's not.

"Do you want me to walk you two back to the hotel? I can come back and watch the fireworks myself."

"Hm. That might actually . . . solve things. So long as you stay away from drunken tourists."

It occurs to me that when the German's body is found, Steven might be held responsible. Won't people show the police their phone videos of the two of them fighting? Those might be going viral already.

If I had corporeality, I'd find the German's discarded body and slide it into the Grand Canal where no one would find it. He might be reported as someone who didn't show up at his next destination, but he was traveling . . . people often take detours and get waylaid.

I turn around and look briefly at Phoebe. I don't want to worry her so I won't mention it. There's nothing we can do about it. If the body's found, it's found. Her family will be back in England by dinnertime tomorrow anyway.

"Should we check out the chapel?" asks Phoebe. "Like we were going to?" Her voice sounds vaguely accusatory, but I shrug it off. I'm not going to feel guilty. If she and Eleanor

want to talk about me, let them. I'm not going to pretend I
didn't notice, though.

"Is everything all right with your sweetheart?" asks
Eleanor.

My sweetheart. I make an unattractive sound from my
nose.

"She's crossed over from sorrow to terror," I say.

"What?" says Phoebe.

"I managed to blow the candle flame a little and it freaked
her out. She ran away."

Phoebe throws her arms around me and almost knocks me
over. "Sorry, Miles," she says.

"But how intriguing that you managed to blow the
flame," Eleanor marvels.

"I could hire out for birthday parties," I say. "A boon for
the lazy and the asthmatic."

"This has possibly important applications," says Eleanor.
"You can manipulate air."

"Lucky me."

"If you're bent on that mood, so be it," snaps Eleanor in a
completely unexpected voice. She stalks off to the row of
manicured miniature trees that frame our horizon.

"I'm going after her," says Phoebe. "And then, let's hit the
chapel. We have to try everything. I'm hoping Mom takes
Steven up on the offer to go back to the hotel. I'll relax once
she and Tabby are away from Giraude."

"Sure," I say. I sit watching with zero interest as Phoebe
catches up with Eleanor and they say girl things to each
other.

I'm done.

I'm exhausted.

If I could wipe my hands and undo everything, go back in time and never meet Phoebe and Eleanor, to the days when I thought of the Arnaud Manor as some crazy decaying mansion I'd never set foot in . . . would I?

I think I would.

I'd love to return to normal.

To return to rolling my eyes at my homework on my desk, to dinners with my parents, to the simple worries of what university I'd attend and whether my grades would get me in or not.

To whether Gillian would go to university with me or not.

To whether I'd care about her in another year. We'd never had our relationship tested. It was exciting and pretty new, and we never moved to the phase where it gets boring.

I knew things got tedious. I knew I'd want to make sure I kept my options open for someone I'd meet at university.

Someone with auburn hair, maybe. An American exchange student. A pretty girl named, oh, say, Phoebe.

I smile at myself, in spite of myself.

I'm tired, all right, and I'd love to exchange this strange reality for the boredom of all my yesterdays.

But . . .

But Phoebe.

Phoebe.

Damn, but I like that girl. I catch her eye from far away and give her a thumbs-up. Chapel it is.

Let's locate those vials of blood and bring them to the centuries-old immortal woman who likes to strangle tourists, shall we?

CHAPTER NINE

It is said that a head once severed from the body maintains awareness and consciousness for a full seven seconds. After guillotining, heads were seen to react and even to bite at others in the basket.

—*The Machine That Fueled a Revolution*

*T*he chapel is vast, like everything else on the Versailles campus. I laugh to myself: "campus." Right.

A place to learn how not to treat peasants, right? A crash course in empathy for breadless folks?

Overhead there are florid scenes painted on the ceiling with blue clouds intermittently between them. It's like the Sistine Chapel on diamonds. Everything here is resplendently golden, amber, light-touched. High up in the rafters, rows of inset, gabled windows bring in the last bits of sun to bathe the marble below.

Since Athénaïs said something about praying, I head first for the altar at the front. It's cordoned off with one of the red ropes that we dead scoff at.

"Today's present chapel site is the fifth on the grounds of the chateau," I overhear a tour guide say, a different person than the one who held forth in Marie-Antoinette's chamber earlier today. "The most recent was located where today's Salon d'Hercule exists, and previous versions have been swallowed by the queen's *salle des gardes*. There were many changes, as

successive kings found the chapel's placement inconvenient
and with typical monarchic whim, simply moved it."

Phoebe stands stock-still, looking at me, horrified. So this
might not be the place Athénaïs referenced after all. We
might have to conduct an archeological dig to locate the
original chapel and its cupboard of blood. I raise an eyebrow
at her. What can we do? It's a silly needle-in-a-haystack mission anyway.

Do we really think we're going to find something that no
one in hundreds of years of cleaning the palace, of restoring
it, of ransacking it, for that matter—that no one else found?
And, uh, also without the benefit of being able to touch
stuff?

We're just like those cops on *Law & Order* who go pay the
house call to the grocery clerk because they have to follow
that lead, all the while knowing it's not going to lead to anything other than a "busy" scene where a kid rolls his eyes and
refuses to stop bagging groceries while chatting with the
cops. (Really? They can't get his manager to let him step
away for a few minutes?)

Oh well, it's something to do other than endlessly regret
the circumstances of my own death.

The chapel was deconsecrated in the 1800s, the guide tells
us, but it still carries an air of solemnity beyond the equally
grand chambers of state. I pause before the altar.

Does it have hidden chambers inside? Where the priests
once stored their wine, wafers, and vestments, is there a
deeper compartment holding glass containers of rusting
blood?

I know I can't touch it, but just to be thorough, I extend
a hand to the altar. It goes right through it. I pause and then

stick my head inside. Highlighted by a shaft of light coming in from a loosely fitting cupboard door, a gray mouse pauses on its hind legs. It can't see me, but it feels me. It squeals and rushes away almost as quickly as I withdraw.

Next I walk the walls, looking at the wooden paneling for some interruption in the pattern, some subtle outline of a door just like the one in Marie-Antoinette's bedroom. I see Phoebe and Eleanor making the same examination of the floor. Maybe a trapdoor will open up and show us a flight of collapsible stairs. The pews are long gone, but I use intention to move to the row of second-story tiers, where noble people could watch the religious proceedings as if they were at the theater. I look carefully but find nothing out of the ordinary.

"In a way I'm relieved," says Phoebe, showing up next to me. "If we don't have the vials, we don't have to wrestle with the ethics of turning them over to Giraude."

"I've been thinking about that," says Eleanor, who appears as Phoebe speaks. "We could give her one and say the cache was depleted. Nothing compels us to give her everything. One vial could hold her over for years, until the next fearless crew comes around, hopefully with more knowledge and power than we have."

"True," says Phoebe. "Or as soon as she takes a swig, we can bat it out of her hands."

"And be back in the same danger we are in now!" protests Eleanor.

"Maybe we could accidentally drop it just as we hand it over to her," I say. "They must be made of glass, right? Who could be mad at someone dropping something?"

We all laugh.

As I look up at the impossible height of the ceiling, as I imagine myself soaring up to the painted clouds and blue sky,

I feel that weightlessness that means I'm about to go some-where. My whole brain is awash in whistling; it feels differ-ent. It's not that the *light* is changing . . . the scene is changing. I'm not indoors anymore, and I sense fresh air coming across my face. There's a roar that's not the quietude of hushed visitors to the chapel . . . it's a gusty yell.

People here are really angry.

We're in Paris. The unmistakable feel of that city washes over me, even though it's not recognizable. It hasn't been Hausmannized yet, and the tumbling, canted medieval archi-tecture is still in place. We're at the back of a crowd pushing through the narrow streets. Phoebe reaches out to grab my hand, and I look wildly around. No Eleanor.

"Let's get to the front of the mob," I say. "And find out what's going on." We use intention to move, and there we see that the crowd has been following a row of horse-drawn tumbrels. Inside, people stand, trying to keep their balance as they jostle side to side on the cobblestones.

They're on their way to execution. The stress and panic rises off them almost like a stink.

"No," says Phoebe. "I can't watch this."

The noblewomen wear gowns of silk with ribbons and in-set panels of brocade, while the men are in fine shirts and well-made breeches, but an overlay of dirt smudges their fin-ery. They've been housed like animals in filthy cells with straw thrown on the floor for their beds. No maid has combed or powdered their hair in weeks. They're bedrag-gled and flea-bitten and sleepless. Their eyes show the beaten-down acceptance of their fate.

Still, if I were in that tumbrel, I'd jump out and see how far I'd get on foot. Those bloodthirsty crowds would doubtless give me a harder death than the clinical speed of the guillotine, but at least I'd feel that I'd tried.

We turn the corner and enter into the square. The smell hits me like a slap. It's blood. Thick, collected blood. The crowd erupts in cheers. "Place du Trône Renversé!" screams the woman ahead of me gleefully. It means the "place of the throne reversed." I remember Phoebe's stepdad talking about this town square that used to be called, simply, Place du Trône—the revolutionaries had turned the name and the concept upside down.

I can see the guillotine elevated above even the tallest men; its platform a stage for open-air theater.

A chilling sight. Nothing in life prepared me to see a device meant to murder as many people as possible, quickly, efficiently. It rises up, wooden and forbidding, with that large, slanted blade poised and ready to drop. A slanted board connects to it, to which one by one, the people in the tumbrels will be fastened, their clothing sticking to the blood there from the former user, and the former, and the former. They'll be lowered into place and the blade dropped. At the base is a board-covered pit to collect blood flowing from the machine. That's what the stench is. It's a pit full of hundreds of people's blood, like a butcher's shop that never cleans its floor.

Terrible enough, but what makes it nauseating is the crowd. They're so happy. So high-energy that their eyes sparkle. Children are here, too, grinning and jubilant. These peasants have been hungry for so long, they've been made as murderous as any serial killer. They can't wait to see these nobles face their deaths while struggling to control their bowels and keep a bit of dignity.

A man is made to lie down on the slanted board, and before I can even blink, he's decapitated.

The crowd loves the thump of the head falling into the basket, a sound I'll never forget. Phoebe shrieks and turns away in anguish. The crowd hoots and hollers like football hooligans when the executioner holds up the head by its hair and the vacant eyes either stare or don't—I can't tell. The jaw drops open, giving this unfortunate man the regrettable look of having been very, very stupid.

The tumbrels arrive now and come to a stop. The people are shuffled out of them, to wait their turn. It's a literal line, I see in horror. They are waiting like cows to the slaughter.

The blade lifts again, the board is swabbed of blood, and the headless body is taken away to lie in a tumbrel so recently vacated by standing people.

The next woman is led up the steps to her death. She's shivering. Her hands move so rapidly it's like she's writing a letter with two hands.

"I can't do it," says Phoebe. We've been holding on to each other this whole time, but I lost track of her in the face of what I'm seeing. She's as panicked as if *she's* about to mount the scaffold and lie down on that wet board.

I nod and use all my strength to intention to the present, to Eleanor and Tabby and her parents.

It doesn't work.

"Okay," I say. "Let's at least try to be somewhere else if we can't leave this time period. How about the plaza in front of Notre Dame?"

"Yes! Anything!" I see her fierce determination and I close my eyes to focus, too, because I can't *be here*, I can't stand this violence and brutality, but the jeers of the sadistic crowd continue in my ears.

"We're meant to watch," says Phoebe grimly.

"You don't have to," I say. "Close your eyes." As I say it, I open mine.

"It's too scary to keep my eyes shut. Even though I'm already dead and they can't hurt me, I don't trust them."

We press ourselves to the back of the crowd to at least be farther away from those forlorn people in the tumbrels and the despicable glee of the peasants.

What makes people want to see others be hurt? They're starving, I get that, but surely they understand that the people in these carts aren't directly responsible?

Phoebe's nails are digging into my wrist.

"Ouch!" I snap my hand away.

"Look, Miles!"

It's Giraude.

She's not associated with the other nobles, and she's dressed in brown, coarse clothing. Her face is stark with determination, and a man pulls at her sleeve, trying to stop her from moving forward. He's dressed simply, like her, and his face shows a lack of courtliness or sophistication.

"My lady, please do not do this. We've risked so much to keep you safe," he implores.

She whirls around and almost snarls at him. "My life is worth nothing. You may save yourself, but I welcome the chance to be delivered from this living hell."

"For my sake?" he pleads.

She's so scornful she doesn't even bother to respond. I see desperation come over his expression.

"I must say this—you know my feelings but I've never dared voice them."

"Don't," she says. "You are my manservant and I value the service you have rendered me over the years. But more than that, you may not proffer."

"I proffer it nonetheless," he says with a boldness I have to admire. "I love you, my lady."

She sighs and permits him to see the derision resting openly on her face. I take a step back from this cruelness.

"I have loved only one man in my life, and he is long dead. You have tried to blackmail me," she says, "protecting me and hiding me as a peasant in return for affection I can never feel. But I don't value my life, so your labors are for naught."

"I did not save you to blackmail you. I saved you because despite your faults and despite the gap in our circumstances, I love you. You believe yourself high above me, but this revolution changes that and evens out our status. *Égalité!*" he shouts.

A few of the women standing near them echo his cry, but then return their attention to the guillotine.

"A revolution does not make us equals," she says. "Dirty peasants killing their betters is nothing but a temporary upturning of the natural order. It is like a flea thinking itself the master of the hound it bites."

"You are a haughty snip," he says, his voice deflated, "and yet I admire you."

"Save yourself, Pierre," she says. "As for me, I crave my spot on that scaffold." She breaks away from him. He no longer pulls at her sleeve, but follows behind her, letting someone get between them, and then a second person. He's resigned.

"What on earth?" asks Phoebe. I translate the gist of their discussion, summarizing it into a few sentences.

Giraude pushes her way to the front of the crowd, and of course we follow, too, a bit behind Pierre. We don't want to return, but we have to learn from this moment. We were flung backward in time by some unknown force to witness it, and it's something important. As we approach the guillotine again, I can smell it: blood has its own distinct tinny smell and it's so profuse it's running in the gutters.

Giraude strides to the base of the scaffold and calls out, "Hark! Here is a noblewoman of the House of Arnaud who turns herself in!"

Everyone turns to gape at her, including the executioner, who forgets his work in the release of weights and cables. But the blade doesn't forget. It flies down resoundingly onto the slender neck of the woman who, too, had turned to look at Giraude and her dramatic announcement. I see in her face multiple surprise as the mystery of Giraude's pronouncement is replaced by the mystery of her own death.

She will become a ghost, I think. Some of these other people will, too, killed in the crush of dread and for no real reason they can discern other than a nation's caprice . . . but this woman was also robbed of the acknowledgment of her final mortal moment. Distracted at the most important second of her life.

I feel awful for her. Her head, bewildered, rolls into the basket, spraying blood as it goes.

This doesn't faze Giraude at all. She climbs the steps even as the executioner belatedly recalls his duty and gathers up the limp body.

"I have hidden myself for months, dressing as you do, eating and behaving as you do," says Giraude loudly as the crowd hushes to hear her. "But I am done with that. I wish to pay the ultimate price for my greed, my wealth, my noble birth. I renounce all that I am and beg you humbly to end my life as it should be ended."

A cheer goes up. I glance at the line of nobles, who seem

dumbfounded. A few look angry. The man who was next to go is visibly sweating. He must've resolved himself and found some courage—and now his death is being delayed by her arrogance. She can't even sacrifice herself in a selfless manner.

"You are correct in all that you suspected of my kind," she informs the peasants. "We supped and busily drank all the night and day that you labored, and we laughed at your plight."

I frown over at Phoebe, although she has no idea what was just said. What does Giraude gain by this? She's just making it worse for people who are going to die anyway. Now I see them swelling with indignation, and one screams out, "That is untrue! I am a minor noble and have barely enough food for my family! It is my name I will die for today, not my wealth!"

Others are shouting now, too, arguing her down. She laughs carelessly and pulls her grimy fichu away from her neck to ready it for the blade. The executioner looks as if he has no idea what to do with her.

"The price of bread? We didn't care what you paid or what you did if you couldn't pay it or if there was no bread," she tells the mob. "I care now, and that is why I ask you to let me die for the excesses of my vile past."

"Is it my fault I am born into the family I am born into?" calls another man. "I landed in a golden cradle as the guest of fate. It could just as easily have been a blanket laid on the floor. None of us control this!"

I glance at Pierre. Silent tears run down his cheeks. Or maybe he's loudly sobbing; I have no idea. I can't hear anything other than the desperate calls of the nobles using this moment to bargain, to try, to throw any reason to the mob calling out chants of hatred.

"My squalid Parisians," Giraude says, "you may not have bread today. But if you do, I invite you to dip it in the blood that will flow from my neck. Let my blood flavor your bread."

I almost swear I can feel the cobblestones under my feet adjusting, tipping, with the crowd's furious stamping of approval—but of course I feel nothing.

Women open up their kerchiefs to take out a bit of bread in readiness, and men check their pockets. "They're seriously going to do it?" I say aloud in disbelief.

The executioner walks the boundary of the platform, his arms open to ask the crowd's . . . what, permission? They roar back at him, throats red and wide, eyes blazing, and Giraude laughs at their vehemence. Satisfied, he completes his circuit and returns to her.

"Citizeness," he says, waving his arm at the guillotine as if he is inviting her to take a seat. He assists her onto the board and secures her. I watch to see if she'll look for Pierre for one last moment with him, but she is so involved in herself she doesn't seem to remember he's here. The board lowers into position and the executioner grins and snaps the rope.

It's done.

Her body pulses and jumps as her artery gushes its last earnest offerings: blood that is unconstrained by the narrow vessels it had kept itself to for decades, now lofting without limits into the air. Her face is satisfied as the executioner holds it aloft for an extended period and parades it around the four sides of the platform.

"Keep her head with her body," he barks to the man who is ferrying bodies from the scaffold to the tumbrels. "She's a special one."

And, yes, women bend to the blood that drips to the

ground below the scaffold. They eat bread soaked in Giraude's blood.

They are vampires.

Blood smears their lips.

"How did Giraude survive this?" Phoebe asks, her eyes frantically searching my face. She's broken, changed. She's never seen anything like this before.

How did she? How do you keep living when your head has been separated from your body?

I watch Pierre's progress as he walks to the tumbrel holding Giraude's body. He has a sense of watchfulness, of protectiveness. So, too, does the young girl standing there next to him. They don't know each other, they say nothing to each other, but they both act like they're standing guard over these murdered bodies.

I remember the story from the Picpus cemetery.

"Pierre is going to dig her back up tonight from the mass grave these people will be thrown into," I say. "He's going to attach her head. She's going to wear a black ribbon around her neck to hide the seam."

"She's the one from the story at the cemetery," says Phoebe slowly.

We look at each other.

"I want my mom," says Phoebe, and we hug each other fiercely. There is no "mom" anymore. There's no comfort. There's just the attempt to feel sensation through the fog.

CHAPTER TEN

Buried at Picpus are the sixteen Carmelite nuns who took courage in their pending executions and sang hymns of joy as the tumbrels brought them to the guillotine. Even as they stood in line they sang, the hymns quieted voice by voice until only one sister continued the thread of the song as she mounted the steps to the scaffold.

—*Catholic Martyrs*

We try to return to the present with more urgency, but some force wants us stuck in this dark evening of death upon death. "Thank God Eleanor's with my family," says Phoebe. Morose, we experiment with how to get as far from the guillotine as possible. We can move a block away, where the people begin to thin out and the cries and cheers are at least, if not muted, not yelled directly into our ears. But as we try to take one extra step, we're immediately blinked back to the foot of the scaffold.

I keep Pierre in my peripheral vision, because it's easier to look at him than the headless body of Giraude . . . and clearly, it's them we're here for. For some reason, we have to see this day out.

Eventually, the tumbrel Giraude shares with a dozen other people, crammed together as if they were sacks of potatoes, no dignity, no sense of their being *people*, begins moving. It's part of a caravan of about ten tumbrels.

Pierre and the young girl follow, but they try to be discreet. The cover of darkness helps their cause. Phoebe and I follow and learn that now we are able to go farther than a city block away. We're part of this strange, secretive funeral procession. Pierre and the girl don't talk to each other, may not even be aware of each other. We walk as the horses pick their way slowly through the streets, turning right, turning left.

The ground is marshy and impedes the wheels' progress, and the cart drivers pass the whip over the horses' heads to make them step faster.

Finally in the distance I see the outlines of the Picpus church. There's no neighborhood around it now; it's a far-flung choice for the leaders of the Revolution. They were smart about it. No one but the four of us is dedicated enough to follow the tumbrels this far on foot.

We enter through a gate in the churchyard's fence. The tumbrels remain in line as the first approaches the edge of a pit. The horseman pulls his horse sharply to the side and then in a curve so that the back of the cart now faces the trench. He gets off his horse and, swearing slightly at the cold we don't feel, the cold that makes his breath a cloud, he tips the cart back on its two wheels . . . and the contents go sliding down into the pit with a sound I can't even begin to describe. He gets back on his horse and the cart moves off, perhaps back to Paris.

The girl is sobbing. Quietly, for she doesn't want to draw attention to herself, but there are people in these tumbrels she loves. Dumped into the earth as if their lives hadn't mattered.

We wait as the carts empty their contents, sometimes urging the horses around to a different part of the trench as the level of the bodies inside approaches the top and we see the pale gleam of arms in strangely graceful positions, rigor mortis arranging them like those of Roman statues forever reaching for a cluster of marble grapes.

The heads go, too, reserved in several red barrels that are dumped indiscriminately.

Finally, the cart we know holds Giraude approaches the lip of the pit. I can't bear to look at Pierre's face. She slides down in an indistinguishable mass, combined in a clump of bodies with strangers, people she may have danced with in the same ballroom at one point, who may have sipped champagne from the same cellar. A few more tumbrels dump their loads, then two men with shovels begin tossing some white material over the bodies as the horses and carts depart. I hear one lone horseman whistling some jaunty tune, its playfulness completely out of place on the thin wind.

"What are they spreading over the bodies?" I ask Phoebe.

"Lime," she says. "I remember reading about it once. It keeps the smell of decomposition down. Pierre will need to be careful. It burns. He can't get it on his skin."

She points to him. He's leaning down on the edge, trying to pull Giraude up. He's got hold of one arm, but a heavier body lies sideways across her, and he can't get her. He lets go and tries to push the man away. He's using all his strength, but the angle is too difficult. I hear harsh cries escape his throat. It's all right to shout and rage now—the tumbrels are gone. The men with shovels broadcast one last load of lime and then retreat to the shadows. It's just us, him, the girl, the silent hundreds reeling.

"I'll help you," says the girl, coming up to Pierre. "Hand me down there." Her voice is unutterably sweet. She's got that small pang of childhood in her voice.

"What did she say?" asks Phoebe, and I translate the French for her. "God, no, she can't go down there!"

She runs toward the girl but we are powerless. We've done nothing but give ourselves a better view of the horror in that pit, the lolled heads and their stricken faces, the bodies that look so crazy, so abjectly wrong, without the balancing head on top. The little girl climbs down into the pit with the assistance of Pierre, who knows he is asking too much of her, but has no other choice.

She stands unevenly, her booted feet astride the torso of an otherwise unseen woman, half buried under others. She's light and lithe and can do the job Pierre can't. She gestures to the body of Giraude, twisted as if she sleeps restlessly, and he nods.

"Yes, this one," he says.

"She was so pretty and so brave," says the girl. "She gave herself up."

She bends and almost falls, her balance dependent on an uneven flooring of corpses. She regains herself and pushes at the large man atop Giraude, her effortful grunt turning triumphant as he rolls off. She grins up at Pierre, who quickly pulls her back up out of that atrocious playground no child should ever witness, let alone set foot in.

And then together, each holding one arm, they pull Giraude's form out and up. She doesn't come easily, but with two working together, they are able to do it. Giraude's head, tucked between her legs by the headman's assistant, her skirts divided for the task, comes with her. Rigor mortis holds her thighs stiff, and it looks in some horrific way as if she were giving birth to her own head.

"Thank you, my sweet," says Pierre to the girl, and he reaches into his pocket to give her a coin. She shakes her head but he insists, and she takes it. I'm glad. She may be an orphan making her own way on the streets . . . no adult has taken an interest in her whereabouts for the last six hours or so we've been here.

"May I help you in turn?" he asks.

Her face is ancient as the pagan stones you find sometimes in an abandoned field. "No," she says. "There's nothing I can do for my father and brother. I just wanted to know where they lie and to say my prayers."

Pierre nods.

"Besides," she adds, "they were in one of the first cartloads. They're deep in; I don't think I could fetch them out even with three men."

"God be with you, girl," he says.

I don't want to watch what Pierre does with Giraude, pulling her head out from between her thighs. I don't want to see him reattach her head or witness whatever stitches he'll be able to sew here in the dark. I don't know how he'll reanimate her . . . Wait.

"Will she need to drink from the vials again to become alive?" I ask Phoebe. "Maybe he has the vials with him?"

"Maybe," she says. "But why would he, a servant, have them? And even if he does, how does it benefit us? We can't touch them or bring them back in time with us."

"If he has them, we can stick with him to find out where he lives, where he keeps them."

"They must be at Versailles," says Phoebe.

"We don't know that for sure," I argue. "It's worth staying with him and observing him."

"Worth it? As if we have any control over it?" asks Phoebe. "We've been stuck in this time period for hours."

"Well, we could try again," I say. Halfheartedly, knowing it won't work, I try to intention myself back to the present day, to Versailles . . . and it *works*.

For a second I look at Eleanor's startled face, the family sprawled on the picnic blanket, Tabby asleep in her mom's arms, the parents chatting—then I instantly return to Picpus.

Phoebe's not there.

No one's there.

What have I done?

What have I *done*? I shout Phoebe's name and run a circuit around the grave pit. I was only gone a second—how did Pierre drag Giraude's body away so quickly?

Unreal.

I go back to the present day. How odd to go from an open pit of bodies to another rectangle: the tartan blanket they're all reclining on. Eleanor rushes to me. "Where's Phoebe?"

"I lost her," I say.

She stares at me, her mouth wide open.

"It was stupid. I just wanted to see if the past would release us—we've been trying all day—but I didn't expect it to work!"

"Go back!" she shouts. "Go get her!"

I return to Picpus, which feels different from even just a few moments ago. More time has passed. I see tumbrels at the gate; it's the new day's load. Based on the sunlight, it seems like early afternoon here.

"Phoebe!" I yell. "Phoebe, where are you?"

I go to the edge of the pit and stare down. I don't remember the layout of bodies enough to know if it's been more than a day. It's just a ghastly assemblage of tortured, murdered people.

I head toward the chapel, a squat white structure with a Germanic-looking clock tower. Maybe Phoebe took shelter in there. I enter and see blood on the stone floor.

Not puddles of blood: smears. As if knives or bayonets were used on people still in motion, fleeing, twisting.

The nuns aren't safe. The priests aren't safe. They're ene-

mies of the state just like the nobles. The reliquaries and statues lie smashed on the floor and the niches for the icons are
empty. I shiver and move to the shadows. "Phoebe?" I call
out again.

I have no idea what to do.

I screwed up.

I don't want to go back and see Eleanor's accusing face. I
can't go back until I have Phoebe. And she's somewhere in
this vicious version of Paris.

I sink to my knees. What can I do? I hear the tumbrel
wheels rolling on the other side of the chapel wall. More
bodies. More death.

God, what am I supposed to do? Find the vials? Some
force sends me back in time and I'm supposed to learn from
everything I witness, right? I'm supposed to be taking notes
like this is some screwed-up version of French History:
1700s to the Present. I scan back through it.

Yolande and Giraude competed for the same lover. He
died for his failure to be true. Yolande tried to take over Giraude's place as firstborn in the family, heir to all the Arnaud
secrets. She used her striking identical-twin similarity to seduce secrets out of Athénaïs, who seemed to know everything. Athénaïs told her the vials were hidden where one
prays. We saw Giraude kill herself with a guillotine and apparently her servant is going to sew her back up and send her
out to continue business as usual with a big ribbon covering
the gaffe in her neck.

And Phoebe's missing.

The light flickers, fades, and changes. Thank God.

Yes, bring on something different, *show me*.

The first thing I notice is an overweight woman in a
bright red fleece. She's wearing khaki shorts and black socks

under her Tevas. It's the present day but I'm still at the Pic-pus chapel.

Things have been fixed up. The niches have statues again. They can't be the originals, but they look old. The blood-stains are gone. There's fluorescent lighting and a buzz of in-terested murmurs. France is a different beast now.

"Phoebe?" I call out at the limits of my voice. I honestly don't think I've ever raised my voice so loudly before. I see the red-fleece woman wince, but it crosses her face so quickly I'm not even sure it was a reaction to me. Maybe gas from the croissant-laden breakfast she's not used to.

I walk back outside and it's the same as it was the day we visited with Phoebe's mum and Tabby in the buggy. Gravel covers the pits and a nice plaque marks the spot where the nobles have shed their tissue and skin and become nothing but skeletons.

"No!" I scream to the sky. "I can't believe this!"

Is it random? I feel like I'm a pinball in the machine, the flippers sending me side to side for no good reason.

". . . the perpetual prayer," murmurs a tourist next to me. "We should put some money in the offering box to fund it."

The perpetual prayer. Right: the nuns have never stopped praying for the victims in this pit. Athénaïs couldn't have known about that—it predated her discussion with the young Yolande—but the chapel has always been a place of prayer, perpetual or otherwise.

I may be slow. But it's dawning on me.

I think the vials are here.

CHAPTER ELEVEN

Washington Irving's short story "The Legend of Sleepy Hollow" tells of a schoolteacher's terrifying horseback ride through the night pursued by a headless Hessian soldier, who throws his head at him. Irving's tale, however, makes it clear that the "ghost" was a rival suitor and the head, found later in shatters, merely a pumpkin.

—A Life in Tarrytown

*N*ow it's pleasurable to look, not like the stupid wanderings through the chapel at Versailles. It's like I know I'm on the right track. This is the place. God only knows why a Catholic church would be the place to hide vials that deliver an unholy immortality to those who drink from them, but this is it.

I go back inside the church and head for the altar. Everything seems in order, so I walk along the edges of the walls and check each paving stone in the floor. I wander into the nave, drift through walls to the areas meant only for the priests, thoroughly search every inch of the structure. I even drift up to the bell tower and check the clapper, the bronze, concave interior of the bell, the whole apparatus that lets it ring.

No dice.

I head back down to the main part of the church again and watch an old woman sit and make the sign of the cross, then begin her prayer. Where? Where could the vials be hidden?

Vials, Phoebe. Phoebe, vials. Things I need to find.

Maybe they're outside in the mass grave, deep in the pit,

I think. Maybe the revolutionaries dug atop an already-excavated vials repository.

Ah! Got it. Digging. Deeper.

The crypt.

How did I miss this? There's a little door (damn, Miles, there's *always* a little door . . . have you learned nothing from Marie-Antoinette's bedroom setup?) behind which is a steep and narrow winding staircase that leads up to the bell tower . . . but it also leads down to the crypt, so long as you're dead and can drift through padlocked doors.

I can feel it.

I take the stairs, sinking into the cool depths of the chapel.

The vials are here. They're almost humming, like they recognize I've come for them. I walk the vaulted undercroft, aware that the musty dead are here, paper-dry, at peace since they died after confession and last rites, assured of everything going their way. No haunting required. I don't know if they actually received that expected final reward, but regardless: there's no regret here.

I close my eyes and follow the low hum or moan or whatever it is that I can sometimes tune into, that undercurrent of energy.

And I crouch in front of a part of the wall that is unremarkable other than the fact that scratched into the wood, worn away by generations of damp, is a symbol.

A special stone! This must be it! This is where the vials are. I *found* them.

The symbol shows a dragon in a cell, its wings outstretched and pressing against his ceiling and walls. He looks like he's trying to break free, and his mouth is open in a miniature roar. Around his feet, his tail winds in an angry twist. Between his claws is a dropped sword.

The image upsets me, even in the midst of my triumph. I can imagine the frustration of being so powerful and then confined to so small a space.

I put my hand to the dragon, but I can't do a darn thing to open the cabinet, to trip the hidden levers, to enact the centuries-old lock that keeps the vials safe. I *could* pass through the wall and look.

I almost don't.

But then I think, *I have to*. This is the source of our quest. I press my face to the stone and move forward. It's so dark in here I can't see a thing, but the scent is intoxicating—a sort of sweet, warm odor, like amber. The humming becomes louder.

Phoebe might be able to open the cabinet. She could touch Arnaud things, and these vials are connected to her family. I'll find her, wherever she is, bring her here, and she'll open the door.

I withdraw and look again at the dragon guarding the hoard behind it. Everything will work itself out. We're so close to understanding everything.

The humming gets agitated. It's like the vials are angry I retreated. "I'll come back," I say.

Reluctantly, I back away from the stone wall. From a distance, the dragon is impossible to see. I close my eyes to leave the crypt and return to Versailles.

I found the vials.

Phoebe's on the blanket with her family and Eleanor. *Thank God.*

I leap on her and nearly knock her over. I nuzzle into her neck, inhaling the sense memory of whatever shampoo she used to use when she was alive: lavender, mint . . .

"You're okay?" I ask.

Instead of hugging me back, she pulls away. "Where the hell did you go?"

"It was stupid. I was just testing the machinery. I came back here and saw Eleanor, and within a second I returned but it was too late. It seemed like it was the next day."

"I spent two days in the past with Giraude's corpse," says Phoebe.

"I'm sorry," I say. "But I've something amazing to tell you."

"I kept trying to pull you to me with intention but it wasn't working."

"This was a different kind of trip," I say. "We traveled geographically, too."

"Sure, blame the trip," says Phoebe.

"Seriously?"

"Yes, seriously!" Her jaw is set and she's staring into the distance: anywhere my face is *not*, it seems. Darkness has settled into the foundations at Versailles, and the fireworks will begin any minute.

"Yeah, that was stupid," I admit. "But I can make up for it by what I have to tell you."

"Can you scrub my eyes? Because that would make up for it. It was all very Frankensteinian, if that's a word. He *sewed her up*. He used *black thread*."

I look at Eleanor, who's biting her lip. I think we're both interested in details, but at the same time don't want to hear them.

"He slumped her body against his legs as he sat, and positioned her head in his lap. He leaned over to sew, and it looked very uncomfortable. He sobbed uncontrollably the whole time."

"Poor man," Eleanor says. "He could've picked a more deserving recipient of his devotion, though."

I'm bursting with my news, but I also figure it can wait. Those vials have been there since Louis was king (one or all of them, who knows?)—and Tabby's right here with us. We're all safe. Plus, Phoebe needs to debrief. We're her ad hoc therapists.

"Did she instantly reanimate?" I ask.

"No, and that made him cry harder than ever. He put her on his bed, laid out nicely, and slept beside her on the floor. The next morning, she was still dead, but she was . . . what's the word?"

Phoebe pauses and she's going through vocabulary lists in her mind, I imagine. "Pliable. That's it. No rigor mortis. He could lift her arms and legs and bend them, and that made him think there was hope. He passed an entire day by her side."

"So he didn't use the vials," I say. I can't help it; I burst into a smile when I say *vials*. Phoebe frowns.

"No, he didn't seem to know anything about that, although he did have faith she would come back to life, as if he understood something about the Sangreçu ways. It wasn't until the next morning that she stirred just as a regular person would, making murmurs and stretching."

Oh my God. I can imagine how that would so profoundly upset Phoebe, seeing a woman whose head was completely severed, now "waking up" and making all the normal sounds of rising.

"You must have *freaked out*," I say.

"I almost threw up. I kept looking at her neck, where those stitches were straining. I kept thinking they would break. I think she was afraid of that, too. She held on to her temples as if she had a big headache, but I think she was making sure her head didn't topple off."

"Were you scared she would see you?"

"I hid in Pierre's kitchen and peered around the corner at the bed."

"Then what happened?" asks Eleanor.

"As soon as she realized she was alive, she sobbed. It was awful. Pierre was devastated. He brought her a mirror and she looked at her stitches and screamed. A little blood came from the stitches then. He cleaned her up. She was like a dog at the vet, struggling to get away."

"He couldn't calm her down?" I ask.

"No. He kept saying things in a comforting voice. I couldn't understand what he said, but she would always shriek 'Non!' I didn't need a translator for that. I actually started to feel bad for her."

I shudder. "She really did want to die that day."

"A servant who completely disregards his instructions," observes Eleanor. "How long did that go on?"

"Hours, I guess. Then she made him hold the mirror while she took a length of ribbon from her garter and wound it around her neck to hide the stitches. She crawled out of bed and left him."

"She . . . left?"

"Yes, walking unsteadily, limping a little until she got used to it. He didn't bother to follow her. She was dressed as a peasant, so I think she thought she'd find some way to walk back to Versailles without calling attention to herself. I walked behind her for a while, but since it was taking forever, I decided to come and check in on Tabby and you guys. That was a story in itself: the past didn't want to let go of me. She struggled to walk, and I struggled to come back to the present."

"You did great, Phoebe," I say.

I see her lips part to say *thanks*, but she stops herself, still sullen about my taking off.

"I'm sorry again about leaving," I say. "It was an accident. I just impulsively came back to the present day because, if you remember, we were talking about whether we *could*—"

"To see Eleanor?" she interrupts.

"Uh, no," I say, with an apologetic look at Eleanor. "I was just testing it, I guess."

"What? Testing what?"

"Whether I could control our traveling or not."

"And meanwhile you stranded me with a very unpleasant task!"

"Please stop, both of you," says Eleanor.

"I didn't mean to!" I say. "I screwed up!"

"Okay," says Phoebe flatly. "It just *sucked.*"

"I don't need any of this," says Eleanor, standing up. She straightens her cap. "I was fine being lonely and haunting an abandoned mansion until you came."

"Listen, I have something good to tell you. While Phoebe was—"

"I'm just as much a victim as you are," Phoebe interrupts. "I didn't ask for this, either."

"Your betrayal caused this," says Eleanor. "You set events in motion long ago."

"Oh my God, Eleanor . . . could you stop with that? I didn't even *know* you. I lived on a completely different continent!"

"Well, look," I say, trying to bring peace. "We do know

that something in our heritage and whatever it is that my ancestors did haunts us," I say. "We have to atone for their
deeds—not Phoebe's—or undo them somehow."

"We'll find the vials and dump them out," says Phoebe.

"Dump them, or drink them," says Eleanor. "I bet you
would."

I drop my face into my hands. What's happening to
Eleanor?

"No," says Phoebe. She gives a tight smile. "There's nothing good in collections of other people's blood."

"Tell that to the bloke in the emergency room bleeding
out," I say, hoping to break the intensity.

"Perfect idea!" exults Phoebe sarcastically. "We can just
donate the vials to a blood bank."

"Problem solved. Have a motorcycle accident and wind
up Sangreçu! Whatever the hell that is," I say.

"Yeah, what is that, really? Just . . . immortality from
drinking magic blood?" Phoebe asks. Eleanor is silent.

"I guess so. But it hasn't seemed to have brought glory or
happiness to any of the Sangreçu we've seen."

"What's your heritage, Eleanor?" Phoebe demands suddenly. "Anybody famous in your background?"

Eleanor laughs, and I take a deep inhale that we seem to
have moved off the testy ground that made everyone angry.
"There aren't many famous servants whose names have
come down from history to us."

"So your family has always been servants?"

"Or farmers, workers of the land."

"They say my family descends from some ancient line of
kings," I offer, and act stung by the withering looks I receive.

"I'm related to Washington Irving, the guy who wrote
'Sleepy Hollow,'" says Phoebe.

"That's promising," I say. "He wrote about a headless Hessian soldier. Was he the original Sangreçu?"

"Although . . ." Eleanor says and stops.

"What?" says Phoebe.

"I thought we'd sort of . . . we'd come around to the idea that your dad . . . that your stepdad is your true dad. That you're an Arnaud, not an Irving."

"Yeah," she says. "It does kind of look that way."

She stares over at Steven, who's pressing a button on his watch to provide a small glow to see what time it is. Even *he's* impatient for the fireworks now.

For the first time, I really get what that means to her. A man she loves, who was her dad when she was small, was betrayed by her mum. Which means a chink in her mum's armor. Phoebe adores her. Admitting Steven is her biological dad means acknowledging her mum ran around on her husband. I try to imagine how I'd feel knowing my mum did that to my dad, or vice versa. It gives me an instant sick feeling in my stomach—or whatever passes for my stomach these days.

"So there's clearly something in your heritage," I say to Phoebe, hoping to move the conversation to objective rather than subjective grounds. "Royalty? Maybe Yolande or Giraude had an illegitimate child from one of the kings who lived here over the centuries?"

"You told us Athénaïs said she was the mistress of the king," says Phoebe. "And that Yolande was asking for advice on how she seduced him. Maybe she crawled right into the royal bed."

I feel kind of stupid saying this. "Which king do you think it is?"

Phoebe laughs lowly and I'm glad she's moved on from

thinking unpleasant things about her mum. "You'd think we should know. There were only three of them, right? All Louis . . . zes?" We all laugh. What is the plural of Louis pronounced Frenchly?

"All of them named Louis," says Eleanor. God, she's sharp.

"Based on what they're wearing, we might be able to tell?"

"Yes, because I'm so up-to-date on ladies' fashions of the past," I say.

"Well, the first Louis was actually a medieval guy, right? Sixteen hundreds? Dammit, we should've listened better when my stepdad was reading from the guidebook and boring us all!"

Stepdad. I let it go.

"Excellent," says Eleanor. "We should surely be able to distinguish medieval garb from later fashions. By the time of the last Louis and the Revolution, we were getting very close to my century."

I try to remember what Giraude was wearing. Did she look more like someone who'd fall subject to the bubonic plague, or someone who ate bonbons off the same tray as Marie-Antoinette?

"But if Giraude never died, she must have adopted the dress of whatever court she was in, right? She would've wanted to fit in," I point out.

"So then how was Athénaïs dressed when she talked about her . . . her . . . bedding the king?" Eleanor asks. She looks shyly at the ground.

"You're asking the wrong person," says Phoebe.

We're not costume scholars or historians. "Well, maybe we should just guess and land in the middle. The middle Louis!" I say.

"The Fifteenth then," says Eleanor.

"Which in Roman numerals is an *X* and then some other letters," says Phoebe with mock authority, and we all grin.

"Many thanks to our Roman-numeral *expert*. Okay, so to recap: Phoebe might be lost royalty, the descendant of Louis the Fifteenth via his mistress. So Versailles actually belongs to her, and all the day's admissions should go to her."

"You know, they can keep it," says Phoebe, waving her hand. "I'm already heir to this oversized manor back in England. I'm good."

"I'll take it," says Eleanor.

"I'll arm-wrestle you for it," I say, rolling up my sleeves.

"I'm a serving girl who's carried many a tray piled high with heavy platters and teapots," says Eleanor. "These forearms are powerful."

"So what are you implying about mine?"

I love flirting with her; she can't handle it. She blushes as deep as . . . as someone can when they've been dead and cold for over a century.

"I believe the palace is large enough for you two to share," says Phoebe.

"True words," says Eleanor primly.

"Glad we settled that."

I take a deep breath. It's time to reveal the golden egg I've been sitting on this whole time.

"Would you two accompany me back to where I think the vials are?"

It's so worth it to see the looks of shock on their faces.

CHAPTER TWELVE

The crypt at Picpus being a strange place, holding the scant consecrated bones that survived the Revolution by virtue of being embedded in stone. Not far from their harmonious rest, a mass grave filled until a second was required to be dug.

—*Morbid Paris*

"You know where the vials are?" Phoebe's face is hard to describe. For a second, I can't answer, too busy memorizing this arrangement of eyebrows and cheekbones and wide, wide eyes.

"I believe so. Pretty flash of me, eh?"

"And why then have we wasted valuable time chatting about kings and nonsense?" Eleanor's face is compelling, too, but she has an element of scolding in her forehead that I'm not a huge fan of.

"Something to do?"

"You!" Eleanor turns her back on me, she's so overcome. I guess this is an important moment. If we figure out the vials, we might be on our way to "graduation."

"So who wants to go?"

Phoebe takes my hand. "This time I'm not stepping away from you so much as an inch."

"Eleanor?"

She doesn't turn around. "Maybe I should stay and keep an eye on Phoebe's family."

"No! Come on, the vials are everything we need to solve things for them."

She turns around to face us, but keeps her eyes down. "I'm not meant to go with you two, or the magic would've taken me."

"No!" I protest. "You weren't close enough when one of us started going."

"Very well," she says.

We all three hold hands.

"Eleanor, come with us. We *want* you," says Phoebe in a rhythmic way, as if she's experimenting with communing with the invisible forces that hurl us around like Ping-Pong balls. Eleanor lifts her head and looks miserably at Phoebe. "We're a *team*," Phoebe adds.

"Okay, so use intention to return to the chapel at Picpus," I say. "We can just meet up in the main part and then I'll show you the staircase down to the crypt."

Phoebe looks at me until I can't help it, I smile. In spite of everything, I admire the hell out of her.

"So, let's *go*," she says. "Intention away!"

I feel time and geography pulling at me with their disastrous potency. I am nothing compared to this force. I have tamed it somewhat so that I can travel where I wish, but I'm like a single seed carried by a tornado. Phoebe's hand tightens on mine, but Eleanor's is instantly gone.

Phoebe and I stand in the chapel, with tourists circulating around us and even through us. That old familiar smell of ancient architecture and the sweat that put the stones in place.

"What happened?" I ask.

"I don't know. Did she pull away or was she not allowed to come?"

"We should go back and check."

We do, even though I can hear the song from the cellars drifting up . . . the vials are calling, or someone is calling us to the vials . . . but we are a team, like Phoebe said.

So we return to the Versailles grounds. I do a quick head-count: three living people, one ghost in distress.

Eleanor's sitting on the grass apart from the family, cross-legged, sobbing. I've never seen her sit in so modern, so casual a position. Her hand props up her forehead as she cries.

"Eleanor?" asks Phoebe gently, crouching down next to her.

She jolts. She hadn't realized we were there. I feel embarrassed for her. "I couldn't go," she says. "I tried, but I'm just not meant to go with you."

She immediately straightens up and adjusts her sitting position to kneeling. I crouch down, too, so we're all down there together.

"You tried as hard as you could? I didn't know if you had gotten scared and let go," says Phoebe.

"No!"

"Sorry."

"We are not equal," says Eleanor in a voice steady despite being threaded through with tears. "You two are the ones of the prophecy. I'm just along for the ride."

"It's all three of us," I insist. "I don't know how it works, but you're part of it."

"I don't think so. I've spent a lot of time thinking about it. I'm a ghost you two encountered during your travels through the Arnaud Manor, but I could've been anyone. Any ghost."

"Stop it!" shouts Phoebe, her hands up in the air. "Oh my

God! Are you forgetting what you did to release the servants? That was *magic* and you were part of it."

"Yes, I agree with you on that," says Eleanor. "But that
was my role, to deal with servants only."

"So why weren't you released?" Phoebe demands.

"I don't know."

"Because you're part of this team!"

"A team member who doesn't have the same power as the
other two."

"Maybe you have the most power of all," Phoebe says.
"Maybe that's why we go on these trips—you're too important to go."

"Wow, good point," I say. It honestly had never occurred
to me. Maybe we were "fetching and carrying" for *her*.

"That can't be the case," she says.

"Why not?" Phoebe asks. "Listen, the luck of why we get
born into certain bodies and not in others . . . it's random
and it's strange and maybe even meaningless. Why was I
born in California with plenty of clean water flowing out
of my faucet, while some poor baby is born in Uganda
and her mom has to walk a mile to bring home a bucket of
water?"

"Don't get her started," I say.

Eleanor kneels, listening to us, her eyes downcast.

"I lucked out, that's why. Although some might say I
didn't luck out, because, look, I died when I was sixteen and
I didn't get to do much with my life . . . but anyway, the fact
that you were born into a household where you had to go
into service, it doesn't mean anything about who you *are*."

"I agree," I say.

"Under other circumstances, you might've been born into

incredible wealth and never had to lift a finger—servants would've served *you*—but you would still be Eleanor."

"Your positions on social status certainly don't match what I was raised with," says Eleanor, and I laugh as I pull her in for a hug.

"The world is changing," says Phoebe. "We all deserve the same chances, but we don't get them."

Eleanor squirms out of my arms, but with a grateful smile up at me.

"Thank you for all that, Phoebe," she says.

"No, don't thank me; it's not some nice thing I'm bestowing on you because I like you. I mean, I *do* like you but even if I didn't it's still the truth that we should all be on equal footing."

"I'm ready to vote Phoebe in as prime minister," I say. Phoebe rolls her eyes at me.

"So, Eleanor, can I ask one favor of you?" she asks.

"Anything."

"Please, can this be the last time you talk about yourself that way?"

Eleanor reaches over to put a hand on Phoebe's shoulder. It looks awkward. She's not used to reaching out in this way. I can see that she, too, knows it's kind of wooden. But she's making an effort.

"I'm going to try," she says simply.

"I think in another life I was a sewerman," I offer up.

"Miles, you are hereby ordered to shut up for the rest of the night," says Phoebe.

"Well, that's a fine way to speak to someone of equal standing!"

"Are you going to show me those damn vials or what?"

"Yes, *go*," says Eleanor. She pulls Phoebe in for a quick, atta-girl hug and then lets go.

In another second, we're back in the chapel, surrounded by stone and oldness, smelling the musty reek of the centuries. I hear the hum of the vials and look to see if Phoebe notices it, too. I can't tell.

"I like all the things you said to Eleanor," I say.

"She's cool."

"There's cool and then there's *cool*." I let my gaze rest right into her eyes, strong and meaningful.

"I do think you care for me a bit," she says in a plummy British accent.

"A Brit after an American?" I scoff.

"Stranger things have happened to guys who abandon their friend with beheaded people."

"Let's be honest," I say. "There was only one beheaded individual."

"Miles?"

"Yeah?"

"I'm so glad I met you."

I fold her into my arms. We hug like it's completely normal to have people walking through you, calling out things to others, and unzipping their fanny packs for their camera. I'm getting better at ignoring the living. For me, right now, the only thing that exists is Phoebe.

Finally, it's a kid that gets us to pull apart. He's about four and he's had it with tromping through the cathedrals of Europe. He emits a squall of such volume that his parents rush to him, through us, and where my hips meet Phoebe's becomes the site of a mum crouching to pick up her kid.

Yeah, kind of a moment killer.

Phoebe walks away, her face shining, her eyes blurred and her lids low. I follow her.

"We're wasting time," she says huskily.

"I like doing that."

"I do, too."

But she's right. The pull of the vials is strong now . . . that buzzing clatter of so many voices . . . is it voices?

"Do you hear it?" I ask.

She listens. "It's coming from below us?"

"Yeah."

I lead her to the small door built for the statures of medieval people, and we enter the stairwell. A second door blocks the staircase that runs downward, and we step through it.

I take her down the dank uneven steps to the crypt. It feels like we're in an upside-down boat, the ceiling curved and vaulted above us, each of the side passageways marked with an archway of stone. If there were windows, this would be an airy and open space, but since we are encased in stone, it feels secretive and the place where nightmares transpire.

"It's really loud down here," she says. She means the vials, calling to us, threading a thin sound through the silent crypt.

She leads me right to the faint carving in the stone. She reaches out and her fingers trace the limits of the dragon's chamber. "Poor thing," she says. "But I can feel it." She lifts her eyes to me in triumph. "The stone lets me touch it."

The song grows louder, as if in response to what she said.

"It recognizes you," I say.

A surge of excitement rides my veins. It's happening. She presses different parts of the etching. I hold my breath.

She leans in closer. "See the markings on its forehead?" she asks.

"No, they're so small I didn't see them before," I say. They look like runes or ancient writing.

She touches the markings, and they are the trigger inlaid by some medieval artisan, a clockmaker who understood gears and pressure. A door coyly opens at just a slant.

The door is the size of a book.

She pulls it and looks, then she moves her head to the side so I can look, too.

One vial rests inside, held in an elaborate wire device intended to hold far more. The rack looks like something fashioned for Versailles, intricate twirls of metal and designs like the dragon's winding tail in the emblem. The enchanting hum exudes from it like a medieval choir sending notes to the top of a cathedral to encircle the bell in its tower. It's irresistible. It's nothing I've ever heard before.

The vial is surprisingly small, made of thick, handblown glass. It looks like a specialty perfume from the most *haute parfumier* of Paris.

It holds a dark viscous liquid.

I immediately feel the fear that someone will take it from us. Greed arises, instant and nauseating. *This belongs to me, and no one shall take it.* We're alone in the crypt, which is locked to the public, but I turn my head and survey the shadows anyway.

"This is it," Phoebe says in a hushed, awed tone.

The vial lets off a babble of buzzing . . . it knows we're looking at it.

She reaches into the space and delicately fastens her fingers around the bottle, which reaches a fever pitch of humming. She struggles to dislodge it from the metal rack it's housed in. The dampness of the crypt seems to have made rust cling to the glass. She uses both hands and the vial leaps out unbroken.

We look at it in wonder. It's singing its luscious, siren song. Is it ancestors, calling out memories and ancient deeds captured in blood? Is the blood a repository of all the long-ago lives?

We stare at it. I can't move. I don't want that glass to break.

Phoebe's thumb and index finger pinch the tiny cork that sits in the bottle's opening.

"No," I say.

But her fingers continue to ease the cork up, and the humming gets so loud I know we both can't stand it. She rocks the cork up until it tumbles onto the stone floor. She lifts the vial to her nose and inhales. A look of supreme gratification comes over her face.

She holds it out to me and I inhale, too. The scent goes to my brain, flooding it with pure ecstatic sensation. I'm somewhere else for a little bit, some memory of skin and water and warmth.

"We shouldn't," I say. "It's the only bottle."

She brings the vial to her lips with a slow and salacious smile. I am powerless to stop her, because I want to drink, too. She lightly tips the glass and a single drop lands on her generous lower lip. She lets it rest there, perfectly round, a half sphere of crimson, while we both adore at its shape, scent, power.

And then her tongue darts out and takes it.

A groan of pleasure comes from her throat like she was never meant to make any other noise, ever. The humming joins her. She is changing as I watch. A spark comes into her eyes: something different, something knowing. Her lips lift to show her teeth, to give air and worship to the single drop she has imbibed.

She drinks again, fully, and her extended cry of pleasure makes me reach out to take it from her, but of course my hands go through the glass.

Yet I'm able to touch the blood on the inside.

It's like touching a heated tear from a lover. It's warm and chills me at the same time. The humming shoots up through my arm and darts into my mind. I'm part of that blood now, and I haven't even drunk yet.

Phoebe, the only one who can touch the glass, tilts the vial so it touches where my mouth would be if I were still living.

We both need to drink. We understand that.

The two of us.

The wash of the blood touches my lips and then subsides.

Oh.

My.

God.

I feel like I'm swooning but instead of losing conscious-ness, I'm *gaining* it. *More* awake, *more* alive. The humming is in my bloodstream now. I regard my arm: there's music flooding through that blue network of veins just under the skin. The veins may not be pumping blood anymore, but they're pumping a gorgeously insane chorus to every inch of my body.

I'm flooded with it.

I'm in it. It's in me.

She pulls the vial away and drinks again, then she tips it for me and gives me the rest of the vial.

In my gluttony, I manage to curb myself. "Save some for Eleanor," I gasp. There's just a bit left there in the bottom for her. Phoebe gives me a look of anguish yet drops to her knees to get the dropped cork and thrust it into the bottle top—just as feeling completely overtakes me.

I hurtle through my mind. I see green, such a painfully saturated color. I rise and see the green is grass, a beautiful meadow from which fog drifts up. It's morning and I'm whole. In the distance I know there is home and a woman who loves me but she is many days' journey away. I walk with a heavy heart and every tree drips with mist, every leaf wearing a stole of dew. I turn back and see the wavering progress I've made through the wet grass. A snake's deceptive trail.

Next it's silver I see, glinting and catching the sun in such a dangerous way—it distracts a man, lets a sword cut your cheek, and I see the eyes behind the helm, full of hatred. The sounds are terrible, the scream of metal on metal, the rough and crude sound of denting and the soft skin beneath denting, too, and the bones and the organs the bones were supposed to protect.

Armor. I'm seeing men in armor. I swivel my gaze down. I'm in armor, too. My feet are in thick metal shoes coming to a sharp point.

Red. Blood on silver. A sword blade with someone else's blood coating it. It's slick and dripping and it hits the grass and the poor beautiful green is soiled by it.

A clanging crash that is so mind-crackingly *loud*. Someone falls. Someone in a full suit of armor hits the ground and every grass blade cries beneath the silver.

I'm back on the crypt floor again, breathing as hard as if I've run for miles, my skin tingling, my whole self tingling. I've been changed and transformed.

I'm Sangreçu.

CHAPTER THIRTEEN

French is the language of heraldry, and *maille*, meaning mesh,
is the foundation of chain mail. Worn as armor, mail consists
of tiny interlocking rings, a beautiful time-consuming art
for the smith.

—*Art of Armor*

*P*hoebe is glowing with it. I stare at her, her skin changed, more vibrant, her eyes fathomless.

"Where were you?" I ask. "Were there colors?"

"Colors . . ." She can't seem to collect herself enough to talk.

"I saw the most incredible green," I said. "It filled my mind."

"I saw stone," she said.

I can see that her experience disturbed her more than mine did.

"Castle walls," she says falteringly.

"And?"

"A well made of stone. There was a man inside."

"Inside the well?"

"Yes. Trapped."

"Trapped . . ." I am lost in that word. I struggle to return to Phoebe. The word makes me feel colors: entrenched grays and blacks so sable no one can ever recover from them.

"Miles, I lowered the stone on top of him," she says, and bends her head so her auburn hair floods down to cover her face. "I placed a cap on the well so he could never escape."

"It wasn't you." But I think, that was me, some version of me, on the field.

"I've done such a terrible thing."

"He must have . . ." I falter. ". . . deserved it? He hurt you?"

"I think he loved me."

"Phoebe, I'm sorry."

"Don't be sorry for me!" she flashes, lifting her head. "I'm a bad person."

"You're not! You could never—" I break off, looking at her hand.

She holds an empty vial. The last drops meant for Eleanor are gone. The cork lies on the ground a distance away, as if thrown.

We both go silent. I hadn't noticed until now: the humming is over.

She replaces the cork and puts the empty vial back into the metal stand. A sob escapes her.

"I really did betray her, just as she said," she says.

I crawl to the cabinet and peer into its depths. Did we miss a vial? But the metal rack was made to hold many vials. There wouldn't be one just lying loose, unprotected. The fact is, someone long ago took the other vials. Just having my head in the space that held the vials is intoxicating; it's like I'm sticking my head into an oven filled with incense and smoke. I really, *really* want another drink.

"I couldn't stop myself. I wanted every last drop."

"It's all right," I say. "I know how powerful it was."

"It's not all right! I drank her only chance to become Sangreçu!"

"She might not want to be," I say.

"You don't believe that."

"If anyone had asked us if we wanted to be, we would've said no. It's only because we saw it and smelled it. You didn't betray her. You were caught up in something you couldn't control."

"I'm a terrible person."

I slam the door to the cupboard closed. "We don't understand anything!" I shout at her. "Someone else makes choices for us, and then we feel guilty for them! It's not your fault, Phoebe!"

She's staring at me like she can't believe what she just saw.

"I'm sorry I yelled," I say quietly.

"Miles—you just slammed that door closed."

Whoa. *That's* why she was looking at me that way.

I reach out and open it again, slam it closed. I inhale with a catch of laughter in my throat. I leap across the room and pick up a reliquary sitting in its somber niche. I set it down carefully, but then run to a wooden bench and kick it. Its clatter across the stone floor is glorious.

I pull Phoebe to standing and whirl her around in a circle. "You're not the only thing I can touch anymore!" I shout.

It's because of the blood. It's the Sangreçu power.

I go on a rampage, up the stairs, through the chapel, touching things. I nudge a pew forward just enough to scare the old woman sitting there going through her rosary. She glares at me, and I *exult* at the sensation of being looked at. She *sees* me. No one but other dead people have seen me since I died.

"Sorry, love," I say. "But the pew was askew! A cockney rhyme; I'm so clever. I'm so real!"

She gestures me away with the worldliness of age. She's seen a million cads and I'm just the most recent one.

I burst outside. Sunshine feels better. My skin is more *real* now, alive to sensation the way it was when I was alive. I'm dizzy with all the feelings.

It feels amazing. I had forgotten what touch really feels like. I had become used to the dampened, limited sensation that I had access to as a ghost.

A thought hits me. How good would this feel if I weren't dead, if I drank this as a living person? I don't know if my nerves could even survive it.

I pace past the memorial site where Pierre dug up Giraude, and Phoebe's laughing behind me. I run as fast as I can and take a flying leap, reveling in the painful thud when I hit the ground.

It's pain.

But I love it.

I'm not about to waste the sensation. There's one amazing thing to do when your skin literally shivers at another's touch. Phoebe and I have kissed a few times and it felt extraordinary and made my pulse go like a train careening around a mountain pass . . . but *now* it's like the train is going too fast and we're going to derail. It feels *so astounding*. My mind is completely blown by what my body can experience now.

And she feels it, too.

"Where do you want to go?" I ask quietly. We can be seen now, and we need somewhere private to be with each other.

We can use intention to go anywhere.

"It would be really cool to go back to my room in California."

I pause. "I don't think it will be the same."

After a moment, she nods. "Someone else must live there now."

"If only we could manipulate time as well as place," I say.

"We could go back to a day when your family was still there."

"A time when I was still alive," she says and shudders.

To distract her from that thought, I start throwing out names, anything. "Want to meet up at the Parthenon? Find a warm room at the Waldorf Astoria? Let's see, a cruise ship?"

"With my luck, we'd land on the deck of the sunken *Titanic*."

"All I know is that I want to touch you until my head explodes," I say. "What's the best place to do that?"

She hesitates for a second. "How about a beach somewhere?"

"A secluded beach. Wait: are we trying to reenact the name of a famous cocktail?"

"Miles, you're a darb but you always make me laugh." She reaches for me, and she guides us there. It's her beach, her decision, and I don't even know where we are, what country, what continent.

All I know is that the surf is a gorgeous rhythmic timekeeper for us, and the sand is powdery and soft.

At first we just sit, watching the waves, totally in tune with the forces that make the waves gather and crest, resonating a little with the bleakness of the receding water and its plaintive pull at the sand underneath.

Then, because it's all I can think about, I reach over and pull her face to mine, and our lips touch. Her mouth is soft, as soft as the sound she makes in her throat when we kiss.

Her arms twine around my neck and her fingers penetrate into the hair on my nape. I shiver.

I press forward and deepen our contact. She surges forward to match my intensity, and I taste inside her mouth, the heat and slight savor of spearmint.

It's like we've never kissed before, because the Sangreçu blood lavishly caressing the inside of my blood vessels makes this feel like nothing ever has, ever. I can hear the blood gathering in my brain, feel the pulse of it everywhere. It makes me dizzy. It makes Phoebe's touch almost unbearably good. I separate from her because the feelings are so forceful I can't breathe . . . whatever counts as breathing for me now, that is . . . and we press our foreheads against each other's, breathing raggedly as if we've run a race.

I touch her shoulder and the heat of her skin burns through the fabric of her shirt. It wasn't like this before. Our skin had been cool, converted to a haunted vestige of what it once was. Now she feels feverish. I unbutton three buttons and push the shirt aside so I can put my cheek against her scorching skin. I kiss from her shoulder to her neck to the back of her ear. Her head lolls to the side to give me more access.

I unbutton the rest of the buttons and slide her shirt off.

Behind us, the surf roars, and my blood roars in response.

Her fingers, deft, remove my shirt, too, and it's going so quickly, too quickly, but it doesn't seem possible to pull away now. Our skin is cauterizing together, like two sides of a wound.

Every part of her is beautiful: her long legs with swimmer's muscles, a dusting of sand clinging to her calf as I run a hand along her thigh; her arched neck and the curve of her breasts and the curve of her waist and her hips and the curve of her shoulders cresting down to the curve of her biceps. Everything about her is rounded, beautiful, and the blood in her veins that I can see so faintly blue at her wrists, at her neck, calls out to me, and my blood is on fire to answer back.

She pulls me down to her and hoists herself so we change positions and now I'm the one on my back in the sand. She rises above me like a figurehead on a ship with her hair whipping in the wind, and undoes my belt buckle. She takes off my belt and throws it aside.

I come up on my elbows so she can ease off my jeans and boxers. I guide her out of what remains of her clothes. Then there's nothing left. Just our skin desperate to fuse.

We pause, looking into each other's eyes. There's a step I've been trained about to the point of nausea. You have to wear a condom. You have to wear a condom. You have to wear a condom.

I ask quietly, "There's no way this could result in anything, right?"

I'm dead; I'm shooting blanks.

She's dead; her womb is a tomb.

Disease doesn't worry me; there's no more worst-case scenario for me. All the things that would've stopped us in real life have no significance now.

"How could it?" she asks.

"I don't know. It couldn't."

"Right. So just . . ."

We both laugh a little. It's my first time. I've never entered another person in this way.

I concentrate on her face, her eyes. The radiance of her skin. I could spend a century gazing at her.

She looks at me, and there's a fragile moment where we nearly sink into each other. I'm there. I'm her. She's everything.

I'm poised at the edge.

"I'm not scared, Miles," she says in a voice crafted of willow. "I'm yours."

And that's enough for me to surge forward until we're joined like I've never been joined before. It is everything. It obliterates me. I don't even exist anymore, it's all just Phoebe, just her and her soft words in my ear and her body moving above me and the way the waves wash over the sand around us and erase their own passage again and again.

Afterward we lie on the sand and drift in our thoughts. Her hair is flung over my neck. Even being Sangreçu, we are still robbed of the solace of sleep. But it's okay. Everything's so okay.

I begin a solitary journey back through the images I saw when I drank from the vials. That grass. That field.

I close my eyes and the metal dances across my vision, a sword sweeping through the air, a body moving through space with slowness and heft, enchained in heavy mail. Those eyes in the break of the helm . . . Who is the person I'm killing? Or is he killing me?

I sigh and try to learn more, see more. Can't I turn my head—what's over there? But my vision is blinded. I think I'm wearing a helm, too. I'm just as held back as he is.

Phoebe rustles and her low voice says, "Shouldn't have trusted me, should you?" There's a musicality to it, a playfulness that contradicts the terrible content of her words. Is this what she said as she lowered the lid onto the well, burying that man?

"Phoebe?"

"That's my name," she says, and her voice still has that

playful tinge. I shudder. Whoever she once was, she was no one to mess with.

"Should we return?"

"No," she says. "I'm never going back."

I laugh, but she doesn't. I sit up and look down at her. "What do you mean?"

"I'm not going back. My sister and my family will be fine. I'm not responsible anymore."

I narrow my eyes. "What about the prophecy? And Eleanor?"

"It will all work itself out."

"You don't sound like yourself," I say.

"Your love has changed me," she says.

"Not for the worse."

"Maybe," she says.

"The Phoebe I know cares about her sister and her safety, and she's a good friend to Eleanor."

"That Phoebe," she says, rolling to her side to give me her back, and then sitting up. "She was a fool."

"Are you kidding me?" I spin her around to face me, my grip maybe a little rougher than I would like.

Her green eyes are somber. "Miles, nothing matters. We betray our friends and the sea keeps bringing brine to the sand."

"It does matter!" I flash.

"Make love to me again."

I stand up and grab my boxers, pull them on. "What's wrong with you?" I ask as I get into my jeans and find my shirt, brought down the beach a bit by the wind.

"The blood makes me see things differently . . . or see things again that I forgot."

"You're not different, Phoebe. You're a member of this team and we have to see things through."

"I love this shore," she says. "The sea is so quiet here. It lets me drift in my thoughts."

"Your thoughts aren't doing you any favors," I say. "Get dressed. We're going back."

"I'd like to stay, but you may go."

"*May* go?" I stand there in disbelief. "I didn't realize I needed your permission."

How did this all go so wrong? Phoebe is the most important person in my life/death, and she's behaving like a stranger. She sits completely naked in the sand, hugging her bent knees, her long hair covering her shoulders and back. She's beautiful, but she isn't the same person.

"Do you remember," she says dreamily, "how much we used to love this?"

My skin goes cold at her words. "We've never been here before, and we've never done this before."

"We're each of us the product of the lives that went before us," she says, still sounding like she's in a trance. "The things your grandfather did reside in your cells. The rudimentary grunts of your ancestor as he built his first fire: that is a memory you experience in a half second as you light a match. Your mother's misery in grade school, your eleven-greats-grandfather's goring by a bull as he tried to pass through his neighbor's field: it all goes into your makeup, Miles. You are the past. And I am, too. I'm just remembering better than you."

"What exactly do you remember?" I ask, although I don't think I want to hear.

"We were linked together," she says. "But we weren't supposed to be."

"Was I supposed to be with Eleanor?" I ask.

She laughs long and low and stands up. Lazily, she walks

the sand looking for her clothes. I help her and she dresses. The timelessness fades when she's back in her Oxford shirt and jeans. Nude, she could be a woman of any era. Now, she's Phoebe Irving in the early twenty-first century.

"*I* was supposed to be with Eleanor," she says.

CHAPTER FOURTEEN

Folklore persists about the Sangreçu despite there being little to buttress the stories. Harder still is it to prove the existence of a society organized to protect or advance the interests of the genus and species. No tangible artifacts exist, no handbook, no secret signal, only an emblem whose provenance seems dubious.

—*Secret Cabals, Societies & Orders*

*I*t takes a while for her strange mood to fade. It's like she's drunk or high—not herself. I know it's the Sangreçu blood, but it's still her and that's so unpleasant . . . like when someone blames something stupid they said on alcohol, and you think, *but you clearly* believe *it; you just wouldn't have* said *it if you were sober.*

A crying jag follows all this. She climbs onto a rock like a mermaid and sobs for things she won't tell me about. I'm halfway committed to leaving her here, but I remember how scary it was when I couldn't find her the last time. She seems to have more power. If she didn't want to be found again, I have no doubt I would never see her. So I stay, worried, fretting, hoping everything is all right at Versailles. For all I know, the fireworks could be over by now or the German tourist could've been found.

Or Giraude could've killed again.

I can't take it any more.

"Phoebe, we have to go back," I say, standing at the foot of her rock. Above me she reclines, looking like a Maxfield Parrish painting.

"What do you mean? Back in time?"

"No, back to your family. Remember, Giraude threatened to kill people. We've wasted time here. She may have already made good on her promise."

"That's her business, not ours," says Phoebe.

"Snap out of it! Your sister needs you. She's too young to be around Giraude without us there to guard her."

"Eleanor's there," she says dismissively.

I have never hated anyone so much as I hate her now. She's not even worth trying to convince. I can't believe I had her in my arms and that we . . .

I was an idiot.

I don't even bother to say good-bye.

I use intention and I'm back at Versailles in a heartbeat.

Tabby is running laps around the blanket her parents sit on, while her mom's face registers the forever-bleak reality of being a bereaved parent. Nearby, the Fountain of Apollo gushes water as the Sun King statue struggles to bring his chariot, pulled by panicked horses, up to the surface.

Eleanor rushes up to me and hugs me. Her touch brings stabbing, startling images to my mind. I can't even describe what I see because the images come crashing in at an incredible speed: like a movie montage that's been sped up too fast. The overwhelming feeling I have is that I *owe* her. She's been incredibly good and generous to me. In the past, in whatever skin we inhabited, she gave much of herself to me.

"You feel different," she says. "What happened?"

I don't know how to tell her. But I'll be beyond redemption if I don't.

"I'm Sangreçu now. We found a vial. And we drank from it."

"My God!" She's appalled. "You *drank* it?"

"It called to us," I say. "It was singing, like a siren in those myths. There wasn't even really a chance for us to resist."

She regards me while her face splinters through changes I see in flashes, like film run through the projector too fast. She's herself, but she's also someone I see with my Sangreçu memory. I try to focus—who am I seeing?

"Is it all gone?" she asks.

I can almost, almost catch that other person on her face, but I can't see past the disappointment, because of course she knows the answer to her question already.

"We meant to save some for you."

Silence.

I want really, really badly to lie. I want to say that it slipped out of our fingers and her portion spilled on the floor.

But I can't do that to her. So I say nothing.

"I'm sure it is for the best," she says. "And where is Phoebe now?"

"For the best? Eleanor, I'm so sorry."

"I have the funniest feeling that her failure to be here now is directly related to the fact that there is nothing in the vial left for me."

"She's changed. She's not who we thought she was. She's not a good person."

"She has a very old practice of betraying me," she says. "And perhaps you as well."

"What do you know?"

"Nothing—just a feeling."

"I'm so sorry."

"It's none of your doing," she says. "And so . . . we wait?"

"I don't think she'll come back," I say. "I think it's up to

us to help Tabby. If we can get through tonight, they'll return to England tomorrow and we'll be fine."

"If we can get through tonight," she repeats. "Tell me,
how does it feel to be Sangreçu?"

I don't want to tell her, because she's so intelligent. She's
going to figure out that I had sex with Phoebe. But I can't
not answer her question. I owe her that much after everything we've been through.

"It heightens all sensation," I say simply.

"Indeed." She blushes. I know she knows. I feel awful for
her. She's been stuck here with a family who doesn't even
know she's here while Phoebe and I did something so bond-
ing, so undoable, so forever.

"And it brings on memories. Images from before. I think
it's what my ancestors saw."

"A key to your heritage."

"I think so."

"And what did Phoebe see?"

I tell her briefly about the man in the well, and she shudders at the part where Phoebe put a stone blocking the entrance. "What a horrible thing to do," she says.

"And I killed a man," I say, "or he killed me."

Suddenly I'm just sick of it all. When I was alive, I was a
decent person. I didn't do anything great, but I didn't do
anything horrible, either. I think I made my parents happy. I
made my friends and my girlfriend happy. I was a good
swimmer on the swim team.

Ta-da, right?

So why am I torturing myself over things other people
did, even if they might be related to me? Why is there a secret society . . . why is some girl visiting my parents when
they just want to be left alone?

It *sucks*. I understand now why Giraude strode to the front of the line and offered up her neck to the guillotine. Sometimes you just want to give up.

Formerly cheerful dead fellow commits suicide.

That could be my obituary.

Which makes me wonder, what did my real obituary say? Too awful to contemplate. My mum must've written it. Or maybe Aunt Ginny, because sometimes she takes charge, like that family reunion where she gave everybody jobs and assignments three months ahead of time. I wonder how she took my death.

"So, drinking from the vial gave you access to old memories and made your skin very sensitive," says Eleanor. "Anything else?"

"Yes. That's right. One very important thing. It gave me corporeality. I was able to touch the cupboard the vial was in."

Her eyes widen. "Why didn't you say so? You can touch things?"

"Yes."

"Miles, don't you see? You can touch Giraude. You can fight her as another human. And you are far taller and stronger than her!" She's almost dancing, she's so excited.

"You're absolutely right," I say. I can take care of Giraude and then Tabby will be safe. Everyone will be safe.

"Let's figure out the best approach," she says. "You should do it now, as quickly as you can. What if the effects wear off over time? The Sangreçu eventually need more to sustain them, and they were *alive* when they drank. And you two shared a vial, whereas they may have drunk an entire one. The effects may be very temporary for you."

I'm suddenly frantic at the thought I could lose all this. I can't bear to go back to a muffled existence where touch feels like I'm wearing five sets of gloves.

"We can use intention to find her, and then you can . . ."

"Right! I can . . ."

"Well . . ."

Big silence.

"Exactly."

There's so much we don't know. But we have made some groundwork into understanding some of the Sangreçu "rules." A death by blood loss can be overcome. Blood can be replenished, even if someone's head is completely severed from the body.

But other kinds of death seem to work. Drowning. Maybe poisoning or suffocation.

I picture myself coming up from behind Giraude and getting her in a choke hold. I shudder. I don't want to do it.

Pick my weapon of choice, I think, except a weapon won't work. Giraude's body will have to work against itself. She'll become her own self-directed weapon.

"What are you thinking?" she asks.

"Unpleasant thoughts."

"It's never pleasant to resolve to kill someone, even when you know it must be done," she says. "I would've never thought myself capable, but I found the strength when I knew I was saving many other lives by destroying a single evil one."

"Tell me how you got ready to do it."

"I planned it out and then I told myself I'd take the best chance I had to do it. I knew if I picked a certain day I might become too scared by the expectation. So although I knew what to do, I didn't decide when to do it. I knew I'd say to myself, 'This is a good night, all the stars are aligned.'"

I nod.

"You're a strong person, Miles," she says. "You can do it. You saw how ruthlessly she killed that man. He may have been a very fine and good person when there isn't rum in his gut. But we'll never know. Anyone who can kill with so much nonchalance—like the way you'd squash a spider in the pantry—she needs to be stopped. It's noble to stop someone like that."

"I know," I say.

"She threatened to kill innocent people."

"I'm beginning to wish I wasn't Sangreçu. It has made expectations for my performance that much higher."

"Which is a grand thing," she says with emphasis. "I wasn't looking forward to devising a manner in which to attack Giraude. Phoebe had some ability, but not to touch Giraude herself. I feared it would be an agonizing showdown."

My jaw drops. Eleanor actually thought we might lose against Giraude?

"But my faith has been completely restored," she says. "I trust you far more than her . . . and now you are strong in this guise as well."

I wonder if I should talk to Phoebe's mum and Steven, staring hard at them sitting there. It could solve some things. It could also lead to him slugging me if I didn't explain fast enough. I know it's not my place to approach them. Either Phoebe does it, or no one.

The first firework launches into the sky and Eleanor runs directionless, shrieking, a zigzag since she can't escape the global noise of the sky. "Come back," I call to soothe her. "They're noisy but harmless."

Thank goodness it's dark—otherwise, to the people here I

would appear to be shouting encouragement to an invisible friend. I'm not used to having corporeality again: it took a while to get used to losing it, but then it became the new normal. Fireworks dazzle the sky overhead and the shrieks of falling sparklers make me jump. Eleanor's bolting like a horse at a gunshot.

Tabby's also screaming. I imagine the dogs of the modern town of Versailles are cowering with their paws over their muzzles. I used to really like fireworks, but what are they good for? Terrifying the young and helpless and making a lot of smoke.

I wonder if Giraude is watching them. Does she enjoy them? Do they remind her of the original fireworks and the applause and envy they earned her king?

If Phoebe's still at that shore, maybe she sees our fireworks from far away, like tiny mushrooms in the sky that light up and dissolve. Is she even thinking of us? Or is she lost to the past, to the man she hated so much that she shut him away for eternity? He must've done something awful to make her do that . . . or she was the one who did the awful thing.

Eleanor calms down enough that I urge her to sit on the grass near the blanket Tabby and her parents are on. We watch the fireworks with our heads tilted back. After a while, Eleanor begins to gasp at the beauty, rather than being scared. The designs of light seem like a rose that blooms too briefly, shedding its petals for longer than it was in flower.

The sky is splintering with rockets, colors, falling man-made stars. Tabby's pointing up, clinging to her mom's arm, the perfect mixture of terrified and excited. I look up at a vast umbrella of white light that spreads as the delayed boom hits our ears and dissipates into trailing diamonds that seem like they will touch the earth.

The sound cracks the heavens open.

It's hard to discern since the sky is black interrupted by patches of blinding color and clouds of resulting smoke, but sure enough: I feel the light change. I'm going away again.

I reach out and take Eleanor's hand. She can't go with me, but at least she'll know I tried. She looks at me questioningly, and I realize it looks like a romantic bid, my taking her hand. "I'm going to—" I start to explain, but it's too late and nearby Tabby makes a squawk of surprise.

Tabby and I are in the past.

CHAPTER FIFTEEN

If anything can call back to me the halcyon pleasures that were once Versailles, it is remembrance of music lifted aloft on a warm summer evening.

—*Memories of a Courtier* (trans. 1811)

*T*here are no fireworks. The sudden release from their thunder and crackle is breathtaking.

Instead, I hear chamber music floating up from a lit tent on the lawns below us. In the shadows, a few people are walking around. The grass is a dark pewter at this hour.

Tabby whimpers as she turns in a slow circle. "Mama?" she calls out tentatively.

Oh, this is bad.

I'd give her a hug . . . but a hug from a stranger might be the worst of her nightmares coming true.

I kneel down so I'm at her level. "Hi, Tabby," I say. "I'm your babysitter tonight, Miles."

Her big gray eyes look terrified.

"It's going to be okay," I say. "Your mom and dad will be back soon."

She gives me a dismissive glance and continues to look around like a deer that knows the wolf is nearby. She's trembling.

This situation sucks. Her parents yanked out from underneath her, the scene changing, darkness becoming twilight, fireworks suddenly disappearing . . . and no one she knows is around. She's a time-traveling toddler.

I reflect that the only saving grace is that she didn't trip to the guillotine in Paris. This just seems to be a placid evening at Versailles.

But if it's such a placid evening . . . why are we here?

I study the figures on the outskirts trying to figure out if I'm seeing Etienne trysting with his twin of choice. Sex in the shadows wouldn't be a great thing for Tabby to witness, but better than heads rolling.

"Mama?" Tabby calls out again.

I feel awful for her. It's not enough to have your sister die on you and have your parents haul you to another country so they can make a new start . . . now you also get to trip all by yourself.

"It's okay, Tabby," I say again. "You're going to be fine. You'll be back with your mom and dad before you know it."

I think my best bet is to keep talking, reassure her by the calmness of my voice. "I'm Miles," I say. "Your sister's friend. Can you say 'Miles'?"

At least she's looking at me now.

"Friend," I say. I remember that she responded best last time to simple sentences.

"Phee friend?" she asks.

Yes!!!! Yes, yes, yes.

"Yes," I say. "Phoebe's friend."

She breaks into a broad smile and I see, really for the first time, the incredible charm of a kid's smile, especially one aimed at me. I always found her cute, but it isn't until this moment that every cell in my body pledges itself to protecting her. I see her just as she finally sees me, the invisible person she's never been aware of.

Behind her, coming toward us, ready to ruin everything, I see trouble. Yup, not a placid evening after all.

I rise to standing. "Let's walk," I say.

She doesn't budge

I bend and say insistently into her face, "Walk?"

Begrudgingly, she comes when I take her hand and pull her. I lead her to the edge of the pathway where the statues and trees provide some cover.

I can't tell if it's Yolande or Giraude. Her cleavage, where I might look for a mole, is covered by something she's carrying: a loudly crying baby wrapped up in a blanket. She keeps looking behind her at the group of about ten people who seem worried and somehow reluctant.

Tabby watches avidly. As the woman approaches, I instinctively reach down and scoop Tabby up, stepping backward so that we are further hidden in the long shadows.

"Faster!" the woman hisses. "You know that if she catches us, she'll kill us!"

They hasten. I notice that they each hold a bag of sorts; they look like they're fleeing. There are men, women, and a few younger children. The kids keep looking back at the chateau: maybe the only home they've ever known?

The baby starts to cry, and the woman's face becomes a snarl.

So Giraude or Yolande had a baby, I think, and now she's leaving under cover of night. All of a sudden, I understand. This must be Yolande, and she's on her way to England where she'll build the Arnaud Manor.

And it looks like her family members are none too enthusiastic to be coming with her. Someone's going to kill them if she catches them: Giraude? But why would Giraude want to kill her family?

I know she's capable of murder; I watched poor Etienne die under a mask of hornet stings. But what would her problem be with these people?

My eyes narrow as Yolande shakes her child—Etienne's baby?—in an attempt to stop the crying. Not the best mother in the world, is she, I find myself thinking.

Someone else thinks that, too: one of the women runs a few steps to catch up with Yolande. "Let me take the baby," she says. "I can stop the crying."

"Indeed," says Yolande. Without a second's hesitation, she hands over her child.

The woman dandles the baby and over her shoulder she throws a look—no, I'd call it a *pang*—to a man still with the family group. The baby almost instantly ceases crying. The child just wanted to be lightly bobbed in some caring arms. Now he or she gurgles and makes happy sounds as the group keeps walking hurriedly.

"You and Henri have had trouble with making babies," says Yolande carelessly, and I feel awful for the look of pain that crosses the other woman's face. "So you can have this one. Congratulations on your effortless delivery."

It's hard to tell how the woman feels, and she says nothing. Is she pleased? Sort of, but she also looks guilty, as if she knows it isn't right to take Yolande's child.

They walk along another few paces until the woman says so quietly that I almost don't hear, "Thank you."

They reach two carriages that have been brought to meet them, white and gold coaches with rounded bodies. Coronets sit on top. Even the wheels have carved decorations, each axle a lion's face. "Quickly now, before we're seen," says Yolande. "Climb in, climb in!"

"Yolande, they're too fine! We'll surely be noticed!" says one of the men in the group.

"We'll switch carriages at Picpus," she says. "Do as I say." The horses snort clouds of moisture from their noses as they wait, dancing from hoof to hoof, for the people to load into the coaches. Their hooves make a crisp clopping sound on the dirt roadway. Yolande was smart to meet the coaches so far away from the chateau, in the dark.

"Horse!" yells Tabby suddenly. She's a tornado in my arms, twisting and hitting me until she's on the ground, running with all her might toward the carriages.

"No!" I shout.

Toddlers are surprisingly fast, especially with the element of surprise. She's zipping right along when—

Oh no no no no no no.

It's changing, the light is changing, and I'm running with everything I've got, my arms reaching out to snatch where no little girl is because I'm not fast enough—

CHAPTER SIXTEEN

Versailles lay abandoned for seven years after the death of Louis XIV; it was only in 1722 that the court returned.

—*Nooks and Crannies of Versailles*

"Oh my God," gasps Eleanor, grabbing my shirt collar. "Where's Tabby?"

The fireworks are over in the present day. Tabby's mom is in hysterics, and over her broken wailing her dad is trying to talk to authorities. A crowd of about ten people has gathered around in a semicircle, watching.

I take a step backward.

It's my fault. I wasn't fast enough.

"She didn't come back with me," I say.

"Go back and get her!" she screams, pushing me, as if she can shove me into the past.

I nod, shaking from my sprint to try to reach Tabby. "I'll try," I say.

I use intention to picture the area on the lawn where I last saw her, and I attempt to pull myself there.

Nothing.

"Go!" insists Eleanor. I've never seen such an intense look on her face. I understand what people mean when they say someone's eyes are blazing.

"I'm trying!" I yell. "I've never been able to control the time-travel part of it! It's out of my hands!"

"Try again. Focus!"

I glare at her. It's easier than paying attention to Tabby's mom sobbing to the point of hyperventilation behind her.

But I try, fiercely, tensing every muscle in my body with the desire to return. "There was a baby there," I start to say. "Yolande was—"

"Tell me that later," she interrupts. "You have to get to Tabby. Her parents can't go through this again."

I visualize the lawn with the carriages with everything I have, but I stay in the present day, where the howl from Tabby's mom is a sound that makes me want to . . . I don't even know.

"You can't do it," says Eleanor. She raises both her hands to her white cap and wrenches it from her head, throwing it on the ground. "Then go get Phoebe—she has more power."

Not what I wanted to do, but before I can talk myself out of it, I move with intention to find Phoebe.

She must want to be found, because I'm there within a second. She's still at the beach, but she's dressed. She's wearing a white eyelet dress I've never seen before.

She's sitting on that same rock, looking out onto the ocean, her long legs bent in a languid triangle in front of her. She turns her head to look at me as I walk toward her.

"Hi," she says.

"Hi. Have you . . . been here the whole time? On this rock?"

She doesn't answer.

"Well, I'm glad you used your time well," I say. "But I need you."

"Yeah?"

I hesitate, wanting to soften the blow but not knowing how to do that. The news is brutal, no matter how it's phrased. "Your sister tripped with me . . . and she didn't come back."

"What?" She's instantly leaping from the rock down onto the sand. "Why didn't you stay with her?"

"She jumped out of my arms and started running right when things started to change."

"And you couldn't grab her?"

"Clearly not," I say.

She's enraged, her eyes venomous. She's almost scary, or she would be if I didn't know her better.

"Eleanor thinks *you* can probably go back and find her," I say.

"How am I supposed to do that?" she demands.

I take a step backward and hold up my hands. "You seem to be the kingpin around all of this," I say. "You can touch things at the Arnaud Manor when no one else can. You're an Arnaud. You have more power."

"Power makes me an unpleasant person," she says.

"I'm not going to argue with that," I say. "But give it a shot. Tabby needs you. You wouldn't believe . . ." I trail off. I was about to tell her how upset her parents are, but although she's a new, awful version of Phoebe, I don't want to hurt her.

"What?"

I don't answer. She shoots more eye venom. Even when I don't like her, she's still beautiful. Her auburn hair lifts in the wind and she looks up at me with an expression that reminds me somewhat of the woman who took over caring for Yolande's baby: elation mixed with guilt.

"Where did you last see her?" she asks.

"On the lawn near the beginning of the Grand Canal. She was running toward horses that were waiting with carriages."

"She loves horses," says Phoebe. She almost smiles and I can tell she's reviewing a split-second memory of afternoons from before she died, when she might've lain on the floor with her sister playing with toy horses, combing their manes.

"Good luck," I say.

I don't expect it to work—tripping has been so out of our control—but she's gone. The beach is empty except for me, the wind, and some gulls. She went somewhere, maybe not where she intended, but she's gone.

I wheel around, looking at the sand and the water. The Sangreçu blood leaps inside of me, a quick hum of activity. Phoebe said we used to like to come here. But I have an aversion to it . . . something linked to my past, not just our badly ended tryst here. The waves rush in and reluctantly scrawl back. They remember me. They are trying to tell me something.

"What happened?" Eleanor demands as soon as I return. I note that Tabby's mom has stopped crying. She's hugging her husband, head lolling on his shoulder. I bet she was given a sedative. Someone has draped a blanket over both of them.

"I saw Phoebe and told her Tabby was stuck in time. She went somewhere—I'm not sure where."

"How was she?"

"Not herself."

"I'm scared, Miles. Everything's falling apart."

"We'll figure it out," I say.

She throws me a look of complete disbelief.

"Phoebe'll find Tabby and stay with her until they come back."

"As if that's a given."

I glare at her. "We've always come back."

"I've always thought the forces guiding us were benevolent," she says. "But what if they were always leading us to this moment? To stealing Tabby?"

"No," I say firmly, and I'm surprised at the sense of authority ringing from my voice. "Tabby could've been snagged a hundred times, here and in England. Her getting stuck in time was just a mistake."

"You truly believe it so?"

God, her quaint language kills me sometimes.

"I think Phoebe and I get sent back in time to witness particular scenes that help us understand stuff, whatever it is. The grand plan. When we get the information we need, we get whisked back. If Tabby hadn't jumped out of my arms, she would've come back with me. It was the damn horses' fault for being so cute."

"That's encouraging, Miles," she says. "Thank you for your words of cheer."

I give her a smile I don't feel, but it seems to do the trick because she gives me a radiant one in return. "We'll have Tabby back in her parents' arms in just a few hours," she says.

I nod, still wearing the manufactured smile.

Who knows where Tabby even is?

Or Phoebe?

"It's time, then, to do the one thing you can do," Eleanor says. "Act while your body is under your command."

Back to that: killing Giraude. I'm a terrible assassin; I'm just not attracted to murder.

Maybe I could put her behind the steering wheel of my car without a seat belt.

"Are you going to use your hands?" she asks.

"I guess so. I hate the idea. But if she's going to keep killing people . . ." I trail off, then gain strength. "She put *us* in this situation."

"That's what I told myself long ago when I went into Madame Arnaud's bedchamber with my knife."

"Right. We're only reacting, as best we can."

"You can do it, Miles," she says, and with my Sangreçu blood stirring, her face changes and she's somebody else, but with the same kindly encouragement in her face. I can *almost* remember, almost hear a different voice filling the air, but in a second it's gone.

If Phoebe were here, we might concoct some kind of snare. She is so much more resourceful than me, so much of a planner, but I honestly can't think of doing this in cold blood. I'll just have to seize the moment, like Eleanor said, and let passion rule my hands.

So, the first question would be: Where is the person I'm supposed to kill?

I say good-bye to Eleanor, who will stay with Tabby's family as an unseen guardian. I do a circle through the bushes, the last place I saw Tabby, just in case she's come back and is too scared to move. She's not there.

I walk the lawns toward the chateau, thinking I might find Giraude in the hallway behind Marie-Antoinette's bedroom. There are no tourists now; the grounds are closed to visitors except American expats talking to police officers about their abducted child named Tabby.

My head aches thinking about what they must be feeling.

They're going to be forever changed by this—as if they weren't already changed by losing their elder daughter. I trudge across the grass until I remember—I'm a dolt—I can just intention myself there.

Easy.

The hallway is dark and empty. I walk it without seeing a glow of candlelight from under any door. I emerge into the oeil-de-boeuf chamber with its oval window and look around. Security lighting provides all the illumination, and the subdued atmosphere makes me feel almost like I've tripped although I haven't.

I take a staircase up to the second floor, where courtiers kept their rooms. Oh yes, there it is . . . the light changing, just as I expected. All the doors have a glow emanating from underneath, and the murmur of voices behind them.

One door draws me.

With deep satisfaction that I am able to do so, I grasp the doorknob and turn it. I silently enter a chamber lit by a candelabra on the round table where Athénaïs sits playing solitaire. Her blond hair is unpowdered, but in a massive construction that doubles her head's size.

The forces brought me to her, not Giraude.

The instant I step into the room, she looks up, eyes wide, nostrils opening. "Sangreçu," she breathes. *"Qui êtes-vous?"*

I scrape back the chair opposite her and sit down. "I'm Miles Whittleby," I answer.

"Friend or foe?" she asks, switching to English. She stares at me, her blue eyes so wide and her skin so pale she resembles one of those china shepherdesses that adorn mantelpieces in certain homes. Her nostrils delicately flare again.

"Friend," I say, although I'm not sure that's the case.

"You look like a friend," she says. "You are so very like someone I once knew."

"Who?" I ask. If Phoebe resembles Yolande and Giraude, who do *I* look like?

"My king."

I frown. Seriously, I look like one of those powdered, frock coat–wearing fops in high heels? One of the Louis dudes? I resist the idea I look like a Bourbon.

"Don't look unhappy. You are quite handsome. What brings you to my chamber?"

"I was looking for Giraude, and something brought me to you instead."

She nods. "I am Athénaïs although I have carried many other names."

"Where is Giraude?"

"At this hour, I imagine in her chambers. The court has abandoned the palace in favor of Paris. Only a few of us still call it home."

"Why?"

"Louis has died"—her face darkens—"after dismissing me. But I've returned. I sometimes sleep in the queen's bed! Nothing to stop me."

"Wait—so there's no king?"

"Your education is sorely lacking. Of course there's a king. There's always a king! He is only five and for now his regent—who adores Paris—is leading our country."

"So the Arnauds have remained in the empty palace?"

"The twins are Sangreçu. It is a healthy thing to withdraw from society and let people forget one's face when it fails to change."

"Giraude is dangerous," I say. "I have to find her. Can you take me to her?"

She laughs lightly. "She's harmless and foolish."

"Why do you say that?"

"She falls in love with the wrong people. She thinks she is important when she's not."

"Is she part of the prophecy?"

Athénaïs raises an eyebrow at me. "I shouldn't be surprised you know of the prophecy, looking as you do." She pauses as if considering whether to divulge confidential information. "I have come to believe she is not."

"Why not?"

She starts to repeat the lines of Old English Phoebe's step-dad read from the book on the train: "On a stronde the king doth slumber, and below the mede the dragon . . ."

"Oh my God," I interrupt. "*That* prophecy? It doesn't make any sense. What does it *mean?*"

She studies my face, and it feels like I don't pass the test, that she was considering telling me but now she won't. "Each generation is born and my hope arises," she says. "But I can't steer the stars."

"You have a lot of power," I say. "You know where the Sangreçu vials are—"

"And now clearly you do, too," she interrupts. "You are expressly forbidden to drink again."

"There was only one vial," I say.

A bleak expression crosses her face. "It seems there are dark times to come," she says. "I have tried to scry in my mirror, but it shows me a void."

It strikes me how strange it is to be sitting with a woman in the past by candlelight, her hair pulled into some towering structure that makes her face piquant, tiny.

"Hard to know who to trust," she mutters. "Yolande is ahead of herself with her pretensions to power . . ."

"Don't trust her," I say. "She's going to run away to England with her baby."

She smiles privately and looks down at her cards. "Thank you for the confidence you have bestowed on me, Miles. I will ensure that does not happen."

"Really? You can stop it?"

The butterfly effect. Will it screw everything up if Madame Arnaud never establishes her manor in England? Will Phoebe never be born? I'm starting to wish I never said anything . . . but then . . . if the Arnaud Manor doesn't exist and Phoebe's family doesn't come to live there, then they wouldn't be visiting Versailles and I wouldn't have to kill Giraude.

But with a sick sense of certainty, I know she won't be able to stop Yolande from leaving. Maybe Yolande has already left—I saw it happen, but time is so fractured, it doesn't seem to correspond to a chronology. Or maybe something will happen to keep Athénaïs from preventing the flight.

Who knows.

"I need more information," I blurt out. "I want to know everything. Tell me what the prophecy means."

She stands up. "Would you like to look in my scrying glass?" she asks. "I can show you better than I can tell you."

"Yes!" I stand up, too, and her eyes flick over my body with appreciation.

"So strong," she says. "Always such a strong man."

She turns and her movement makes the candelabra flicker—but that's not it. It wasn't her. It was the very air glimmering.

"No," I cry, and the last thing I see is her look of shock as I vanish from her view.

I'm back in an abandoned section of the palace, dark and

cold. I stumble my way back out to the hall. Why couldn't I see? Why did I get whisked away just as she was about to tell me everything?

I punch the wall and it makes a satisfying dent. *There.* I ruined a national monument.

"Come back!" I shout as loud as I can. I realize I'm dangerous to myself: any guard who comes across me now can see me, can arrest me.

Using my corporeality to spend the night in jail would be an insane waste.

"Athénaïs?" I whisper.

These halls have not had living people dwelling in them for a long time.

Intention still works. I find Eleanor.

She's in the hotel room where Phoebe's mum is lying on the bed sideways, black mascara trails running down her face and staining the pillowcase. She must've cried herself to sleep. Steven sits in the chair, rigidly upright yet slumbering. Good thing they're out of it or they'd lose their minds seeing a strange person suddenly appear in their room.

What a change, coming from the warmth of Athénaïs's compelling personality. Eleanor stands and comes to look at me assessingly.

"Did you find Giraude?" she asks.

"No. Did Phoebe come back with Tabby?" Stupid, but I had to ask.

She shakes her head.

"None of the jobs have been done," she says.

"I'll go back out again. I just wanted to check in."

"We're fine. If you consider this fine." We both turn and regard the monumental sadness that fills the room with grief so deep it is almost tangible. I swear the air is thicker in this gloomy room.

"Okay," I say. "I'm off, then."

"Good luck," she says, but her voice sounds tinny and insincere.

I'm about to go, but I pause and look her deep into the eyes.

"Not like that," I say. "Eleanor, I need to hear it like you mean it. Like you always used to mean it."

Her face, a different face, her words of wisdom, her guidance for me across the stretch of centuries. She was once my advisor, my counselor, my head on my shoulders.

"Miles," she says. *"Good luck."*

CHAPTER SEVENTEEN

The trouble with prophecies is that if they give a timeline,
often that timeline comes and goes without the world
quivering or even pausing. Belief in divination becomes an
act of fervent if misguided faith.

—*Failed Prophecies throughout the Ages*

I choose the part of the lawn where I last saw Tabby. She's not there . . . but . . .

Around the corner of a bush, skirts are disappearing, thick and dragging on the moist night grass. I surge after them and catch up with Giraude.

"Hello!" I greet her.

She frowns and steps aside to allow me to pass as if I'm any other jerky tourist who stayed within the grounds past closing time. I can see the very instant she senses I'm Sangreçu. I'm full of blood and sensation—my veins roaring with the Sangreçu blood and the job I have to do.

"My God!" she says. "Who are you?"

"Miles Whittleby."

"I smell it on you."

"I don't have it," I say.

She looks me up and down, and in turn I stare at the black ribbon of velvet around her neck. I may be imagining things, but I think I see a slight crease in the middle where the velvet indents into her wound. "You are modern," she comments.

"But dead."

She reels for a second but then accepts it. She's seen a ton of death already. The fact that I'm talking to her is probably not that startling given she lived through her own beheading.

"Where do you come from?" she asks.

"England."

"I didn't think you were French," she says haughtily. "I meant, why are you here and where did you find the vials?"

"One vial," I correct her.

"Where?" she demands.

There's no reason not to tell her. "The chapel at Picpus."

"Of course." Her eyes close in a private moment of self-remonstration. "Athénaïs loved that little chapel. Why didn't I think of that?"

She reaches up to touch the ribbon on her neck. I look away.

"Let's walk," I say. I enjoy seeing the indignation that crosses her face. She's used to calling the shots, not taking direction from outsiders she encounters on the lawn.

"How did you find the vial?" she says, standing stock-still.

Eleanor was right; I am stronger than Giraude. She resists, but I am able to make her walk with me as I pull her along. It's so heady, this sensation of touching another person. Her corset under the silk is stiff, and my hand marvels at how the fabric slides up and down over the corset.

She's significantly shorter than I am and her hair is right in my face, practically up my nose. I smell the horrible powder that she uses to make it white, and I try to resist sneezing, knowing I may lose my grip on her if I do.

"This is the end for you," I say. "You've had a good couple hundred years, right?"

She snatches herself out of my grip and whirls away. "Who on earth are you?"

"I told you. Weren't you listening?"

I smile at her and her eyes mark it uneasily. "Why do you threaten me so? I am Sangreçu and can never die."

"Not quite right," I say.

"*Absolutely* right," she proclaims. "Not even the guillotine could kill me!"

"I know, I saw," I say, and she looks up at me, surprised. "Well, whatever you've gone through, it's over now. You killed a man just for being in your way—what's wrong with you?"

She doesn't even react. "I value very little. There are some whose excellence shines, but he was a peasant."

"Peasant or prince, he didn't deserve to be killed."

I resume walking, pulling her with me. I need to get her somewhere concealed so I can complete my mission. Plus, it feels amazing to walk. I can actually feel my lungs getting tight from the effort. I haven't felt anything strenuous since . . . well, since I died.

Because my skin is hypersensitive, I immediately notice when she runs her fingers down the arm that's pulling her along. What's that about?

"Come into my chamber," she says. "We can talk there in comfort. Sangreçu should offer hospitality to other Sangreçu."

I get it now. The coquette never stops believing in her charms. She thinks she can seduce me out of killing her.

Good luck with that.

"I'd like to tell you some things you should know, as one of our special assembly, those who have tasted of the vials. I have been the victim of the most despicable deceit. I have been wronged in the worst way possible. My only hope now is to achieve my destiny, to fulfill the prophecy."

"What destiny is that?" I ask. "Can you fill me in?"

"I'll tell you everything," she says, "because I'm meant for great things. I just need more elixir from the vials to sustain me until the conditions of the prophecy are met."

I say nothing.

She looks up at me, and her face is suddenly coy. She looks like her sister when she spoke to Athénaïs, using her sexual power as a ruse. "And if you help me," she says, "there will be great reward for you, too."

"I don't want that kind of reward," I say.

We're now at the wall of the chateau, a facing of weathered blond stone. "Press the second stone before you," she says. "This was an entrance Athénaïs created for herself. Did you know Athénaïs?"

"A little," I say. "Which stone?"

"Unhand me, and I'll show you."

I let go of her, knowing she can never outrun me. My hands feel bereft suddenly, without the heat of her waist. Maybe I'm not as immune to her as I think. The minute I think that, my body responds and I'm angry at myself. That is not what I need to be thinking about now.

She reaches out a hand that I'm now noticing is graceful, and presses a stone that is shaped slightly differently from the others around it. I hear grinding rock, and a door reveals itself, ajar with minimal space between it and the wall.

"Come in," she says, throwing a certain look over her shoulder at me. Can she tell, does she notice? Crap. Suddenly I sense Eleanor behind me.

I turn my head and smile at her. Even if Giraude can't see her, she'll keep me on the straight and narrow.

We enter a hallway of heavy stone . . . so medieval, it must be part of the earlier architecture of the chateau. Two of our three sets of footsteps make a muffled thud. She leads us until the darkness is almost unbearable, and we reach a door.

"This is my chamber," she says.

Inside, there is welcome warmth and light. Her room is lavish, with carpeting and tapestries of rich maroon hues. Her bed is draped with fabrics, and a fire flickers in her fireplace, with a few lamps of flame behind glass globes set on different tables throughout the room.

"Please look," she says, and leads me to a cradle tucked between her bed and the wall. The blankets within are in disarray. "I haven't changed anything since that day," she says.

"What . . . what do you mean?"

"My child was stolen from me," she says. "By someone you might've trusted."

It takes me a minute.

When Yolande met the carriages in the dark of night, she was not holding her own child. She plucked her sister's straight out of the cradle and fled.

"A woman who steals a child," she says, "is the most despicable of women. You cannot trust her."

Pity rushes through me. The cradle is painted with lambs and fleur-de-lis, and the blankets appear to have been ravaged in distress by the mother who woke to find her beloved baby gone. I see a withered rose lying in the panic of linens—her memorial for the child whose fate she never learned.

"Is she the one who gave you to drink of the vials?" she asks.

"No," I say.

"Then who?"

"Phoebe," I say truthfully.

"Who is that?"

"The person you told that you would murder 'everyone you care about.'"

She doesn't even flinch. "The one who looks just like my sister. And thus, like me. Only clothed from another era as you are."

"Exactly," I say.

"And how did she gain access to the cache?"

"I told her where it was."

Her eyes widen. "And how did you know?"

"I stumbled on it. So what happened after Yolande stole your baby?"

"I sent messengers to all corners of the world," she says. "I was never able to find my baby."

"Did you send messengers to the north corner of England?"

"Every corner!" she says fiercely.

"I think they missed one."

"What do you know?"

"I think your sister raised him, and he lived to have his own children. I think Phoebe is his descendant."

"My baby was a daughter," she says.

Dark emotions cross her face, and this time I can't read them. "I can't even focus on what you've told me," she says, sitting down on the large bed framed by thick tapestries. "All I can think about is the smell of the Sangreçu blood in you now."

"Right, the vials." I bite my tongue.

"Athénaïs told me I'd have my due someday, and not to worry. But she's been gone, too, all these many centuries."

Hm.

"I have seen everyone go," she says. "My responsibility has been even mightier than that of a king. I have borne my duty without complaint and held my head high, for the prophecy is awaiting that . . ."

"That what?"

"That perfect moment," she says.

She looks up at me and her eyes hold such strong belief that I feel compassion for her for this as well. I've hated her since the moment I saw her and mistook her for her twin, but I haven't been able to acknowledge that she's been duped by fate, too.

She thinks all this suffering is going to pay off. She's going to have a grand ascension to the stars, just as soon as that prophecy kicks in. She's lost her child, was so forlorn she wanted to be beheaded, and she's lived alone in a back hallway of Versailles for hundreds of years. But she thinks it'll be worth it.

"And what if you're not the one?"

Her eyes immediately fill with tears and I feel like a jerk.

"Look, Giraude," I say. "I saw you kill someone just because he was in the wrong place at the wrong time. And you've threatened to kill others."

She doesn't say anything.

"What am I supposed to do?" I ask. "You're dangerous. You're unpredictable."

A single tear rolls down her cheek, and I stalk off, catching Eleanor's bewildered face from about five paces off. I open the door and stand in the dark hallway, trying to master my emotions.

How am I supposed to strangle a woman who's crying?

★ ★ ★

Eleanor's at me in an instant. "Miles, don't let her fool you," she says. "Her tears are manufactured to bring you under her spell."

I keep my back turned to Giraude in case she's watching through the open door, so that she doesn't know I'm having a conversation with a ghost she can't see. "I know, I know," I whisper. "I wanted to step away to clear my head."

"She's evil. As bad as her twin."

"Maybe," I say.

"*Maybe?*"

"Okay, she is! It's just I haven't heard legends about any silver straw connected to her!"

"If she were plain as dishwater, you'd have your hands around her neck already," she mutters.

Not fair. Giraude is pretty and she looks like Phoebe, but that's not why I'm loath to kill her.

It's because she's a person. She's real and she has emotions and vulnerability and her destiny is a great, monstrous downfall.

"I'd happily hand her over to you if I could, Madame Executioner," I say.

Her jaw sets.

Ouch. Bad move, Miles. The reason I can't hand her over is that Phoebe was a total glutton with the vials.

"I'm not bloodthirsty," she says. "But I accept my duty."

I look over my shoulder back into the chamber. Giraude has risen from her bed and is standing in the doorway, staring over at me. She's no longer crying.

"Miles, you can do this," Eleanor says. "You are strong, you are right. You must lead us."

"I . . . what?" I whirl back around, my attention firmly on Eleanor.

"You must be strong and do this," she says.

My head spins. She's told me this before, with other words in another voice.

"Are you all right?" she asks.

"I'm okay," I say in a hushed voice, pushing around the corner so Giraude can't see me. "I'm just having another one of those memory blips. It's like a déjà vu, you telling me that."

"How odd," she says quietly. "Me telling *you* things. The most powerless advisor you have ever had."

"No," I say. "You were powerful."

I hear encouraging words from a husky, low voice, and see afresh the glint of silver flashing into the sun, a roar of pain from me or my adversary. The Sangreçu blood in me is trying to clue me in, help me remember the once-lived life.

I am physically strong, but it's my mind that needs fortification. I need to believe in my own worthiness to lead.

Eleanor's simple face, broad and honest, pins me with its expectation. "She is dangerous. You must act *now.*"

I square myself up, feeling residual emotions from that other life. I can do this. I almost feel for the scabbard at my hip. No, I don't have a scabbard; *he* did. That other self.

"I shall," I say, and she narrows her eyes at my antiquated language. "I mean, I can do it."

"Yes," she says resolutely. "You can."

"Okay, then," I say. I turn around and take a deep breath. From the doorway, Giraude gazes at me with a plaintive look of deep longing and sadness and perplexity, all at the same time.

My strength could so easily overcome her. If only there

were a way to make her kill herself, in essence. I could take a page out of Phoebe's playbook. Trickery.

Phoebe was always good at trickery.

How might I trick such a woman as Giraude? She's got hundreds of years of experience on me. She's seen it all.

She's lost more than I ever even *had*.

Oh yeah.

I think I know what might work.

CHAPTER EIGHTEEN

And so it is that ancient man dangled his head back upon its broad neck to survey the pantheon of stars and began to form loosely woven connections between them. He imaginatively straightened the jagged to become the shaft of an arrow or the belt of the archer, doing his best to impose some sense of familiarity onto the vast incomprehensibility that terrified him.

—Constellations with a Cultural Overlay

I walk over to her and catch her in a sideways hug. After a moment of hesitation, she curls her head onto my chest.

"You've been through a lot," I say.

"With no one to comfort me," she says.

"I'm here now," I say.

She reacts with a shudder of pleasure that would have been completely delicious coming from anyone else.

"You never saw your baby again. Do you think your sister killed her?"

She stiffens. "I knew she'd keep her alive," she says. "Yolande stole my destiny, but she was uncertain if it would work. With my daughter at her side, on her side, she had the benefit of my heir."

"Or she had her own heir and murdered yours," I suggest.

Her face goes blank.

"It's surely occurred to you," I say, "that she was pregnant when she left."

"It did," she says tightly.

"She stole your child and never paid recompense."

She convulses and I hug her more closely. An odor, like

that of ancient oranges, a rudimentary perfume, arises from her body.

"While you've been here lonely, she's been surrounded by family and good fortune. It must be so galling that you can never get your revenge," I say.

"Oh, I will," she says. "The prophecy is my revenge."

I let her go and step back into the bedroom. I walk straight over to the cradle and make a point of looking at it. She follows me with soft footsteps in her satin slippers.

"Tell me about the Revolution," I say.

"It was sheer madness," she says. "Everyone went mad."

"And you tried to get yourself guillotined," I say. It sounds so horrible out loud.

"You say you saw me?" she asks. She takes a heavy inhale, and I see that her porcelain teeth are pretty, are still intact, like tiny chips of white candy.

"I travel through time," I tell her. "I was there. I saw you push your way to the front of the crowd. You wanted to die."

I try to put my arm back around her but she pushes it off.

"I wanted to die most fiercely," she says, and her voice is a pure shadow of itself, frail and pained.

"Because of your daughter?" I press. I feel like an A-level jerkwad doing it, but it's part of my plan.

"Because of her, because so many years had passed. My lover gone, the only man I ever loved."

My eyes narrow and I quickly turn my head so she can't see. I remember quite well how that lover was made "gone," by her own hornet's nest of fury.

"Because everything I cared about or knew about was vanishing. Because the prophecy wasn't taking place, and I thought maybe if I tested it by trying to die, it would enact."

That hadn't occurred to me—that she had thought her suicide attempt wouldn't really *work*. That the prophecy would jump right in and make sure she didn't actually die. And . . . come to think of it . . . she *hadn't* died. Permanently, anyway.

"What was it like directly after?" I ask.

"Like I saw the world through seven layers of glass," she says. "Remote and hazy, barely visible. I welcomed the glass going dark but it didn't. I saw everything until the dirt was shoveled onto my face. Did you see that, too?"

"Yes," I say. "I followed the tumbrel."

"And then I waited. I lay there, my body twisted, another woman's arm tossed across my cheek, and for the other part of me, someone else's hip digging into mine. The smell of blood in my nostrils, a thick mélange of all our spilled essence. I waited, listening for the song of the Sangreçu to stop. It grew dim, but it never truly went away."

"You can't die a blood death," I say quietly.

"What do you mean?"

"Once you are Sangreçu, the spilling of blood can't kill you. There will always be a way to return the blood. But you can die other ways."

She looks at me sharply. "What other ways?"

"Suffocation, drowning, strangulation . . ."

For a long time, she stands there thinking, no doubt remembering that day in the Place du Trône Renversé and everything she felt then. Very French, she laughs bitterly. "So it was just my bad luck the Revolution chose the guillotine rather than simple hanging."

I look behind us at Eleanor, waiting solemnly, visible only to me.

"You must've been frantic."

"Frantic? That is not the right word," she says. "I craved death."

"I can understand," I say.

"No. You can't. Do you have a child?"

I shake my head.

"I didn't think so. You can't know what it feels like. One moment you are staring down at your slumbering child in the cradle, in love with every eyelash resting on her cheeks, and the next you are howling with pain because she has vanished."

"Betrayed by your own sister," I say.

"My family went with her. I had no one left. *No one.* Athénaïs left to find her and never returned."

"You must've felt so alone."

Tears flow down her cheeks, making rivulets in the thick makeup I hadn't realized she was wearing. Underneath is a lighter flesh tone. She rubs at the tears with the heel of her hand and a blotch appears. It's like she is cleaning a filthy window with a rag, revealing the clean glass beneath.

"But did later years bring peace?" I ask, knowing the answer.

"Peace!" she spits out. "There is no peace. I hate every day, every moment, I must continue to breathe this air. I want the prophecy to unfold."

I pause, wondering how to respond. Should I lie, act like I know more than I do? But what if I'm wrong—what if she *is* the object of the prophecy and I screw everything up by convincing her she's not?

"Don't you wonder sometimes if the prophecy is real?" I finally manage to ask.

"Of course it's real! It has to be! There must be—"

She can't continue on, bent double by her sobs. I put my

hand on her back, rubbing in gentle circles with distaste, feeling the knobs of her vertebrae through the silk gown above the line of the corset.

"It would be too cruel if it wasn't real," I say.

She sinks to her knees, and so I do, too.

"My life has been nothing but cruel," she says when she can speak. She leans back and raises her face to the ceiling. "I've counted. I had seventeen years of happiness and three hundred and twelve years of bitterness. It is not a pleasant accounting."

"And the only thing that has kept you living was the thought of the prophecy?"

There's a long silence in which she contemplates the cradle. "No," she says in an altered voice that makes me wonder if all along she's been talking the way the court of Versailles trained its courtiers to speak. This voice is raw, real.

"No," she says again. "The only thing that kept me living was the fact that I couldn't die."

My hand stills on her back.

"But you tell me that I can," she says.

She rises to her feet and begins walking, her head held high. She seems filled with resolve. "The prophecy is a thin thread I've held on to," she says. "But you have come with your broom and swept it away like a cobweb."

She walks to the doorway and without saying a word, passes through it. Eleanor stares at me with wide eyes.

"Where are you going?" I ask.

"To try for a second time."

"All right," I say.

I'm terrified all of a sudden. She's a monster, but I don't need to be the suicide hotline's worst nightmare.

We walk silently through the passageway and back out to

the exterior of the chateau. The moon regards us impassively as we make our way to the Hameau pond. So far away. It takes forever. I wish I could offer her moving by intention, but she's not dead.

She looks up at the sky while we walk, her face moving left to right, recognizing the constellations that have been here throughout all her miseries, and that will continue long after she passes.

The moon has seen so many others give up throughout the centuries. It has never reached out a silvery hand to stop anyone. This is its duty: to watch with remote disinterest.

Giraude stops and looks around at the quaint buildings, once happy, once a place where Marie-Antoinette ran and danced with her children. I look to the field where we saw the queen and her daughter cut flowers, but they are not here. Are they only a daytime haunting? Does the sun awaken their endless replay of a happy afternoon?

"Joy is always undone," Giraude says. "We frolic like children, but then must bow to the black master when he shows us the foolishness of our pleasure."

She bends and picks up a stone. Instantly, I dodge to the side, an innate suspicion in me, and she laughs.

"I'm not going to throw it at you," she says. "Will you help me gather them?"

"What for?"

"For my pockets," she says.

I stand there a long time watching her pick up stones until it dawns on me. She's going to weight down her dress with the rocks, then walk into the pond.

"I can't help you," I say quietly.

Eleanor comes to my side and together we pay silent homage to the woman preparing for her own death.

Stone by stone, she fills her pockets until her gown bulges at the hips like the elongated hoop skirts women of her era wore anyway. Finally it seems she can't fit any more in. She becomes a statue as she looks at the flat mirror of the pond, with the moon reflected in its center. She turns to look at me.

"What will I do if this doesn't work?" she says, her eyes on mine, but really she's asking herself.

She takes her first steps toward the pond. Because it's artificial, there's no gradual entry. She'll just have to step off the tufted grass into the water whose depth is unknown.

"Hold my hand?" she asks quietly, stretching her arm to me.

"Don't touch her," says Eleanor. "She'll take you with her, and you don't know how things work now that you are Sangreçu."

But I know that I can intention myself away, so I'm fearless as I take Giraude's pale fingers. She lifts one lavender-colored shoe so it peeks out from beneath her skirts, fragile and soft as a ballet slipper. We both know she's waiting to see if the prophecy will unleash lightning on our heads or bring dark clouds to encircle the moon, but nothing happens.

She steps in.

A minor splash, and she's in up to her thighs. I steady her as she lurches, and she gives me a grateful smile. She lets go of my hand and her lips open. She's about to say something but then thinks better of it. She walks into deeper water, her fingertips touching the surface and then her whole hand disappearing into the water. She doesn't hesitate, but she walks with a certain sense of slow ceremony.

Ripples spread out from her progress and I hear the water lapping the farther shore. She walks until her dress is wet above the surface, the silk taking on water like a towel. She never once turns back to look at me.

She goes deeper until her head sits atop the water. It seems like the surface of the pond is its own horizontal guillotine.

And then, as if I dreamed her, she is gone.

"That's it?" I say in disbelief. "That's all we had to do?"

"What a tortured soul," says Eleanor. "You did her a great service."

Bubbles come to the surface in a riot, and I picture Giraude on her hands and knees at the bottom of the pond, her last lungful of air escaping up to the surface. If she changes her mind, she won't be able to rise. The stones and her heavy skirts will keep her down. She must be struggling for air, but all we see are bubbles breaking under the calm moon.

"Well done, Miles," says Eleanor. "Your hands are clean."

"I'm a regular Pontius Pilate," I say.

"I tormented myself over what I did," she says. "And all you did was . . . talk to her."

I shudder. "It wasn't an easy talk."

We stand guard until the bubbles stop and the pond is glass again. Tension drains from me, and I wish for the solace of sleep. The inability to close my eyes and drift away for eight hours is one of the true hardships of death. Things just don't end.

"What do we do now?" I ask.

"We take a deep breath and then we find Tabby and Phoebe."

"And after that?"

"God only knows."

She faces me and her arms come around my shoulders. I step closer and we hug, a long, heartfelt hug.

"You're a good man, Miles."

Her words give me a jolt. I'm not used to thinking of myself as a man. "Thanks," I say, and we step apart.

Then I feel *her* at my back and whirl around.

Phoebe.

She's dressed in a black vintage dress with gray tights and black combat boots. Not the style I'm used to seeing her in.

"Hi," she says. She won't meet my eyes.

"Tabby's not with you?"

"I couldn't find her."

"You've been looking for her all this time?"

She looks away.

"I'll go with you," I say.

"If you promise not to let go of her this time."

I inhale sharply.

Eleanor reaches out and squeezes my hand. "I'm going to wander off for a while," she says.

"No, don't," I say.

"You need to talk," she says, and walks away.

I refuse to say anything first, so I wait, looking at Phoebe's averted gaze. She sneaks a glance up at me, and I don't think she likes what she sees on my face.

"I'm sorry, Miles," she says.

"I wish I could say, 'It's all right.'"

"I know it's not."

I'm not sure what she's talking about: losing track of Tabby or how she treated me on that beach after we made love.

"Let's try together. I'll go with you. Giraude is dead."

She gives a wan smile. "Nicely done."

I wait for her to ask me details, how I managed it. She

seems incredibly nonchalant about something that was intense and *huge*. But she doesn't ask.

"We don't have to worry about her killing anyone else," I say, "Let alone your sister."

She nods. If she were a man, I'd slug her.

"Now all we have to do is rescue Tabby, and your family returns to England and everything's fine again."

"Nothing's fine when my parents have spent hours thinking they lost their second child."

"Then it's all the more important that we go now."

"Sure."

"God, Phoebe!" I explode. "Stop acting that way. We have to believe in this and make it happen."

"The trouble is, I don't think I believe."

"You think your sister's forever stuck in time," I say. "She's going to find someone to give her a long skirt and put her hair up in a bun and teach her to speak French."

No response.

"I don't need this," I say. "You're giving me all this attitude, but actually you're the source of the problem."

"I know," she says. "That's why the attitude."

I soften. "It's okay. As soon as your parents get Tabby back, everything's going to be fine."

"If you say so."

"It's at least going to be a lot more fine than if we never go get her, right? Let's do it."

She doesn't respond. I turn around and shout to Eleanor, "We'll be back soon, with Tabby!"

She smiles at me but her smile fades when she looks at Phoebe. "I'll expect you back shortly," she says.

"Okay, bye!"

I feel like I'm some ridiculous cheerleader still bouncing

on the balls of her feet while the entire team has been slaughtered and lies in fly-encrusted heaps on the field.

"A leader leads," I hear Eleanor say under her breath.

"Got it," I say. "Let's go, back into the past." I close my eyes, firmly grasping Phoebe's hand. I'm picturing that entourage on the lawn, Yolande scurrying along, her family following, Giraude's baby passed along to another family member, the horses pawing the ground, the beautiful carriages waiting to take them away.

But instead we land on the beach again. The rock rises up against the horizon, and the waves come to the shore and recede again.

"See what I mean?" says Phoebe.

"Is this what happened last time?"

"Yes." She nods miserably. "I tried and tried and could only wind up here."

"No wonder you were so upset."

She lets out a sob, and I press her to me. "It's going to be okay," I say into her hair, which smells of salt air. "Phoebe, honestly, we will find her. I know we will."

"I wish I had your faith."

"You know what else I think, though? I think Tabby has a lot of your spirit in her. I think no matter where she is, she's fine. She's a smart girl."

"But she's surrounded by evil people."

"She's smart. I left her in the shadows, and I bet she stayed there until it was safe to go. Trust her a little."

"She's *two!*"

"But she's from an extraordinary family," I say. "She's an Arnaud."

"I don't have much respect for the Arnauds, including myself."

"Listen, this could all turn out brilliant. There's a prophecy, and we're part of it."

"We think."

"Athénaïs seems to agree."

"Well, can Athénaïs get me to my sister?"

I stare at her.

And smile.

"Maybe?" I say.

I intention us back to the hallway above the staircase. It's dark and I don't even know which chamber was Athénaïs's.

"All we can do is hope that it happens again," I say.

We wait there long moments, but no light appears from under any of the doors. I guess at which door is hers and open it. Can't see anything. I push my way to the window and look out. The moon shows the vast lawns and . . . in the distance . . . Eleanor. She's walking back to the chateau from the Hameau.

"Let's try any of the places we've ever tripped to," I suggest. "Maybe it will trigger something."

"Okay," says Phoebe in a lackluster tone.

"So . . . let's skip the guillotine scene for now. How about Etienne and Giraude running through the trees?"

"Sure."

"At least it's outside. We last saw Tabby outside."

"*You* did," she says, and there's something unpleasant in her tone.

I look squarely at where I know her face is. "I refuse to beat myself up for a kid wiggling out of my arms. I don't know how toddlers act. I'm an only child."

She says nothing.

"And if I were really a bastard, I might point out that if you hadn't spent so much time looking morosely out to sea on a beach by yourself, you might've been the one holding on to Tabby." As soon as I've said it, I wish I could take it back.

"Don't you think I know that?" she says, and I hear the tears in her voice. "Miles, have you ever really hated yourself?"

"At times."

"You've gotten mad at things you did. Stupid things."

"Yeah, that's right."

"Well, the Sangreçu blood showed me that I was someone very unlikable. I hated what I saw. What I was."

"It's not really you," I say.

"It's me *somehow*. I've been fighting with who I am. I couldn't bear to see you. I'm so ashamed at how I treated you after we—"

She breaks off, too embarrassed to come up with a verb, it seems.

"Why are you responsible for things some former self did?" I ask. "I was in some field fighting someone I don't even know. It was like a dream."

"I don't really understand," she says. "But I have to undo some things."

"Like what?"

"That man I trapped. I have to release him."

"Okayyyy," I say. "And where is he?"

"I don't know. I think I have to drink more Sangreçu blood to understand. Don't you feel like it's already lessening?"

Stunned, I realize she's right. To test it, without thinking I reach out to touch her face.

I hadn't wanted to be so forgiving. But here I am caressing her face while her hand reaches up to cup mine.

"We don't have much time," I say. "We're wasting it as we speak. We *have* to find Tabby." I pull her back out into the hallway. Maybe another door leads to Athénaïs's room. I walk down the passage, trying to see anything familiar in the dimness.

"How? *How*, Miles? I've been going back to that beach every time I try!"

"We have to control something we can't control," I say.

"That's what's so frustrating. It's like we're chess pieces on a board, and someone's moving us around, but only when they feel like it. Meanwhile, Tabby's all by herself in another century."

I look up at the ceiling. Not sure why: it seems like prayer always drifts upward, right? There's some force nestled in the sky above us?

"If you were waiting for us to get desperate," I tell the ceiling, "we're there now."

"I want my sister!" screams Phoebe, her voice filled with agony.

I look at her, biting my lip.

If there's any vestige of human kindness, anything left of compassion or sorrow to the force that let Yolande steal her sister's child, that let Yolande kill the children of Grenshire . . . this would be its moment to kick in and save the day.

"I command it!" I yell.

And the light changes.

CHAPTER NINETEEN

Athénaïs was known to have consulted with a witch called La Voisin in 1665 to create love potions for the king out of the blood and pulverized bones of newborns. For thirteen years, she secretly plied the king with this foul concoction. This, and black masses, performed naked, kept her in his favor.

—The Fine Art of the Concubine

A slit of light appears under the door, growing, I imagine as Athénaïs lights taper after taper in her candelabra.

"Miles, you made that happen," says Phoebe in awe.

"No, it was a coincidence," I say. "My timing was perfect, wouldn't you say?"

I rap on the door.

"Is she going to think I'm Yolande?" asks Phoebe, just as Athénaïs opens the door.

She stands there outlined in a rectangle of light so bright I have to clap my hands over my eyes. I hear some kind of electrical zing, and an unearthly silence.

I take my hands off my face to see that Phoebe is frozen, her arm raised in the motion of trying to stop whatever magic was thrust at her.

"You've found her!" Athénaïs exults.

"It's not her," I say. "It's Phoebe, my friend. She's an Arnaud descendant."

I see her eye go to the mole in Phoebe's cleavage.

"Look at her clothes," I beg. "She's from my time."

"And so she is, now that I look closer. Her face is very close to the twins' face, but not precise. Just as you are similar to my king."

She takes her time, though, looking Phoebe over from head to toe. "She's Sangreçu," she says. "And does she have other powers?"

"No. We're . . . normal. Please undo whatever you did."

She hesitates, loath to release Phoebe, held in a defensive pose, her feet in their combat boots caught in the very moment of stepping backward.

"She's not Yolande," I say. "Please let her go."

Athénaïs says a few words in another language—not French, I can tell, but something else. She makes an arcane gesture with her hands, and Phoebe is again in motion. She falters backward until I catch her.

"Apologies, my dear," says Athénaïs.

"She doesn't speak French," I say, and turn to tell Phoebe in English, "She's sorry."

"She can do whatever she wants," says Phoebe in a wondering voice. "I'm hers forever. I saw her before, but I wasn't Sangreçu then."

Uh, what?

She steps closer to Athénaïs and they gaze at each other, frank, open, deeply interested.

"Oh my sweet Lord," breathes Athénaïs. "I feel it."

"What do you feel?" I ask.

They ignore me, lost in each other's eyes. "This is extraordinary," says Athénaïs. "Perhaps we shouldn't meet."

"It almost hurts," says Phoebe.

"You are pulling, and I am pulling," says Athénaïs. They both close their eyes and look like they're in ecstasy or a drug-induced state.

"Hullo?" I say. "What's going on?"

They don't react.

"Open your eyes!" I shout, shaking Phoebe. "We have to get your sister."

Phoebe opens her eyes and seems to have to force herself to look away from Athénaïs. "Can you help us?" she asks in a purely docile voice. "My sister has disappeared into the past."

"Ah, that bright, noisy finch," says Athénaïs. "She has certainly caused turmoil, running around the empty palace, calling for her mother."

"You've seen her?" Phoebe cries.

"She's here," says Athénaïs. She steps aside and we can see past her, where Tabby sits at Athénaïs's table, moving playing cards around and wiping her nose, which is running from all her crying.

Phoebe makes a sound I've never heard her make before and rushes in to hug her sister.

I rub my jaw, feeling the rough whiskers, as I see the reaction from Tabby.

It's the first time she's *seen* her sister since she died.

Her little body can't seem to hold all the emotion inside; she cries and shrieks over and over as Phoebe kneels at her feet and gives her entire self over to her sister. They hug, Tabby twisting side to side with her emotions. She can't sit still. She pulls away to look at Phoebe's face. Her eyes are red with tears but she's laughing.

"Fee!" she yells.

"Tabby, Tabby, Tabby, Tabby, Tabby," Phoebe says, her voice raw.

"Love," says Tabby.

"Oh my God, yes, I love you, too!"

"*Love*," says Tabby. Phoebe runs a shaking hand over the cornflower fluff of Tabby's hair. It springs back up when her hand passes.

I feel a prickle behind my own eyes. I never felt this kind of love; I didn't get a sister or brother. But it also means I never *lost* a brother or sister.

Tabby's eyes are full of adoration; she sits and gazes at Phoebe, drinking her in. The fervent, unselfconscious stare of a child.

"I love you, Fee," she says slowly, each word carefully framed. It's the longest sentence I've ever heard her say.

"Thank you, Tabby," says Phoebe. "Thank you for saying that. I'll remember it forever." She kisses her sister's cheek with her eyes closed.

"You have no idea how much I love you," she whispers, and in Phoebe's voice I hear longing that makes my throat ache with unshed tears. She won't be in Tabby's life other than the wraith without a voice. After the Sangreçu effect fades, she'll just be a hunch that Tabby has that will make her twist around sharply in a seemingly empty room because she thinks she senses something.

Their trance of union is almost like prayer. It's so sacred, so private. I have no place here.

I turn and catch Athénaïs's eyes on my face. She beckons me to join her at the armchairs near the fireplace. She adds twigs so sparks catch and a new fire begins. She sits and we regard the growing flames while the two sisters behind us murmur and cry their gratefulness.

"What is your connection with Phoebe?" I ask when I have schooled myself to be calm again.

"She is me," Athénaïs says. "I sit here marveling at the bending of the universe's rules to see her in the flesh."

"She is you?"

"Yes."

"How is that possible?"

"You will have to consult the universe."

"I don't have that number in my speed dial."

She throws me an amused but perplexed look.

"I don't know how long we will be permitted to share the same space together," she says. "It seems a fleeting gift."

"Is she your reincarnation?" It feels so queer to use that word.

"How can she be? I am yet alive."

"So how is she you?"

"We are sharing our soul. I feel the pull of her spirit and I am pushing some of myself into her at the same time."

I look over at Phoebe, happily talking to her sister . . . and apparently playing some invisible game of soul tug-of-war with Athénaïs.

"Is this related to the prophecy?" I ask. "Do you know Eleanor?"

"Not by such a name," she says. "But what are names? I have had many myself."

"Eleanor's a servant from the Arnaud Manor in England, where we all met. Yolande established a home there after she snuck out of Versailles with Giraude's baby." I'm talking quickly, nervous because our time together is momentary. "I don't think you stopped her, did you? Is it the same evening as when we last met?"

"It is. You were here a few hours ago. I wasn't able to stop her. She was long gone."

"Does Giraude know yet?"

"She hasn't raised an alarm."

I rush through my next words. "Phoebe's an Arnaud, and

I have nothing to do with any of this except Phoebe and I met because we had both recently died—at least that's what we think, but we're not sure—and we fought Madame Arnaud—I mean, Yolande."

"You're dead?" she repeats.

"Yes."

"But you're Sangreçu."

"I drank after I died."

She frowns and smiles at the same time, shaking her head. "It's a marvel and a testament to the power of that blood."

"So it's not typical for people to become Sangreçu after they've died?"

"You're the only one."

"Phoebe, too," I say.

"Phoebe can't be dead," she says.

"She is very much so," I say. "But she was always different. Even before drinking the Sangreçu blood, she could touch things at the Arnaud manor. She had more . . . well, I don't know. She wasn't wispy."

She smiles thoughtfully to herself. "She has a lot of power. She is special."

"How do you know? What are we supposed to do?"

"I'm not certain about the details, although I understand the overall aim of your existence. My glass shows me a void for the future: Dark. Solitary. I don't know what is going to happen to me. It is most unfortunate, when I have spent so much of my life obtaining sorcery knowledge. But this last important facet—my own fate—is lost to me."

The fire is talking now in its languid, bright tongues, so she stands to add a log. I turn around and grab a quick glance at Phoebe and Tabby. They are so quiet and motionless it almost seems they have fallen asleep in each other's arms. Maybe Tabby has: she's found solace in her sister's embrace and can relax enough to do that most magic of tricks—falling asleep.

"Is Tabby important?" I ask quietly. "It seems like all we do is save her."

Athénaïs sighs in a worldly way. "She is important in that her family treasures her. Throughout history, that has been the ambition most people strive for."

"But in a larger sense? In terms of the prophecy?"

"She is not important in that way," says Athénaïs gently. "She's a very ordinary child. It's her family's love for her that makes her swell with seeming importance."

I feel guilty thinking it, but maybe that's why we had such a hard time finding Tabby. She wasn't important to the prophecy, so it wasn't cooperating in helping us locate her. *Until I commanded it.*

"But you rescued her and brought her to your chambers," I say. "She could be with any common nursemaid now, but you took her in."

"There are no nursemaids," she says. "The chateau is vacant. Yet you're right. I have a sympathy for children, especially those found far from home without protection. Decades ago, I was talked of, accused of despicable acts regarding poison and children, but it was nothing but falsehoods. My heart is tender toward children, although it can be as a stone to adults."

"Then you didn't instruct Yolande to drink children's blood?"

"Great God, no!" She looks genuinely disturbed. "She developed theories and misinformation on her own. I won't confide my knowledge to her because she is not the first-born. Yet she insists on vying for the chance of filling her basket with half-heard admonitions."

"She will terrorize a small English town for centuries," I say bleakly. "For no good reason."

"That sounds like her. Most unfortunate for your countrymen. I'll go to England and stop her."

I stare, face hot from the fire, mind spinning. It was all a mistake, Yolande replenishing her powers—so she thought—by draining the village children of their blood.

"Don't go to England," I say abruptly.

"I must right the wrong," says Athénaïs. "Collect Giraude's child. Stop this bloodshed you tell me of."

"I've been told you disappear."

In the silence that falls between Athénaïs and me, I hear again the delighted babble of sisters reuniting.

I don't know if I've done the right thing.

I stand up. "Phoebe," I call across to her. "We need to go. Our powers are waning. If we go back before we lose them, you can tell your parents everything."

She stands. Tabby clings to her like a koala bear. They're fused together and I don't think either will ever let go so long as their touching is possible.

"I don't know if I could do that to them," she says, coming over to me by the fire.

"You have the chance to tell them Tabby's okay and that she's been okay the whole time she was missing. To tell them you're missing, too, in a way."

"I can't tell my mom that Tabby has time-traveled," says Phoebe. "It's too much."

"She needs to know. What if Tabby does it again?"

"It never happened in England. If we can just get her back there, she'll be safe."

"Phoebe, you have a chance to explain everything without trying to get your message through Tabby's mouth."

She looks down at her sister in her arms, who has a look of bald worship on her toddler face. "I know! I just . . . wasn't expecting it. I'm not prepared. Up until a few minutes ago, the only people I could talk to were you and Eleanor."

"Where might we find this Eleanor?" says Athénaïs to me, recognizing the name in the babble of English. "I should like to meet her."

"She's on her way to the chateau in another time frame," I say. "Eleanor was never able to trip with us. We tried."

"And she is also dead?"

"Yes. We're a great team. The Power Corpses."

I snicker, but Athénaïs looks appalled.

"Well, anyway, we should return Tabby to her parents before we do anything else. We've got to put them out of their misery," I say. I turn to Phoebe and ask in English, "Are you ready to go?"

"Ready!" says Phoebe. "So let's go!" She looks brightly, sarcastically at me.

"Athénaïs, can you help us?" I ask in French. "Send us back to our time?"

She smiles regretfully. "I have no idea how to do that or I might've changed my own luck several times."

"So you're not the one sending us back and forth?"

"No."

She kisses Tabby in Phoebe's arms. "*Au revoir, ma petite.* In case you leave abruptly, I've enjoyed our time together," she says. Tabby smiles, understanding the kindness underneath the foreign words.

"What do you think the force is?" I ask Athénaïs. I feel like every moment before we trip is a chance to learn more.

"The ancient ones."

"And who would that be?"

"The old rule. My king."

"Louis?"

"That fool? No. May God rest his soul, but he was a buffoon with negligible power."

I recall her earlier pride and sensuality, talking about her turns in his bed. How many years ago was that for her?

"But then who do you—"

"Miles," interrupts Phoebe, who can't understand our conversation. "Ask her why we can't graduate."

"That's exactly what I'm trying to do, isn't it?" I turn back to Athénaïs. "Who is the force behind all this?"

But even as I'm asking, dread fills me because I see the shadow across Athénaïs's face. I lost the moment, and the light is changing. Phoebe grabs my shoulder and Tabby squeals as Phoebe squeezes her close.

I don't even get a chance to say good-bye.

We're now in a cold furnitureless room with no fire in the long-dormant fireplace. Because I now have corporeality, something odd happens: since my weight truly rests on a chair, when it vanishes—or rather, when I vanish—I tumble to the ground. Surprise provides a surge of adrenaline: to be startled, to land on the floor with an *ooph* . . . this is something I've missed.

Phoebe and I move into a pool of moonlight from the window so we can see her sister's face. She's fine, absolutely fine, smiling at both of us like this is the biggest adventure.

"Can we use intention with her?" Phoebe asks. "Why don't you stay here in case it doesn't work, so she's not alone?"

"I will," I say. I kiss her on the lips and Tabby on the cheek, and they are gone before I finish straightening from bending over.

So I miss the incredible reunion of the family. I linger instead to see the silver light on the lawn below the window and Eleanor standing by herself waiting, surrounded by gleaming white statues, and a thick silver ribbon of water that stretches into the distance.

I wait until I'm sure Phoebe and Tabby must be with their parents, then I intention myself next to Eleanor.

I'm rewarded with a smile that any queen would've wished to add to her arsenal.

"Are you all right?" I ask her.

"The real question is, are you and is Tabby?"

"Tabby's great. She got to see her sister, really see her. Phoebe's like me now, at least for as long as it lasts."

I see the flicker of envy cross her face just for a flash, but she continues smiling through it.

"I'm sure they're with their parents now."

"We can afford them some privacy," she says.

I had been intending to join them; I wanted to see Tabby fly into the arms of her relieved parents. But Eleanor's right. It's their moment. They don't even know me. How terrified would they be to see a strange bloke appear in their hotel room just as they're wrapping their mind around the fact that their daughter is somehow—but not really—back from the dead?

So instead, Eleanor and I stroll.

We promenade as languidly as any courtiers of days gone by, the sky recovering from the smoke of the fireworks, the moon sorting things out. We pass ghosts as we go, people sobbing, men roaring through their attacks as they run so quickly their heels are a blur.

"It feels good to be peaceful again," says Eleanor.

"It does."

We continue walking. I can only imagine what's happening at the hotel. Phoebe will tell us later. For now: the lawns are ours.

The moon is ours.

I have a job to do before we leave Versailles. During our walk, Eleanor pointed out the bush where the German tourist's body still lay from this afternoon. We're worried that when he's found—as he doubtless will be—Tabby's father will be blamed for his murder. After all, several people caught him on video fighting the man.

While Eleanor keeps guard, I pull the German from the bushes and drag him toward the canal. It's the perfect time to do it. No one's around; the fireworks are over, and the grounds are closed. As I look at his slack, five-o'clock-shadowed face, I feel terrible. No one should die just for being drunk and a jerk.

"Let's hope he was a really dreadful man," says Eleanor. "Maybe he was drinking out of guilt for the terrible deeds he'd committed."

"I agree. Let's keep thinking that," I say grimly.

I've got him now so his feet are dangling into the canal water. I pause. I could just tip him in, but we need him to stay on the bottom.

"How will we keep him from rising?" asks Eleanor. "Stones in his pockets like Giraude?"

"Sure, let's do that." As I bend over to pick up a stone, I

notice that I have trouble picking it up. My fingers wrestle with the surface a little, like I'm trying to pick up a wet balloon. "Eleanor . . . I think I'm starting to lose my corporeality."

She bites her lip. "Then we have to work quickly. Roll him in. Then we'll work on keeping him down."

I nod. She's right. We can't leave him here on the edge of the canal. We'll have to take our chances that we can secure him underwater before I completely lose my strength. He's wearing oversized jeans and a navy hoodie; my fingers feel and then don't feel the fabric, then feel it again. I'm fading in and out. I push him into the canal and he sinks.

I jump in after him. We sink together through the dark water to the bottom. As he hits, a dim light emerges from his hip. It turns out he has a flashlight attached to his belt. I have no idea how long the batteries will last underwater—much like me, its power could flee any second.

I take it from his belt and shine it around.

There's a lot of detritus here on the bottom. Rusted metal and broken things. Shapes I can't truly discern with the weak light from his torch. It's almost dangerous to be down here with the sharp edges, or it would be if I were a different sort of person.

At first I think the trash is just what people have thrown in the canal for years, but then I see the glint of a fine golden tray, dented as if from prior violence, and I wonder if these are things the revolutionaries hurled in the canal in anger and outrage. All around me are objects half buried in the canal floor: candelabra, heads of statues, marble arms reaching imploringly.

I see curved lines in the near distance, almost like the ribs of a large animal, and as I approach I see it's the skeleton of a carriage, turned on its side. Perhaps it's even the same carriage that once took Yolande away from Versailles, returned, whose horses so captivated Tabby. Now it's an underwater hulk whose lacquered sides are peeling and swelling.

It's the perfect place to secure the German. I hold the flashlight in my teeth so I can pick him up, the water helping with his weight, and bring him to the carriage. My fingers press against him and then through him. My power's waning. I thrust his body halfway through the wrecked carriage and push his legs in until I can latch the swollen door again. Hopefully the weight of the mass will keep him down here until he's no longer recognizable.

I'm relieved Giraude is in the Hameau pond, far away, slumped with a hundred stones. I don't think I could handle seeing her down here in the torch beam.

I close my eyes and let myself feel the cold, brackish water on my skin, the back of my neck, my hair wet and lightly floating.

And then I don't feel it any longer. If I hadn't known I was dead, I might've invented sensation to fill in the gaps, but I know—and the gaps are gaps. There's just no feeling. And then . . . momentarily, it returns. It's like trying to catch a radio signal in the car—strong and loud one second, staticky the next, wholly vanished the next.

I rise to the surface and see Eleanor, worried.

"Done," I say, and she jumps. "Sorry. He's secured down there. Just wanted to let you know we can cross one more thing off our checklist."

"No stone left unturned," she says, but then I think the inadvertent reference to Giraude makes us both uncomfortable.

I join her and we sigh deeply, looking at each other. I

think if Phoebe saw us, she would think there was more to that shared look, but it's really just battle-hardened warriors acknowledging the end of one war.

"Where'd you like to watch the moon set and the sun rise?" I ask her.

"I know where *I'll* sit, but you have one more thing to do."

I look into her forthright gaze, and I know exactly what she means. I've been thinking the same thing in the back of my mind all night. I just don't want to do it.

But I have to.

I intention with her to the meadow at the Hameau so she can wait for the dawn to come and for its warmth to arouse the ghosts of the happy queen and her daughter, frolicking in the flowers before the world tore everything apart for them.

And me?

I go home.

CHAPTER TWENTY

Every culture has a scrying practice, whether by mirror, water, oil, or polished stone . . . a way for the future to show images of what will come to pass.

—Divination Practices

I stop by Gillian's house first. She's asleep, thank God. Ideal for both of us. I go to her pencil cup and grab one, open drawers until I find the miniature sketch pad I gave her. I flip past her drawings, including that hat she wanted to buy, to get to a blank page. I write as fast as I can, my fingers fumbling as the pencil is alternately firmly in my grasp and not there—or rather, *I'm* not there.

> *Dear Gillian,*
> *I wish you every happiness. It's fine to be with Chad: I release you. I'm sorry I scared you that day with the candle. Please no more séances. Love, Miles*

I leave the notebook with the pencil cup on it to prop it open to the right page. I walk to where she lies sleeping and jolt at the sight of her new hair color: purple. Grief by way of hair dye. I blow her a kiss. I want to stay, but I have to rush because I know my time is limited.

I intention to my living room.

Mum and Dad sit there watching some inane show, whatever's on, to fill the house with noise.

I arrive behind the sofa so they don't see me. I linger there, so scared to walk around to the front and show myself, but I'm also aware that it's now or never, because my body is losing visibility and corporeality by the minute.

How to do it? What to do?

I'm going to scare the trousers off them (or in Mum's case, the knee-length tweed skirt).

I wonder how Phoebe did it . . . but it was probably a cacophony of loudness produced by Tabby, and Phoebe helplessly swept along in all the relief and tears and madness. I don't have a noisy toddler with me, so I have a chance to somehow soften the "news" of my appearance.

On the spur of the moment, I think it might be good to whistle a tune to get their attention. Something that they gradually become aware of as they watch the telly.

I start with the first few notes of "Blowin' in the Wind," an old Bob Dylan song both my parents love. *How many roads must a man walk down—*

I've dramatically underestimated my mum's ability to be startled by strangers whistling in her house.

She screams and is instantly on her feet in some sort of martial-arts pose (nice one, Mum!) and staring at me for a second in which I think she's going to attack me. Then the fact that it's *me* registers.

I see relief cross her face, then horror and confusion make her mouth into a gaping panorama of teeth where I can see the amalgam in her molars.

"I'm not supposed to be here," I say. Gillian prepared me for this: I'm terrifying my own mother. She believes in heaven, and not seeing me again until she dies.

Now my father's on his feet, too, making some sort of roaring sound. I feel like the clueless tourist in a Jeep, surrounded by rhinos and elephants preparing to stampede.

"I'm sorry I'm upsetting you," I say.

"Miles!" says Mum, and there are acres of longing in her voice . . . but she doesn't move. She's stricken. I wonder if she thinks I'm a demon or some other trick of the eye.

"I'm a ghost," I say. "I've been a ghost since the accident." I add after the long silence, "I'm sorry."

"Miles," says my mum again, and she finally takes a few steps toward me. I run to her and am encircled in those sturdy, warm arms that smell of bath salts and the lotions she uses each day.

"I miss you," I say. For a second, I feel her arms collapse around me, because the body she's holding on to is wavering and disappearing. "I don't have much time. I'm going to disappear again."

"Are you all right, son?" asks my father. He and I never hugged much in life, so I offer him my hand and we shake. How insane to again feel that warm palm, those large knuckles. My father's hand is a work of art, a warm, priceless sculpture. I never really looked at it before.

"That's a complicated question," I say. "There's so much to tell you, but I think I'm going to wink out any moment. There's . . . there's no other way to put this, but there's a lot of magic at the Arnaud Manor. A family's living there now and I met their daughter—"

It's happening and it's more frustrating than any of the trips. I'm losing myself. I'm fading. I look down at my own arm and its glow seems substantially less.

"Can you still hear me?" I ask, but they don't answer. Everyone's attention turns to the bottom of the staircase, where the girl from the secret society stands with her mouth open, looking at me in shock.

"You're not dead?" Raven says. "My God, Miles, we have to—"

"Tell them everything!" I shout rapid-fire. "Work with the Arnaud family; they will have some answers!"

"Miles!" shrieks Mum in a newly panicked tone.

I think the Sangreçu spell has ended. I wish I had the code to renew.

"He's gone," cries my father and he runs to where I am, windmilling his arms through my ephemeral body. "He's coming back, isn't he? We'll see our lad again?"

I totally blew it. I didn't get the chance to say anything worthwhile, and all I did was distress them. Better to have left them watching the telly like zombies.

I'm not sure if anyone heard my last words, either.

The only good thing was the hug and the handshake.

Actually . . . those were both pretty damn good.

"I'm going now," I announce, but I'm ignored. "Great seeing you. Glad we connected. I'm going back to Versailles if that's cool with you. Because I'm sure you have no further questions or concerns."

A stronger man would've stayed and observed his parents recovering. I tell myself that Eleanor needs me more.

Yeah, right.

She needs me like a cod needs a scooter.

I've always hated crying. I'm just not *good* with tears, my own or anyone else's. So it's really best for all involved if I . . . just . . . go.

Bye, Mum and Dad.

I'm sorry.

★   ★   ★

I rejoin Eleanor at the meadow and sit in darkness with her. It's a long night. It's okay.

Eternity is long, too.

In the morning, Phoebe comes to us. I can tell the Sangreçu is dim within her, too, slowly crawling in her veins. We both lost our bodies, but we can still touch each other like always. She melts into my arms, and she's serene, bolstered with happiness. She whispers into my ear, "Thank you," and then hugs Eleanor.

"How did it go?" asks Eleanor when they disengage.

"Wonderfully."

"You were able to talk with your parents?" Eleanor asks.

"I did. They're okay," says Phoebe

I raise my eyebrow. "Only okay?"

"Well, it was intense. Imagine seeing your dead daughter show up in the middle of the hotel room with the child you believe has been abducted. But we sorted things out, and I got to tell them about the Arnaud twins."

"They must've been reeling."

"They were. Big-time. And just as I was telling them about the secret society and the girl who visited your house, Miles, I started to fade. So we all hugged together in one clump until I just wasn't part of it anymore."

"How beautiful," says Eleanor. "I would have welcomed that chance myself. Miles availed himself."

"You did?" Phoebe looks at me in surprise.

"I did, and it was quite the what-the-eff-is-my-son-doing-back-from-the-dead? kind of moment. And then shortly thereafter, I disappeared."

She takes my hand. "I'm so sorry. That sounds awful."

"Yeah. I don't think anyone got much out of it. But I did

leave a reverse-love note for Gillian, so she can relax about her relationship choices."

I see Phoebe and Eleanor exchange a glance. "I'm not bitter!" I protest. "I'm just . . . it was a lot."

"I know," says Phoebe. "Believe me, I know."

"A lot," agrees Eleanor. "You're both handling this so very well. It's quite the shake-up."

"Well put," I say, and burst out laughing.

"It's really, really good," says Phoebe. "My stepdad . . . my dad? . . . what on earth do I call him? . . . anyway, he'll help us with research. He agreed that whatever he finds, he'll leave it on the kitchen table for us open to the right page so we can read it, too."

"And Tabby's fine?"

"Always."

"And your mum?"

Phoebe's face darkens momentarily. "It's the hardest on her, but I tried to be really positive, like the afterlife is all upbeat and awesome."

"This isn't the afterlife," says Eleanor. "At least, I hope not."

"Well, it came after my life ended," says Phoebe. "*Afterlife* sort of sums it up."

"Whatever it is, it's quite the grind," I say. "Assassinations, victim burials, time and place switching at a head-spinning speed . . ."

"I need a vacation from my eternal vacation," says Phoebe.

"You lot should've tried life in service in the eighteen hundreds," says Eleanor. "You wouldn't be complaining a bit now."

"Ah, Eleanor, put your feet up and we'll bring *you* a spot of tea," I say.

"A really big spot!" says Phoebe. "Like, a sphere!"

"How lovely," says Eleanor. "I won't say no."

"Now, to find that tea . . ." I say.

"Tea comes from England," Phoebe announces. "It's their thing."

"Well, brewed in England," amends Eleanor. "*Appreciated* in England."

"There's only one thing to do, then," I say. "Let's head back to the Arnaud Manor!" I wait, grinning. "Are you not enthused, then? You're wanting to stay where the gold and shiny things are?"

We look over together at the queen in the meadow, now adjusting the brim of her daughter's straw sunbonnet. Mustn't get the sun in one's eyes. The least of their troubles, and they'll wish they'd stayed there in that meadow and stared at that bright orb until they went blind.

We can't control our fate, none of us.

Nor even predict it. Even Athénaïs's magic glass balked at showing her everything.

It's out of our hands.

The Arnaud Manor. I can't say I'm fond of its dark stone walls and fortresslike attitude. It was built as a bit of a mimic of Versailles, but somehow the lightness and imperialness of the original palace didn't carry over.

The Sangreçu in me is gone, and I waft through walls like any time-honored ghost, but there is some vestige of its influence that lets me feel how different the estate is now. I'm tuned into the ancientness of the site in a way I wasn't before. It all feels so *old*.

"Do you notice the manor feels different now?" I ask Phoebe.

"Yeah," she says, her face marveling. We're standing in the courtyard just outside the doors to the modern part of the home, watching while Phoebe's family unpacks the car. "It's like there's another shadow layer I can sense now. Something that was underneath the way it felt before."

"It doesn't feel different to me," says Eleanor. "It must be the Sangreçu in you."

I close my eyes so I can focus on that buzz or hum or whatever it is. It's not unlike the sound the vials made in the Picpus chapel.

Ancient souls and their music, I conclude.

"You with us, Phoebe?" her stepdad asks the air, pausing with a suitcase in each hand.

"Right here," she says, but he doesn't hear.

"I'm here, too!" I call out. "Sheesh, he really just doesn't care about me, does he?"

"No one's asking after me, either," Eleanor huffs.

"Seriously, though, you did tell him about us, right?" I ask.

"Of course! That was a very key detail, friend."

"Thank you, Phoebe."

We troop inside with the family as they turn the heat on and start a fire in the fireplace. "Hard to believe it's only October in such a drafty place as this," says Phoebe's mum.

"It's just because we were gone so long and the air got cold," says Steven. "It'll be nice again soon."

"It's not California," she says.

"Nothing will ever be California again." He gives her a long look. As if hearing an audible reminder, they busy themselves with all their living tasks and we wander around looking at stuff, tickling Tabby as practice to see if she can feel it.

It almost feels normal. It's like I'm just hanging out at Phoebe's after school and after a while I'll go home.

If only.

After a few hours, the family settles down to dinner, napkins in their laps and Tabby clicked into her high chair. They've taken only a few bites of their chicken Alfredo when the doorbell rings.

"Who on earth?" asks Phoebe's mum. "No one's rung that doorbell before."

Steven goes to the door, and we ghosts go with him. A man in his sixties stands there, dressed in a gray wool suit. His hair is thin and unkempt.

"Hello?" says Phoebe's stepdad.

"Hello. Allow me to introduce myself. My name is Reginald Boswick. I've been a Grenshire resident all my life."

"Oh, how nice!" says Phoebe's mum from behind us. She took the time to get Tabby out of her high chair, apparently too curious to sit waiting in the dining room. "Thank you for coming to welcome us!"

He seems taken aback by this. "We do . . . welcome you," he stumbles. "I'm here on quite another matter, it seems. We've noted that you are preparing to make renovations here at the manor house. We hear of carpenters and gardeners being lined up?"

"Yes!" Steven beams. "We want to bring some life to this old shack."

The man winces.

"No reason we can't spend a little money and bring her back to some of her former glory."

"Well, we in the village . . . I'm not going to mince words. We don't welcome attention paid to the manor. You notice you weren't able to hire labor in the village and had to go farther out?"

Steven pauses, then says, "Everyone said they were too busy."

" 'Busy,' " repeats the man with a nasty smile.

"Well, it's fine," says Steven brightly. "I found who I needed."

"Please let them go," says the man. "I have here a good bit we've put together to ask you to halt the renovations." He holds out a thick envelope. No one takes it.

"Who is the 'we'?" Phoebe's mum asks icily.

"All of us," he says simply.

"You're telling me the whole village has put up money so we won't fix the manor," says Steven.

"A good bit. Count it," says Reginald, still holding out the envelope.

"Why? I can only think this would be a wonderful thing for Grenshire," says Phoebe's mum. "Bringing money into the economy, providing jobs for laborers . . ."

"We hear you've been talking with the National Trust for Historic Preservation," he says.

"Yes, they're very interested in our plans!"

"We don't want outsiders coming in. The intrusion will be severe. This is a small village and we like it that way. I insist you look at the contents of the envelope."

"You can put that envelope away," says Steven. "We're not interested."

"Did ye not see the wall that was built across the drive? Puttin' that up was a long-ago message to stay out! I don't even know how ye managed to buy the house; the estate agents are quite put to worryin', too—" In his vim, he's lapsing into country language, dropping his *g*'s and saying "ye."

"I didn't buy it," interrupts Steven flatly. "I own it. I'm an Arnaud. This is my family's home."

The man literally takes a step back. His gaze moves from Steven to Phoebe's mum and finally to Tabby. "A young one," he says softly. He must not have noticed her before. "You really shouldn't be living here."

There's this silence that just grows and grows, and I know Phoebe's family is considering everything she told them last night in the hotel room in France.

"Madame Arnaud doesn't drink children's blood anymore, thank you very much," says Steven crisply.

The man gasps and drops the envelope.

"She's been taken care of," adds Phoebe's mum. "So tell everyone not to worry! We're bringing sunshine to the manor!"

He kneels and picks up the envelope, putting it into his interior coat pocket without taking his eyes off Steven.

"Perhaps I took the wrong tack at first," he says in a softer voice. "It's of course your home to do with as you wish. But there's more to this property than just old wives' tales. You really should not be bringing the world in on a tourist bus. We need to keep the property undisturbed."

"Describe 'undisturbed,'" says Phoebe's mum. "The fact is, I've lost my elder daughter. A project like this is exactly what I need to pour my energies and my hopefulness into. *I'm* disturbed."

He looks surprised. "I do offer you every condolence for your loss," he says gruffly. "I beg you to leave this as it is. The status quo where we all can relax at night."

"We'll never respond to bribes," says Steven.

"I beg your pardon for that," says Reginald. "But I do wish I could impress upon you the *deep* sincerity of our wish that the property be undisturbed." He's wincing. He's turning to go in defeat, but he doesn't want to leave. His feet are facing a different direction when he turns back to Steve and Phoebe's mum as if struck with inspiration. "I'd like to leave you with my business card so you may reach me at any time."

He pulls out his wallet. He gives a separate business card to each of them, as if he thinks he may divide and conquer.

They take their cards without comment.

"I know I did start out wrong," he says. "But there's no call to be fixing up this old manor house. It's been fine here all this time being lonely. Wouldn't you prefer to be in town yourselves? We've some very fine homes closer to the village center where I think you'd be far less drafty and gloomy. We could set you up quite nicely and with a mind-spinning discount to boot!"

"Thank you for your input and we'll consider it," says Steven in a clipped tone.

Reginald concedes defeat. As he turns to go, he gives one last glance to Tabby. "There was another born before her, the one that passed on?" he asks.

"Yes," says Steven.

I look over at Phoebe. Reginald knows the firstborn is the important one.

"My sympathies again," says Reginald, and he begins to walk to his car, parked in the courtyard.

"What was that all about?" asks Phoebe's mum before the door even shuts.

"It must have to do with what Phoebe was telling us. There are pagan roots to this land, old stories we have to figure out," says Steven.

"I feel like I'm on an episode of *Scooby-Doo*, with the old man telling us to stay off his property."

"Which usually means there's a treasure buried somewhere," he replies.

"Okay, I'm going to start looking for that hoard tomorrow," says Phoebe's mum. "In the meantime, I'm looking forward to dinner and our first night back at what I think is starting to qualify as 'home.'"

"Sounds great," says Steven. He throws Reginald's business card onto the table in the entry, and they head back to the dining room. I linger to talk to Phoebe and Eleanor about the man's weird insistence that the family not let in outsiders.

Eleanor makes a sharp whistle when she inhales.

"What?" I ask.

She's pointing to the card on the table. I come closer to look.

Along with the typical printed information about Reginald, his office, and how to contact him, it shows the dragon design from Picpus.

"This emblem," says Eleanor. "It was carved onto the door at Austin's house."

"Oh my God!" says Phoebe. "It was also carved onto the stone that hid the vial!"

I look once more at that helpless, enraged dragon, his wings spread almost to their utmost, but not quite. On Reginald's card, the design is in color, and the markings on the dragon's forehead are embossed in gold leaf.

We all three look at one another with exhilaration. The lines are connecting up. Austin's family studied pagan lore, and Reginald has something to do with it. We'll get answers someday. We'll graduate somehow.

But in the meantime, the renovations are going to be a lot of fun.

AUTHOR'S NOTE

Spoiler Alert! Read only after you've finished the book.

As a history buff, I've enjoyed threading into this narrative many historical facts. The inhabitants of Versailles and Paris were fascinating people, and the Revolution a horrific event. Many of the historical references in this novel are true, such as descriptions of Paris, Versailles, the Hameau, and the places where the guillotine administered its grisly, misguided justice. There is indeed a secret passageway next to Marie-Antoinette's bed. Picpus, with Lafayette's grave and the two mass pit graves, can be visited. However, I did alter history a bit on two occasions that I'll discuss below.

The chapel on the Picpus grounds dates only to 1814 and thus Athénaïs would not have been able to visit and leave something in the crypt. There was an active convent at Picpus predating the Revolution, but unfortunately for my fictional purposes, it no longer exists. So I made the choice to transform the Picpus chapel into a far older structure.

Second, Yolande and Etienne could have never trysted in the grotto, because it was built 1778–82 for Marie-Antoinette, long after Yolande left for England.

Athénaïs, Madame de Montespan, was an actual historical figure who played an important role in the story of Versailles. For over a decade, she was mistress to Louis XIV

(Miles guessed wrong!). After the poison affair very lightly referenced here, coinciding with his tiring of her and choosing another mistress, she withdrew to a convent in Paris. She reportedly died in 1707 while taking the waters—but that was simply her plan to go underground and reinvent herself. After Louis XIV died, she secretly returned to Versailles during the seven years the palace was deserted and resumed her connection with the Arnaud family.

Avenged, Book 3 of the Arnaud Legacy, will let you know what happened after that . . .

ACKNOWLEDGMENTS

I owe a debt of gratitude to Alison McMahan, who suggested that with a triad of characters enacting within a trilogy, perhaps it might make sense to let each of them narrate their own volume. I also heartily thank her for pointing out that letting the characters time-slip would permit me to more efficiently deliver the ponderous backstory. Thank you for receiving panicked phone calls and for judicious advice.

Jordan Rosenfeld, you continue to be an amazing reader and I value your input.

Thanks also to Ariana Rosado-Fernández, Heather Johnson, and Jenny D. Williams. For naming rights, I'm deeply grateful to Richard Spees and the Gellerman family for supporting Chabot Space & Science Center and Lake Forest.

For wonderful blurbs that adorned Book 1, warm gratitude goes to two writers I adore: Danielle Paige and Michelle Gagnon. For help with Britishisms, I thank Essie Fox, who read the manuscript overnight and whose writing is so deliciously eerie. Christian Labau very nicely went over the French phrases for me.

Many thanks to the fantastic team that supports me and makes all this possible: Michaela Hamilton, Morgan Elwell, Lauren Jernigan, Randie Lipkin, Arthur Maisel, Marly Rusoff, and Michael Radulescu.

Don't miss the next novel in the Arnaud Legacy series by
Lynn Carthage

Avenged

Coming from Kensington in 2017!